Praise for *Mackinac Murder*

Mackinac Murder is a relentlessly page-turning story and a good mystery. Warning: Before cracking the cover, find a comfortable chair. You're going to be there for a while. Vizard, an award-winning journalist, is a natural-born storyteller.
—Tom Powers, Michigan in Books blog

Mackinac Murder is an engaging and suspenseful story, told with the details for which Dave Vizard is known. It contains humor, compassion and current events. He gives a nod to Bay City, MI, including streets, landmarks and restaurants. This next book in the Nick Steele series is a must read.
—Karen Kolb, Michigan Book Snobs, a social media group

A storyteller extraordinaire, Dave Vizard is quickly becoming a Michigan favorite! With a captivating storyline, multiple sub-plots, and interesting characters, Vizard has mastered a rarity in the writing world—crafting a novel that is both plot-driven and character-driven. Readers will not be able to put this page-turner down!
—Janis Stein, Michigan award-winning author, editor, and speaker

Author Dave Vizard has outdone himself with *Mackinac Murder*, his latest work in his series featuring investigative reporter Nick Steele. Vizard paints vivid images of the many characters through his descriptive writing and clever imagination. I couldn't put the book down and I think *Mackinac Murder* would make an excellent movie!
—Dave Maurer, retired broadcast journalist and radio programmer

Mackinac Murder is a new take on the old genre of hard-hitting detective stories. It's wonderful, fast-paced reading and I highly recommend going on the ride. An excellent novel. This is a stand-alone story but part of a highly entertaining series. You will love it.
—Dave Lemaster, broadcaster and radio-show host

Dave Vizard has done it again. *Mackinac Murder*, the latest installment in his Nick Steele murder mystery series, starts out fast and never slows down. Beautiful Mackinac island is an unlikely place for a murder, but that just makes the story more intriguing. The characters are well drawn, and there's plenty not to like about them. The plot is full of twists and turns, and Nick has his hands full from start to finish. *Mackinac Murder* is a first rate murder mystery and a great read.
—Charles Cutter

Mackinac Murder has an interesting protagonist, a puzzling mystery and a setting worth exploring. What more do you want?
—Jeffrey Cohen, author of six mystery series, a screenwriter, and college professor

Praise for *Mackinac Murder*

Over the years I've read several of Dave Vizard's stories. They've all been good, but *Mackinac Murder* clearly raises the bar. The characters are crisp and believable, and the plot captures the reader. Bravo!
—Dennis Collins, author of *Nightmare* and *The First Domino*

Praise for *Murder for Treasure: Booty is in the Eye of the Beholder*

This book was a fast-paced, tons of fun, adventure to read! I easily became caught in the story and didn't want to put it down! Looking forward to more!
—Amber K., Goodreads

Enjoyed this easy-to-read mystery. Likable characters and interesting plot.
—Donna, Goodreads

Praise for *Murder, So Sweet*

I love a good mystery story with a twist thrown in.
—Carol, Goodreads

Page for page one of the most original and entirely involving books I read this year.
—Michigan in Books blog

Praise for *Murder, Key West Style*

Enlightening and intriguing. Spent a week in Key West recently which is why I was drawn to this book. The story is interesting and well written. I will have more compassion for the homeless in the future.
—Janet Griffin, Goodreads

Praise for *A Place for Murder*

Fast paced and entertaining! Enjoyable read! I really like the development of the characters. Exciting and definitely a page turner. Can't wait to see what Nick stumbles into next.
—Angela, Goodreads

Intriguing plot began with steam and rolled right along. Characters are interesting and defined. Clean, carefully structured and recommended for mystery fans and those looking for a good bed, beach, or waiting-for-my-appointment read.
—Cindy B., Goodreads

Praise for *Murder in the Wind*

Tangled web of suspense. Characters are believable and plot is interesting.
—Lisa Klein, Amazon

A fun twisty mystery placed in the Thumb area of Michigan. Newspaper reporter Nick Steele bumps into a mystery when a half-frozen ice fisherman stumbles into the interview he is conducting and says that his father is lost on the ice of Lake Huron.
—Diane Kohn, Amazon

Praise for *A Grand Murder*

A great story about a murder investigation by reporter Nick Steele and his companions from the *Blade*. Well worth the read for the armchair detective.
—Frederick Danysh, Goodreads

A great read, especially if you are familiar or want to be familiar with Mackinac Island and/or Michigan. The characters feel like they could be your neighbors; they are well developed and believable.
—Connor, Goodreads

Praise for *A Formula for Murder*

Be careful when you purchase this book. Make sure you have a day with nothing else planned. I started reading on Saturday morning and absolutely could not put it down until I finished it late afternoon. A spellbinding, extremely well written book.
—Konnie Gill, Amazon

A great story. Well written, good plot with enough twists, you only think (several times) that you've solved the mystery.
—Dee, Goodreads

Other books by Dave Vizard in the Nick Steele series:

A Formula for Murder
A Grand Murder
Murder in the Wind
A Place for Murder
Murder, Key West Style
Murder, So Sweet
Murder for Treasure: Booty is in the Eye of the Beholder

Mackinac Murder

Crude Intentions

For Sister S, Rosie, and Calypso

Copyright ©2024 by Dave Vizard

All world rights reserved

This is a work of fiction. Names, places, and incidents are the products of the author's imagination or are used fictitiously. Any resemblance to actual events or locales or persons, living or dead, is entirely coincidental.

No part of this book may be reproduced, stored in a retrieval system, or transmitted in any form or by any means electronic, mechanical, photocopying, recording or otherwise, without the prior consent of the publisher.

Readers are encouraged to go to www.MissionPointPress.com to contact the author or to find information on how to buy this book in bulk at a discounted rate.

MISSION POINT PRESS

Published by Mission Point Press
2554 Chandler Rd.
Traverse City, MI 49696

(231) 421-9513
www.MissionPointPress.com

ISBN: 978-1-961302-85-3 (Hardcover)
ISBN: 978-1-965278-18-5 (Softcover)

Library of Congress Control Number: 2024915322

Printed in the United States of America

MACKINAC MURDER
CRUDE INTENTIONS

By Dave Vizard

MISSION POINT PRESS

Chapter 1
Monday Morning
Bay City Blade

Nick Steele ditched his jacket in the hallway leading to *The Blade* newsroom from the back entrance. He hoped to disguise the fact that he was running late for work—again. Like usual, it didn't work.

The C-Man, boss Drayton Clapper, spotted Nick slinking toward his desk, acting nonchalant and indifferent. The managing editor grabbed a printout and a file from the pile atop his desk and confronted the reporter.

"Steele, who the hell do you think you're kidding?" he barked while marching toward the tardy employee's desk. "I've been waiting for you for twenty minutes. Don't bother sitting down and stuff your lame excuse for being late. I've got a story for you to jump on right now."

Nick looked up just in time to see the C-Man stuff the printout into his face. It was an Associated Press news story, fresh off the morning wire, about a Bay City man who died in a reported accident on Mackinac Island Sunday afternoon. The reporter squinted to read the first few paragraphs of the news story. The name of the deceased, Eric Stapleton, sounded familiar to Nick.

Clapper tossed a clippings file on the reporter's desk. "The name should ring a bell. That's his fat file from our library. Read the story, check the file, make some calls, and give me a piece for today's paper. You've got 90 minutes before first-edition deadline. Clock is ticking."

Nick eased into his chair as he studied the AP news story, opening the morgue file without looking at it. Stapleton died during a horse-riding accident on the famous resort island in Lake Huron between Michigan's upper and lower peninsulas. The wire service reported that Stapleton, who worked for the maintenance company that took care of the underwater Line 5 oil pipeline between the peninsulas, broke his neck from falling off a horse on the island.

As Nick turned to the morgue file, his buddy, Dave Balz—also late for work—strolled into the newsroom, unconcerned about hiding his tardiness. But today, Balz entered quietly, reserving his usual bluster and bravado. His timorous appearance prompted Nick to look up from the library file that he'd just finished scanning. He was about to speak but bit his tongue when he noticed that his friend sported a swollen, black eye.

"Whoa, what happened to you?" he asked from across the newsroom, tossing out the question on the lips of every reporter and editor within sight. The usual chatter and clamor lightened as eyes focused on the burley-but-bruised reporter. Nick considered adding a smart-ass remark about Dave crossing his current girlfriend but thought better of it; he could see that Dave was in no mood for levity, which ran against his usual flashy nature.

"I'll fill you in later," Dave said quietly, averting his eyes and moving slowly toward his desk. No one else pushed him for an explanation. Newsroom buzz rose back to normal. Clearly, something was wrong and troubling; Balz's spirit and panache were not damped easily.

Nick grabbed the Stapleton clip file and his coffee cup and hustled toward the breakroom, exchanging banter with other reporters on the way. As usual, the coffee stunk—way too strong and burned—but he needed his caffeine and resigned himself to blow against the steamy cup as he broke open the file. Instantly, the history of Eric "The Nutjob" flashed back to mind. The clips offered a wild tale.

Stapleton, the files declared, was the single dad who allowed his teen daughter to host a slumber party—alcohol included—in his apartment. Five fifteen-year-old girls from Central High School brought the hard-liquor beverage of their choice to his place for a sleepover. They ordered pizza and chips, turned up the music, and flirted with boyfriends on their phones.

In the morning, Stapleton counted heads, he'd told police, and discovered one girl, Sherry Conaway, was missing. She would not be seen again. That was just over three months ago. Nick shook his head. No wonder the police referred to Stapleton as The Nutjob. How stupid. How utterly irresponsible.

The rest of the news reports in the file described the fruitless search for Sherry. Police, family members, friends, Central High students, and the general public turned up no leads on the disappearance of Sherry Conaway. The clips indicated that everyone was mystified by what happened to the teen. It was as if she simply vanished. Stapleton was vilified by media, first for hosting an underage drinking party and then for losing track of Sherry. Nick folded the news clips neatly and put them back in the morgue file.

As he headed back to his desk, Nick thought about the calls he would have to make to localize the AP wire story about Stapleton's death on Mackinac Island. The C-Man's words, "clock is ticking," spurred him to get moving and work the phones.

But a rousing clatter in the newsroom reception area froze him at his desk. It was 8:31 a.m. and the front door of The *Blade* building was now open to the public. Nick could see that Helen, the frail 74-year-old newsroom receptionist, had assumed a karate defensive stance. She shuffled backward as the security guard came into view. He pushed against an advancing hulk of a man like an offensive lineman trying to protect an NFL quarterback. Phil, the security guard, fought furiously to hold off the intruder.

"Hold it right there," Phil demanded, pushing with both hands and leaning into the monster, who looked like Paul Bunyan—super tall, thick, and wide with short black hair and matching beard. He wore a red flannel shirt and well-worn jeans. The only things missing were an ax on his shoulder and a blue ox. "You are not authorized to enter the newsroom. I will be forced to call the police."

Lumbering Paul brushed Phil off with a sweep of his right arm like swiping at a toy. Helen continued shuffling backward, shifting her martial-arts stance and shrieking as forcefully as an aging grandma could. The big man paid her no attention and barked into the stunned and silent newsroom.

"My name is Ben Conaway and I want to talk to the person in charge. My daughter has been missing for more than three months and no one—not the cops or the press—gives a shit. And now the last man who saw my Sherry is dead."

No one responded. Reporters looked at each other, then turned to copy editors. Both groups looked for the C-Man, the person in charge. Lumbering Paul's booming rant grabbed his full attention. He rushed to Nick's desk.

"Steele, you're a big guy. Go see what he wants," Clapper said, light perspiration beading on his shiny forehead. His noggin swiveled back and forth from Nick to the giant standing next to Helen. "Calm him down and I'll call the police from my office."

Nick shook his head. "I'm not that big, and I'm not in charge. He wants you, not me."

Lumbering Paul growled and advanced closer, fists clenched and veins bulging from his neck. "I'm not going to ask again. My daughter is missing, and I need help. Don't make me start tossing desks out the windows. I'm not leaving until you hear me out."

That was enough. Nick stepped forward and held up his hand. At 6'2" and 220 pounds, the reporter was dwarfed by the Bunyan look-alike. "I will help you. There's no need for violence. You're frightening Helen and the rest of us. Let's talk. I'll get my notebook. Let's go to the conference room."

The big man's massive chest and shoulders eased like air slowly hissing out of a balloon. His fists opened, revealing thick fingers as long and sturdy as wrenches. He surveyed the newsroom and realized he'd spread terror.

"I'm sorry Helen," he said in an even voice, looking down at the trembling receptionist. "I didn't mean to scare you. I just want to find my Sherry. She's still out there somewhere. I know it. My wife is a crying wreck. I haven't slept in weeks. I gotta find her."

Helen dropped her karate chop hands and moved close to Lumbering Paul. She reached up and patted his bulging forearm. "You're Ben, right? Don't worry, Ben. If Nick Steele says he will help you, then you're going to be alright. Nick will know what to do."

For the first time, Conaway smiled. He thanked Helen and apologized again. Reporters and editors returned to their work. Nick asked the big man to follow him to the conference room. As they passed Phil, Conaway told the security guard he was sorry and asked if he was OK. Phil nodded, straightening his necktie.

Nick looked over his shoulder and told Conaway he was out of town on assignment when Sherry went missing. "You'll have to fill me in on the search. Give me the details. Everything you can remember."

They entered the conference room and Helen offered coffee. She disappeared and returned in minutes with a tray—two steaming cups and a box of Girl Scout cookies. "Double chocolate and mint, from my granddaughter," she declared proudly.

Nick jotted down all of Ben Conaway's contact information as well as the important numbers for his wife, Danielle, Sherry's mom. He asked who the family worked with at the Bay City Public Safety Department.

"That's been one of the problems," Ben said, staring into his coffee as if searching for answers. "We keep getting shuffled between detectives. It's like checkers only with cops moving on a board. Seems like each month, as we get further from when Sherry went missing, a new cop gets the case. I feel like we're slipping down a greased pole in terms of police priority. They keep saying they're doing everything possible to find her, but they've made zero progress. All I know is my Sherry is gone and I've got to find her."

What about Eric Stapleton? Nick wanted to know if the big guy believed Stapleton's story. Did he think the dad who hosted the party was on the level? Had Conaway dealt with Stapleton—dad to dad—before the fateful night?

"Yes, Sherry had been to slumber parties at his place before, going back to when the girls were in sixth grade," Conaway said. "But this was the first time, as far as we can tell, that booze was allowed. We were absolutely shocked when we learned about the pot and random guys showing up that night. We believed she was safe. We believed Sherry would be protected. Turns out, we were fools."

"And since your daughter went missing," Nick asked, "what has your relationship with Stapleton been like?"

"Honestly, I wanted to kill him," Conaway said flatly, no emotion in his voice whatsoever. "But I restrained myself because I think he's been the key to this whole thing. I believe he knows more than he's saying. He monitored the party. He knew how drunk the girls were. Hell, he even joined in—he admitted that to the cops. And he was the last one to see her. He swore that he saw her in a sleeping bag, drifting off to sleep. Then he crashes, with his snoot full of alcohol and pot, and Sherry goes missing.

"It stinks like a hog pen," he continued, "and now the bastard is dead. I heard it on WSGW this morning. That's when I did a U-turn on Center Avenue and drove straight here. You're my last hope."

Lumbering Paul paused and asked Nick a question. He wanted to know what the reporter had learned about Stapleton's death beyond the basic report he'd heard on his car radio. "What was he doing on Mackinac Island? They called it an accident—what kind of accident?"

Nick replied that he'd just begun looking into the basic report and had no details to share. "I was reviewing Stapleton's file when you roared into the newsroom," he said, chuckling. "You definitely know how to make your presence known. I need to get back to work so I can get you some answers."

The big guy's face reddened, and he folded his hands on the table. "I'm embarrassed by my behavior. I apologize for going ape shit out there, but you have to try and understand what this has done to me and Danielle. We're going nuts over our missing daughter. I refuse to give up. You gotta help us find her."

The reporter stood up and assured the ailing dad he would do his best. "I'm all over this now. I promise I'll dig into it and let you know what I find out as soon as I can."

Conaway offered his hand, swallowing Nick's right mitt as they shook. He walked Lumbering Paul to the stairway exit and returned to the newsroom. Thirty minutes had passed. He had one hour to deadline.

While Nick was tied up interviewing Ben Conaway, Clapper had directed Dave Balz to make the initial calls on Stapleton's death. Dave was on hold with the Mackinac Island police, a small unit of peace officers who had the monumental task of serving the community and thousands of tourists every day. Dave would collect all the details he could from the police.

Nick checked the big newsroom deadline clock just as Dave sent him a file with notes from his interviews. The two reporters had worked together for years and communicated with minimal words; they understood each other's thinking as well as their shorthand notes.

Before Nick started writing, he caught another glimpse of Dave's bruised and swollen eye. It made him wince, feeling his pain.

"Are you going to tell me what happened or am I going to have to guess?" he asked his longtime friend.

"I got clobbered by a cane," Dave said, averting his eyes. "You're not going to believe who clocked me. Let's grab a beer later for details."

Chapter 2

Monday Afternoon
Bay City's West Side

Nick discovered Eric Stapleton's duplex apartment tucked in a cozy neighborhood four blocks west of Euclid Avenue. He slowed his gold '68 Firebird down as he cruised past the two-story brick and aluminum building. Lights on, front door open slightly. A silhouette darted across the front picture window.

Great, Nick thought, perhaps a relative or friend of the dead man is checking out his place. He parked in front of the duplex and knocked on the front storm door. High heels clicked across the hardwood floor toward the front entry. A middle-aged woman with long dark hair grabbed the inside door handle and gripped it tight. She wore a light tan jacket, powder blue sweater, and dark jeans.

"Yes, how can I help you?" she asked, grimacing, her hand firmly holding the storm door.

Nick smiled and introduced himself as a reporter with the *Blade*. "I've been assigned to look into the death of Eric Stapleton. Are you a friend of his?"

"No, I'm his mother," she said, relaxing slightly. "Can I see some ID?"

Nick reached inside the breast pocket of his brown corduroy jacket and produced an identification card with his photo on it. He understood her hesitancy—can't be too careful when dealing with strangers. He heard the woman unlock the aluminum door and open it. She stood to the side, motioning him into the apartment's living room.

"I'm Louise Stapleton," she said softly. "I know I look like a mess, but I just heard from the police this morning about my son. I cried for two hours then thought I should come to his place to pick up some things.

A funeral home in St. Ignace will bring him back to Bay City tomorrow, or the next day."

Nick offered his condolences. He thought Louise looked as though she was fighting off another bout of tears.

"I understand this may not be a good time," he said, watching her face carefully. "I could reach out to you at another time if you like, but I just have a few questions about your son."

The woman forced a small smile. She had coal-black eyes, her pale skin smooth save for a few etched creases at the corners of her eyes. She wore no makeup. Black barrettes on each side of her head held back long, dark, uncombed hair.

"No, now is fine," she said, gesturing for Nick to take a seat on the small couch in the apartment's living room. Louise sat across from him in a wooden rocker. "It might be good for me to talk about it. My mind has been racing all morning, trying to sort out what happened and make sense of it."

Nick repeated the basic facts he and Dave had gleaned about her son's death from inquiries in the morning. He mentioned that the *Blade* would carry a basic news story in that day's paper. He said he was seeking additional detailed information for a more in-depth follow-up article. Louise nodded.

"Do the police have the report finished yet?" Nick asked. "Anything from the county medical examiner? I believe the island shares one with St. Ignace."

"Not yet," she responded, looking down at folded hands in her lap. "They said the medical examiner went to the accident scene on the island yesterday. They told me the report will take a bit; it's got to be reviewed and authorized before they release my son's body. They don't have many deaths on the island, so they have to go through all the procedures. The officer I talked with—they only have a handful of police up there—was kind and respectful."

The reporter asked if Louise knew where her son was staying on the island. He said he had learned Eric's company had a rental unit for employees to use.

"Yes, it's called the Jupiter Lodge," she replied. "He sent photos. Beautiful little place. So nice of his company to do that for workers."

Nick added the cottage name to his notes. "Now about your son's company … our files show he worked for a company called Underwater Solutions, based in Detroit. Is that true? What was his job and how long had he worked for them?"

"He was a supervisor, going on five years with Underwater Solutions. His company was under contract with Enbridge, the Canadian oil company that owns the pipelines between the two peninsulas. Eric and his team of divers and techs monitored the lines and helped with maintenance. It was a spring-to-fall job, so they were up there all summer. This was his third summer. I visited him up there, so did his daughter."

The mention of Jada offered Nick the opportunity to shift the interview from Mackinac Island to Bay City and the slumber party.

"Ah, yes, his daughter, Jada," he said, pausing from his notebook scribbling. "Do you happen to know if Jada invited friends to her dad's place for sleepovers? Was that common?"

"After Stephanie and Eric separated," she said, "he tried to strengthen the bond with his daughter. Eric's visitation weekends were all about her. He tried to do whatever she wanted. Her friends visited here quite frequently."

Nick leaned back in his chair, looking around the spacious living room. Large wraparound couch. Bean-bag chairs, rocker. Small game table on one wall with two chairs. Mega flatscreen on another wall. Coffee table on wheels. Everything but the couch was portable.

"So, this is where the girls spread out their sleeping bags?" he asked, gesturing toward the center of the room. "Combined kitchen and dining area on this floor, bedrooms upstairs?"

Louise nodded, adding that each floor had its own small bathroom. She stood up and walked to the large picture window, looking out at the small pines in the front yard. Jada's grandmother didn't say anything. Nick let the silence work for a few minutes, then pushed ahead.

"Did you happen to be here the weekend of the slumber party—the night Sherry Conaway went missing?"

Louise turned and faced Nick. "I was out of town and didn't hear about it until the day after. Eric and Jada were in a panic. The police were here and at Jada's mom's place. The Conaways, as you can imagine, were going crazy. And Sherry's dad—have you met him yet? He's as big and loud as a firetruck."

Nick nodded. He wanted to keep her talking about the aftermath of the slumber party. "Eric must have been horrified," he stated, then paused before making a second comment that worked as a question. "Asleep upstairs, it must have been shocking to see Sherry's empty sleeping bag in the morning."

Louise placed her fingers on her forehead. "Eric was beside himself. He told me how guilty he felt about not hearing Sherry leave. She left through the front door and left it unlocked. At first, he thought she woke up early and walked to the convenience store up the street for doughnuts. Then, the other girls woke up. When Sherry didn't return, her best friend revealed her plan to meet her boyfriend. That's when all hell broke loose and the search for Sherry was on."

The reporter recorded her words in his notebook, looking up as often as he could to study Louise's expressions as she spoke. She appeared truly troubled by what had occurred. He decided not to press her too hard for more details. Instead, he asked her for contact information so he could follow up with her after the investigation into Eric's death was complete.

Eric's mom gave Nick her cell number and said he could call anytime. He thanked her and said he planned to walk the neighborhood.

As he left the duplex, he noticed a set of eyes in parted curtains at a ranch-style home across the street. Nick could feel the eyes follow him as he walked toward Euclid Avenue, the main West Side Bay City highway. It was also where Sherry was supposedly going to meet her boyfriend. He hoped he'd remembered to lock up the Firebird when he parked it. He checked his watch to time the walk.

The fall air was cool, causing him to button his sports jacket. When Sherry went missing, it would likely have been a warm summer night. He made a note to check the record for the weather that night.

Today, it was cloudy. He hoped the forecast of mid-afternoon rain showers was wrong. The neighborhood, a mix of middle-class dwellings in good repair, was quiet except for a yipping dog in a fenced yard. He wondered if the dog had been outside during the night of the slumber party. Surely, it would have yapped at Sherry that night.

Nick also noticed that most of the homes had yard lights, probably motion-sensitive. No streetlights between the duplex and Euclid. He looked for surveillance cameras but spotted none. He figured the police would have checked for video when they canvassed the neighborhood after Sherry went missing, but he made a note to ask the cops about it.

Nick walked at a steady but unhurried pace. He guessed that Sherry, intoxicated and unfamiliar with the street—especially in the dark—would have been slow-footed. Some sections of the sidewalk had heaved, treacherous for a teen full of booze. When he arrived at Euclid, a fully lit thoroughfare with muffler shops and fast-food neon signs, the gas station where Sherry's boyfriend was supposed to have been waiting for her came into view. Twelve minutes from Eric's place.

As Nick strolled back to the Firebird, he surveyed the street. In the four-block stretch, he could see only one alley, designed for trash pickup and utility service. Could someone have been lurking in the alley when Sherry stumbled past? His mind raced. In less than 15 minutes, a tipsy teen vanished. Who watched her? Who snatched her so smoothly and cleanly that no ruckus occurred? No one heard? No one noticed? He had a boatload of questions for police.

Eric's duplex was now dark with curtains drawn, windows and doors shut. Louise had left. Nick looked across the street where, earlier, the ranch home had a set of eyes stuck in the front curtains. They were gone, but the entry door was open. Was it an invitation? The reporter's curiosity would not allow him to leave without inquiring. He crossed the street and approached the front door.

The aroma of hot apple pie slapped his face and instantly made him hungry. This was definitely an invitation. He reached for the doorbell but was stopped cold before he could push it. An aging woman, who could double for Betty Crocker complete with a flowery bib apron, appeared in the entryway. Her smile was as warm and sweet as the fragrance of the fruit pastry.

"Are you a police officer?" she asked. "I couldn't help but notice you meeting with Louise and then walking toward Euclid."

Nick identified himself and said he was working on a follow-up story for the *Blade*. He asked if he could ask her a few questions about her neighbor and the people on the block. She nodded eagerly, never allowing the smile to fade from her face. She pushed the door open and invited the reporter into her home.

"I'm Bea," she said, extending a tiny hand covered with white powder. Long, sandy-silver hair sat atop her head twirled into a bun. "Bea McDonald. Shocking about Eric. So much drama and trauma in that place."

She turned and marched toward the back of the home. The daisy-covered apron protected a powder blue dress. It was held tight with strings tied in a rabbit-ears knot in the middle of her back. "Follow me. I'm baking. Got to keep an eye on my pies."

The home felt toasty, like grandma's place. Overstuffed furniture, large family photos in husky wood frames. Hardwood flooring in the dining room with an enormous multicolor, rope area rug. An oak dining table with four chairs anchored the rug and center of the room. A matching oak buffet stood against a wall under a rectangular mirror.

The smell of hot apple pie intensified as they reached the country-style kitchen. Nick felt a smile stretch across his face as the sight of 14 pies covered a large butcher block in the center of the yellow room. Tucked in a corner were a tiny table and two bar stools. Bea used her apron, bunched in her right hand, to dust flour from a seat. She offered it to Nick.

"Would you like coffee?" she asked, still smiling. Her cheeks were naturally rosy, the same hue as her unpainted lips. "My last two pies are just about done."

"Coffee sounds good," Nick responded, settling onto the stool. He watched her pour a cup of steamy brew and set it in front of him. She then turned to her oven, using the apron with its thick front pockets as potholders to open the heavy metal door. A wave of warm air, scented with simmering apple and cinnamon, rolled across the kitchen. "That smells so good. You've got a real bakery in the works here."

Bea closed the oven. She told Nick she baked 16 pies—four cherry, four peach, four blueberry, and four apple—three times a week for the West Side Grocery over on Euclid. "When these have cooled, I'll box them for Ed, my hubby, to run to the store."

Moisture puddled under Nick's tongue. He fought off the urge to ask her if she and Ed owned a farm, surmising that it was corny, and she'd probably heard it a million times given their last name.

"Is Ed at work?" Nick asked, gulping down the puddle of saliva.

Bea nodded. "He helps out on his nephew's crop farm up near Kawkawlin three days a week."

"Wow, you two are busy," he said, loving the idea that the elderly McDonalds indeed had a farm. "Surprised you're not kicking your heels up in a Florida condo."

"Soon," she said. **Ding!** The oven timer chimed for attention. "We're finishing off our last child's student loan. We put three through college. We didn't want them to start their families under the weight of heavy debt. Next year, we're all done."

Bea used her apron to rescue the pies from the oven. Brown nectar oozed lightly from slits in dark golden crusts. She placed the last pie in its place on the butcher block, bumping the oven door closed with her hip. She stood up to admire her steamy fare.

"Now, I know where to buy fresh-baked pies," Nick said. "My wife, Tanya, would love all your fruit pies. Coming out of the oven, they're simply intoxicating."

Bea used the flowery apron to wipe her hands and went to a cupboard, pulling out a tall, sealed plastic pie holder. She opened it, revealing an apple pie with two slices missing. "Would you like a piece? It's from my last batch. I can warm it if you like."

Nick nodded, afraid he would drool if he opened his mouth. He swallowed hard and suggested they could talk over pie and coffee.

"It really saddened me to hear of Eric's accident," she said, placing two plates of warm pie and forks on the table. "Especially considering what poor Jada has gone through."

"Were you and Ed home the night of the slumber party?" He shoveled a fork full in his mouth. The flaky crust delicious, the fruit filling divine.

"We called the police," Bea said. "We're not prudes, but the party rose to a new level after midnight. Boys were coming and going, driving while drinking. They sat on the front step passing a jug and joints around. It got louder. We were afraid. We thought it was dangerous."

A little girl with curly brown hair barreled into the kitchen, burying her head in the apron. She turned her head to peek at Nick with one eye. "Gama, who's eating your pie?"

"It's OK, Calypso. This is Nick," she cooed, gently patting the preschooler on her back. She offered the youngster a forkful of pie. "He's just visiting. Are you done playing upstairs?"

The bite of pie disappeared from the fork, and Calypso bolted from the kitchen. She clamored up the stairs.

"How sweet," Nick said, sipping coffee. "How many grandkids?"

Bea held up four fingers, smiling as she chewed.

Nick nodded, then returned to the party. "Did you and Ed stay awake after the cops cooled down the action?"

"We went right to sleep once the music came down and the boys disappeared," she said, looking out the window over the kitchen sink. A large birch tree with golden leaves stood just in view outside. "We thought that was the end of it. When the police showed up in the morning, we were shocked. Then we were told a girl was missing."

Nick asked about Eric. Was he a good neighbor? Did the McDonalds like him? Was he friendly and helpful?

Bea nodded, using the apron to wipe her lips before speaking. "Yes, generally. Now, don't quote me in the paper on this because I would never speak poorly of the dead. But Eric had the oddest of visitors when Jada wasn't there.

"The men looked like they just crawled out of the woods—long greasy hair, untrimmed beards, pickup trucks with Confederate flags and gun racks in the back window," she continued, pushing wrinkles out of the apron in her lap. "The women were, shall I say, provocative."

Nick asked what she meant by provocative. "You mean like tight jeans, sweaters?"

Bea studied the reporter. "No, I won't mince words. They were whores. They looked like sluts and we watched him walk them to their cars and hand them money. Ed said I was jumping to conclusions, but I know a tramp when I see one."

Nick let that settle for a bit, then continued. "Were they all different? Any repeats?"

"More than a dozen different women, but one repeat," she said, eyeing the last chunk of pie on her plate. "She was a big girl, early 20s. Long, curly hair. Big gazongas, no bra. Big bottom. Tight jeans, multi-color hair."

Good detail, the reporter thought.

He scooped up the last crumb of crust onto his fork before nudging the plate away and scribbling in his notebook. He thanked Bea for the delicious treat and the information, giving her his card and asking her to call if she thought of anything else or noticed suspicious activity at Eric's place.

Nick checked his watch as he hustled across the street to the Firebird. He'd scored a key interview at the Bay City cop shop and didn't want to be late for the appointment.

Nick left the McDonalds' home with three impressions: Bea was keenly observant, she knew how to bake great pie, and the woman used her apron like it was the Swiss Army knife of kitchen ware.

The Bay City Public Safety Department was located just a few blocks from the *Blade* building. Nick parked in his usual place and walked to the cop shop. It had rained lightly, and sunshine now warmed the cool, fall afternoon.

Lieutenant Barbara Winkler was the latest officer who'd had the Sherry Conaway file land on her desk. It had been passed to her through a long line of succession: first a sick leave, then a retirement, and finally a transfer. It was one of a dozen active Missing Persons filed on her cluttered desk. She had agreed to meet Nick for 15 minutes.

"How did you end up with the Conaway story?" Winkler asked, looking away from her computer screen. Even sitting down she looked tall and lanky. Her braided blonde hair was pinned to the back of her head, only a faint trace of makeup. Nick guessed she was about 50. "What happened to Sheila Belford? She was chasing this story and doing a good job with it."

"Maternity leave," Nick responded, "and I was standing nearby when Ben Conaway stormed into our newsroom, demanding action for his missing daughter."

Winkler grunted. She'd been on the receiving end of Conaway's wrath herself. "He's a load. Can't say as I blame him. This case has everybody scratching their heads. Sherry simply disappeared that night and we've got nothing."

Nick said he'd read all the *Blade's* news stories about her disappearance and the investigation. He asked the lieutenant if she could share any more information on a background, not-for-publication basis.

The officer shook her head, her face as solemn as a gravedigger's. "Sorry to say, but there's really not much more. The boyfriend Sherry was supposed to meet had been the prime suspect, but he checks out and so does his story. No cameras in that neighborhood and the ones at businesses on Euclid don't show her walking to the gas station.

"We talked to every neighbor and came up empty-handed," Winkler continued. "The girls at the slumber party were all pretty drunk and high and remember nothing, except that Sherry had whispered and giggled about meeting her boyfriend. The party host, Eric Stapleton, had joined in on the drinking and toking—said he was asleep upstairs when the girl slipped out of the house. We got nothing that says different. And now he's dead."

"What about the tip hotline or the searches—anything promising?"

Winkler formed a big zero with her fingers.

A far-fetched question caught in Nick's mind. "Any chance you think Sherry Conaway was a runaway? Could she have created the meeting-boyfriend scenario to divert attention away from her meeting someone to bolt from town?"

"That theory was considered, but we couldn't find any preparation by Sherry to support the idea. The girl didn't even take her purse when she left. Just grabbed her cell phone and walked out wearing sweats and flip-flops. Left the front door unlocked like she was coming back. She walked into the night and fell off the radar."

Winkler checked her watch, telling Nick without words that his allotted time was about to expire. He pushed harder, hoping to get the internal police thinking about the case. "So, if she's not a runaway, then what's your working theory? How are you working it now that a quarter year has lapsed?"

The cop gave Nick a hard look, sizing him up. She pushed her chair away from her desk and stood up as if she was ready for a summation.

"What I'm about to say is not for publication," she said, crossing her arms.

"Feels like a kidnapping, and the longer Sherry remains missing the grimmer it gets for her. If she was snatched off the street, she may not even be in the state anymore. And, of course, there's always the possibility she's no longer alive. The family has been involved in more than a dozen searches in every corner of the county with no evidence—not even a flip-flop found. We're staying positive and chasing every lead but we're at a dead end right now."

Nick nodded and thanked her. He said the Conaways had asked him to look into the disappearance. He added that he'd just begun to dig into it and would stay in touch with her.

As he left the cop, the reporter tossed what he'd learned from Winkler around in his mind. Kidnapped and long gone, or dead? He was surprised that the police were not getting more tips from the public—not even dead-end tips—and the searches had produced nothing. No trace of Sherry Conaway.

Nick's cell phone pinged. It was a text from Dave. "Meet me at Jake's Corner Bar. Got a tip for you. I'm thirsty." The note produced a smile. The two buddies had worked together on dozens of stories at the *Blade* over the past 20 years. Dave had great reporting instincts and he knew everybody in town. If he had a tip, Nick wanted to hear it.

Jake's, a rehabbed hole-in-the-wall bar, had become a popular East Side, after-work watering hole, located just two blocks off the Saginaw River. Nick quickened his pace as it started to rain lightly, his breath forming clouds in the chilly air. He sent Tanya a text that he planned to meet Dave and invited her to join them at Jake's. As a student counselor at Bay City Central High, she would have the latest on Sherry Conaway's disappearance from the school.

Jake's was dim and noisy. Tables filled as the clock ticked toward 5 o'clock, the stools at the bar already filled. The chatter and laughter drowned out the jukebox, which featured classic oldies. Nick paused in the doorway, allowing his eyes to adjust to the lack of light. He spotted Dave at a small table near the front.

A bottle of Labatt stood guard in front of an empty chair. Nick filled it and asked Dave what was up. "What's your hot tip?"

Dave held his beer bottle against the side of his swollen eye.

"Hey, this cold beer is therapy for my bruised face—any doctor would surely approve," he said.

"Here's to more therapy," Nick responded, raising his beer in a toast of clinking bottles. "So, what have you picked up?"

"Not sure how hot the tip is but I got it from my never-been-wrong 9-1-1 dispatcher," Dave said, rolling the bottle to a new part of the shiner. "She says the cops will never say it publicly, but they believe Sherry Conaway is dead. Privately, they're just waiting for her body to wash up on shore somewhere."

Nick took a long sip from his beer. "Hmmm. Why are they so sour on her not being found? Why does your contact say they think she's dead?"

Dave took a long chug from his therapy device. "Two reasons. If Sherry was kidnapped for ransom, the family would have received a list of demands by now. They've heard nothing. And second, Sherry's trail is stone cold. No sightings. No evidence has turned up. Absolutely nothing from family or friends."

Nick nodded, disheartened by Dave's information. The dispatcher

Dave whispered with had always proven reliable. He hoped she was wrong this time.

As the two friends talked, Tanya entered Jake's through a side door. Instantly, a hush fell across the area of the bar as she glided through it—dressed in white, matching high heels, her blonde hair bouncing with every move. Stunning. Nick held a chair for her and gave her a peck on the cheek.

Tanya greeted Dave and said she was sorry about his injury. "That eye hurts me just looking at it."

Immediately, a server stopped by to take her order. Nick had seen this a dozen times in places where guys waited tables. They wanted to assist her, hear her voice, see her smile. She obliged with a wide grin and asked for a vodka martini on the rocks, extra dry.

Nick told Tanya about what Dave had learned from his dispatch source, then recounted his afternoon collecting information in Stapleton's neighborhood.

Tanya's martini arrived and she took a sip, savoring the cold vodka. Dave asked her for the latest word from Central on the disappearance of Sherry Conaway. She said news of the accidental death of Jada Stapleton's dad had rekindled discussion of the slumber party and Sherry Conaway.

"It's funny. Now, students are wondering out loud if Sherry didn't take off on her own," Tanya said. "Some said she'll probably turn up in a rock band out in Seattle, or on a surfboard in California. They seem to think she will reappear after going on some incredible adventure. They don't seem to understand that so many missing persons end up in a bad way—especially after this much time."

"My mind keeps coming back to the boyfriend," Nick said, taking a long swig from his beer. "Supposedly his story checks out. Maybe we should look at him and his friends a little harder. Could you do that Dave? I'm heading up to Mackinac Island in the morning."

Dave nodded. "Love to. I gotta hunch this is going to be another good story. Can you clear it with the C-Man? I don't have the patience to deal with Clapper right now. I'm already battered and bruised—I don't need the verbal abuse."

Nick decided the time was right to ask Dave about what happened with his swollen, multicolored eye. "You mentioned you got hit by a cane. Please explain."

Dave's face turned sullen as if he had been suddenly defeated. He looked his dear friends in the eyes and leveled them with a blow of his own. "My mom clobbered me. She had another moment when she didn't recognize me. I was at her place helping her, and she just hauled off and smacked me with her cane. She screamed that I was an intruder attacking her."

Dave went silent, staring at his half-empty beer, scratching at its label with his thumbnail. Nick and Tanya looked at each other at a loss for words.

Mrs. Balz had recently turned 92. Physically, she was still in good shape, but she had begun to slip mentally, prompting her move from her home to an assisted-care facility. Dave's late sister had been their mom's primary caretaker until her passing from a heart attack at 75 a year ago. Since then, the decline in his mom had been steep.

"She hasn't called me by name in months," Dave said, his voice cracking. "Now, it's, 'Hey, you!' or, 'Hey, buddy!' Can you imagine? She doesn't even know who I am anymore. Clubbing me because she thought I wanted to hurt her is a new low.

"I need some air," Dave said, standing up suddenly and bolting for the door. Tanya urged Nick to go to his friend.

Outside, Dave leaned against a street sign and wept into the palm of his hand. Nick reached for his friend's shoulder.

"Your mom doesn't mean it, Dave," he said, pulling him close. "She's not herself. I know it hurts, but she still loves you. She's just struggling with herself right now."

Dave cried openly, turning to face Nick. They hugged, tears now welling from Nick's eyes. Dave sniffed hard and blubbered: "She's never hit me, in my whole life, besides maybe a swat on the bottom. It's killing me to see her like this."

Tanya joined the guys, hugging them both on the sidewalk in full public view. She had not seen the two pals hurting like this before. She tried to console Dave and support her husband. The three huddled, swaying slightly.

After several minutes of this group hug, Mrs. Balz's son took a huge breath, sniffing up tears and frustration about his mom. That's when the old Dave returned: "OK, OK, thank you so much. Can't tell you how much your support means to me. But our beers are getting warm in there and we're getting cold out here. Back to the party!"

The threesome rushed inside, toasted their friendship, and ordered food.

"Hang in there, my friend," Nick said. "Your mom is not the same, but enjoy her as much as you can while she's still with us. And keep us posted. We're here for you."

Chapter 3

Tuesday Morning
Mackinac Island

The nearly three-hour drive from Bay City to Mackinaw City on Interstate 75 can be long and somewhat monotonous until reaching the rolling hills and heavily wooded stretches of highway after passing through West Branch.

Nick used the early and tedious stretch of this drive to set up interviews on Mackinac Island for the afternoon. He also decided to try and interview Eric Stapleton's ex-wife, Stephanie, who still carried her married name despite the fact that she'd been divorced from Stapleton for nearly a year and separated for two. Her contact information had been on file in the newsroom since the search for Sherry Conaway began.

It was early in the morning, but the reporter hoped he could catch Stephanie before she left for work. She answered her cell phone on the second ring. Nick identified himself and told her he was working on a follow-up story about her ex-husband's death.

"May I ask you a few questions about Eric?" Before she could respond, Nick inquired about Jada. "How's your daughter doing? She's so young, this has all got to be difficult for her."

"She's having a tough time," Stephanie said without hesitation, quickly adding, "First her girlfriend ends up missing from a disastrous slumber party and now her dad, who everybody in town attacked for allowing the party, dies in a freak accident on a resort island. That's a lot for a teen to handle. She's been crying all morning."

Nick sensed that Stephanie wanted to talk. He asked about the freak accident. Could she reveal what island police had told her? Was her ex-husband vacationing when he died?

The reporter could hear a lighter igniting, then a long inhale before

Stephanie continued. "His company has a long-term rental cottage on the island that employees take turns using while they're up there working in the Straits," she said, exhaling long and slow. "Her dad told Jada he had the place for the next two weeks. She was going to visit him up there this coming weekend. I don't know anything else about the cottage."

Nick pressed her for details about the accident. "Did the police give you details?"

"What I've gotten so far is sketchy," she said, adding that she remained skeptical. "I mean, who dies on Mackinac Island? You go there, you eat fudge, get a carriage ride, buy some trinkets, and come home. Eric liked to ride and was good at it. How does he die falling off a horse?"

She was talkative, and he decided to press for more, asking Stephanie about their marriage. "Sounds as though you still have feelings for Eric. Was your divorce difficult? Must have been hard for Jada."

Stephanie did not respond immediately, and the reporter did not push. After a few moments, she gushed.

"I'm going to say something here, but I don't want to see it in print. Do you understand me? Acknowledge, please."

"Yes, I hear you."

"Sure it was difficult for our daughter, but I had to get away from Eric for Jada's sake. He's got a dark side. He's kinky—I mean, sicko kinky and cruel. Bad friends, bottom feeders. Yuck! I didn't want Jada growing up in the same house with that. I couldn't risk it, so we split."

"Thanks for your candor," he said, hoping she would volunteer more.

"Now, I don't want to see that in the paper—you got that? I don't want to read that Jada's mom says her dead dad was a deranged, sick puppy."

"Yup, I got it."

"I'm only saying this because there's some weird shit going on here with Eric and somebody has got to get to the bottom of it. I'm trying to help you, but don't screw me—don't violate the trust I put in you."

Stephanie then went silent.

Nick thanked her and asked if he could call her again to talk more.

"I'll think about it, but don't press your luck."

"Good luck with Jada," he responded. "I wish the best for both of you."

It was a good interview and Nick was glad he was able to connect with Stephanie. He took it as a good omen for the day ahead and continued setting up interviews as the Firebird rumbled up I-75.

Authorities contacted by cell were friendly and cooperative, which came as a bit of a surprise. Island bigwigs had a notoriously protective attitude when it came to the resort's image and reputation. They spend millions of bucks every year putting a spit shine on the island's reputation as a fabulous and luxurious refuge. It's a place for great fun, food, lodging, vistas, and memories—not a place where people die while at play.

The new island police chief agreed to meet Nick as soon as he arrived. Debra Westover, a retired captain from the police force in Lansing, Michigan's capital, said the official report on Eric Stapleton's death was still being compiled but she would present the information gathered so far for the reporter.

A manager from Underwater Solutions had also agreed to chat with Nick at the cottage the company rented for employees while they worked in the Straits of Mackinac. Jerry Meade said he planned to gather Stapleton's personal effects at the cottage to send to the deceased's mother.

Following that, there was the interview with the day manager of the horseback-riding stable Stapleton regularly used when he was on the island. The manager, who knew Stapleton from his frequent visits and rentals, said she would show Nick where the fatal accident took place.

And, finally, before Nick caught the ferry back to the mainland at the end of the day, he would meet Hank, the horse handler and old friend he'd met during the last island story he wrote ten years ago, for a cold beer at the Mustang Lounge.

As the ferry to Mackinac Island sped out of Mackinaw City, Nick settled into his seat for the twenty-minute boat ride. Vacationers on the ferry jostled in their seats to take photos of the majestic five-mile Mackinac Bridge, linking Michigan's upper and lower peninsulas. Families, couples, friends of all ages—just one boatload of an estimated one million visitors per season—wiggled in their seats with anticipation.

Nick winced as a man with an Ann Arbor shirt held onto a woman's waist as she hung over the ferry's bulkhead trying for a lifetime picture of Mighty Mac. At the same time, Ann Arbor man's clone, age about six, worked busily at his feet tying his sneaker shoes together. The reporter grinned, thinking about how that was going to end.

A mist of cold Lake Huron water shot off the bow of the ferry, giving Nick a chill and drenching his graying moustache. He brushed the fresh water away with a finger and moved toward the center of the ferry for the remainder of the ride.

Chief Westover, a stout woman dressed in a blue and yellow uniform of short-sleeve polo shirt and khaki dress shorts, greeted Nick on the ferry dock. She straddled a bicycle with two helmets dangling from the handlebars. At his request, she rented Nick a three-speed with a flat carriage rack over the rear wheel. The island was famous for its non-motorized vehicle status (except for emergency equipment and winter snow machines). Part of the Mackinac charm is the notion that transportation is limited to walking, biking, or horses, so no noisy, smelly engines at work on the streets.

The two dodged tourists as they rode toward police headquarters, home to a single jail cell and seven full-time officers who spend most of their time chasing shoplifters, pickpockets, and street scammers.

"Come on inside," the top cop said, her voice husky and her breath short. A pack of Marlboros poked out from her shorts pocket. She strode to her desk and picked up a spiral notebook. "I don't have a lot for you, but I'll give you what I've got."

Nick reached inside his sports jacket breast pocket and clicked on his recorder. The chief dug around in the lap drawer of her desk and produced black-rimmed glasses, so thick the bifocals were detectable.

She flipped open the notebook, ticking off a list of facts she felt comfortable sharing:

- Deceased is Eric D. Stapleton, age 46, of Bay City.
- Mr. Stapleton rented a saddle horse at the Sunny Day riding stable at 10 a.m. on Sunday. The stable is located next to the Mackinac State Historic Park. It was a horse the deceased had ridden several times in the past. He was presented with a list of riding rules and encouraged to wear a riding helmet.

- Mr. Stapleton was one of six individual riders who was escorted into the state park by a guide from the stable. Once inside, each rider followed a different trail.
- At about 12:30 p.m. horseback riders discovered the accident. They called 9-1-1 and notified the stable.
- Emergency rescue personnel and a police officer responded at 12:50 p.m. to the call and discovered Mr. Stapleton, his right ankle tangled in the saddle's stirrup, unresponsive. A blood trail indicated he'd been dragged about 100 feet.
- The area of the accident was secured, and the medical examiner in St. Ignace was called to the scene.
- The medical examiner arrived at 2 p.m. and observed the accident scene. He examined Mr. Stapleton. It was determined the deceased fell from the horse and suffered a broken neck and fractured shoulder blade. Mr. Stapleton was declared dead at the scene. An abrasion to the head occurred when the deceased was dragged by the horse.

Chief Westover closed the notebook and set it on her desk. "That's it in a nutshell. Final report still under review."

"I made my own notes from your narrative, but a copy would make them accurate," Nick said.

The chief shook her head. "These are my personal notes. I can't give you a copy. When the final report is completed, I'll make sure you get it. If you like, you can read your notes back to me and I can confirm or correct them."

Odd, Nick thought, but he was glad to get what he could. He started to read back his notes when the chief interrupted. She suggested they go outside to a shaded picnic table where she could smoke a cigarette while they talked.

The chief fired up a crooked cigarette pulled from the crunched pack in her pocket, a warm, light breeze from Lake Huron whisking the smoke away from the two-bench table. Nick went back through his notes and asked questions as he made corrections and side notes.

"Tell me about the horse," he said. "Was it big? Young? Familiar with the trail? You indicated Stapleton had rented it before. Do you know how many times?"

"You can get more detailed information from the stable. I'm sticking with my notes and not elaborating on that."

The reporter continued. "You said Stapleton was given a helmet. Was he wearing the helmet when his body was discovered?"

The chief flipped the notebook back open and studied the pages, pausing to draw on the cigarette. She blew smoke out the side of her mouth. "Says here the helmet was tied to the saddle by its straps. Again, he was a frequent rider. The stable can give you more on that."

"You said the riders split up once inside the park. Did any riders see Stapleton between the time they went into the park and when his body was discovered 90 minutes later?"

"We have no reports of anyone encountering the deceased while he was riding. I'm not surprised—there's 2,500 acres of trails and roads. Have one of the guides take you out there. Beautiful and wide open."

"One hundred feet of blood trail from an abrasion sounds like a lot to me. That's a heck of a scrape to the head. Were there any other injuries that would produce blood and contribute to the trail?"

The chief stubbed out her smoke on the heel of her shoe and reached for another one in her pocket. She cupped her hand around her lighter as she held it to the tip of yet another crooked cigarette. She puffed hard, smoke flooding through her nostrils as she exhaled.

"Don't have anything more on that," she said, examining the cigarette as if it wasn't working well. "I gotta stick with what I gave you."

"What about the body?" the reporter asked, closing his notebook, and sticking it in his pocket. "Where is Mr. Stapleton's body now? Was an autopsy completed?"

The chief did not consult her notes to respond. "An autopsy was not deemed necessary—the body was transported to the Farewell Funeral Home in St. Ignace where arrangements are being made to send it to Bay City."

Nick thanked her and asked if he could call her with follow-up questions.

"Sure, you can ask, and I'll do my best to get what you need," she said, flicking ashes off the cigarette. "Leave a message if you can't get me direct. We'll be pretty busy from now until things start shutting down here in late October."

"How long before the official report is completed and released?"

"Dunno. It's got to go through channels," she said. "Once everyone is satisfied, it will go out."

Nick hopped on his bike and asked the top cop for directions to the cottage Stapleton's company rented.

The chief produced a tourists' map from her hip pocket. She pointed to the west side of the four-square-mile island.

"The cottage is on a trail just off the eight-mile paved road that encircles the island. It'll be a fifteen-minute ride if you don't run into much foot or horse traffic and the headwind off the lake isn't too stiff."

Nick pedaled through the main-street commercial district, dodging horse carriages, walkers, bikers, and gawkers funneling in and out of high-end gift stores, restaurants, pubs, and fudge shops, which dot the thoroughfare.

As he rode, Nick thought about the research he'd done the night before on Eric Stapleton's company, Underwater Solutions, and the oil pipelines that run along the bottom of the lake between the upper and lower peninsulas.

The four-mile-long pipelines, called Line 5 and owned by a Canadian company, have been ensnarled in controversy for years. Millions of barrels of oil and natural gas flow through Line 5. Located west of Mighty Mac, they were built in the early 1950s. Native American tribes in northern Michigan have regularly opposed the pipelines because they feared a potential leak would foul the Straits of Mackinac, considered a sacred region, and the fisheries. Clean-water advocates, sometimes called the water lovers, joined the tribes in opposition to the pipelines as they aged and outlived their projected life expectancies.

When an anchor from a passing ship dented, but did not rupture, the pipelines in 1989, the controversy erupted, and tree-hugging environmentalists joined the water lovers in protest. In reaction, the oil company increased pipeline inspections, maintenance protocols, and monitoring, declaring the pipelines safe and necessary for the economies of Canada and the United States.

Underwater Solutions, a Detroit company, was contracted by the oil company to help as part of its 24/7, year-around plan for upkeep. Stapleton was hired by Underwater Solutions five years ago, first as a frogman, surveying the lakebed under the pipeline, and was later promoted to supervisor.

Stapleton and Jerry Meade were hired about the same time. They had been co-workers and friends since they first started diving together to monitor the pipeline, a precarious job. The depth of the water varies in the Straits, running from 50 to 250 feet. The lakebed is not flat like a pool table; it has many peaks and valleys, and the pipeline needs strong support structures in many areas between the peninsulas. Additionally, critics say the vigorous water currents of the Straits have eroded the lake bottom under the pipeline in several areas over the decades, causing severe stress on it.

As Nick rolled up, Meade stepped out on the front deck of the cottage. Dressed in shorts, sandals, and a light blue fleece pullover, he smiled and waved his right hand.

"Hey, buckaroo—you Nick?" he asked as a gusty wind fluffed his shaggy blonde hair. The reporter thought he looked like Ryan Gosling in need of a haircut and a major trim of bushy sideburns. Dangling from his neck were enough gold chains to make a rap star jealous. "I've been waiting for you. Thought you got lost."

Nick leaned his three-speed up against a purple plum tree in the front yard. He greeted Meade and said he took his time, enjoying the bike ride. He said he circled the Grand Hotel twice just to absorb its majesty and magnitude.

"Haven't visited the Grand in years and forgot just how terrific the place is. The grounds are fabulous," he said, pausing to take in the view from the cottage, set up on a ridge in a wooded area overlooking Lake Huron and the Mackinac Bridge. "Wow! This is like a postcard. I can see why you like it."

The smile remained riveted to Meade's face. "Yup. Nice benny from the company. They gave us a choice of rentals in Mackinaw City, Escanaba, or here. We picked here. Great place for the fams and a great place to party with the girlies when the fams go home."

Nick climbed the steps to the deck. The two men shook hands and Meade invited Nick inside. "Right this way, buckaroo. I'll show you around. I've just about got all of Eric's personal stuff packed up. Not that much really. Made me sad," he continued, the big grin fading.

A small suitcase rested atop the dining table, its top open. Clothing and a bulging shaving kit topped the bag filled with papers and personal effects. Meade pulled a framed photo of he and Stapleton off the fireplace mantel. It was a summer scene of the two outside the cottage, happy with drinks in hand toasting each other, Mighty Mac in the background. He showed it to Nick, who handed it back and asked about the tall walking stick in Meade's hand. "Hand-carved hickory?"

"Yup, a beauty. Great for hiking hills. Lot of great times up here," he said. "This is from just a few months ago. And now, poor Eric is gone. What a horrible accident."

Nick studied the photo. "Just curious. Why is Eric wearing a turtleneck in mid-summer? Looks out of place."

The grin returned. "Me and Eric, well, we're what you might call chick magnets. The turtleneck is covering up collateral damage—if you know what I mean."

Nick felt his stomach turn. Chick magnets? Collateral damage? Nasty—suddenly a shower seemed appropriate. He didn't respond, placing the photo on top of the pile in the suitcase. He followed Gold Chains on a tour through the rest of the cottage.

As they walked, Meade pointed out features of the place. He snagged items he thought should be added to Stapleton's suitcase. "I told Eric's mom I'd get Eric's stuff to her as soon as I could. I'm almost done packing. Would you mind taking it with you back to Bay City?"

The reporter said he'd be happy to make the delivery. "I met Louise yesterday. Understandably, news of her son's death devastated her. I'd be happy to help. She's a very nice lady. I figured we'd talk again."

The two stopped in the kitchen near the side entry when Meade spotted two hoop key chains hanging on hooks next to the door. One chain contained six keys, the other one a solitary key.

"Now, the six keys are for the cottage and the two sheds out back," he said. Then he plucked the hoop with the single key off the hook. "This one here I'm not familiar with—must be Eric's." He tossed it into the suitcase. It clunked when it hit the framed photo.

"As a supervisor, what did Stapleton oversee?" Nick asked.

Gold Chains said his friend organized the maintenance schedule for divers and made sure they followed strict protocols. "It's hour-by-hour observation of a four-mile expanse—all at various depths underwater. Everything had to be documented. Pressure packed. Lots of people watching every move we made."

Nick nodded. "Sounds like a pretty stressful job. Did Stapleton seem satisfied?"

The grin returned. "The pay is great, and the bennies terrific," he said looking around the cottage. "Who wouldn't want to be here on your downtime in spring, summer, and fall? Beauty and privacy."

Nick strode to the massive picture window overlooking the lake. "I get it. Sweet. This place is remote and quiet. No neighbors within view."

"You got that right, buckaroo," Gold Chains said, joining the reporter at the window. "The chicks can cry and scream all they want, and nobody hears a thing."

Stunned, Nick turned and faced Meade. Was he joshing, or speaking from experience? Braggadocio, or statement of fact?

Meade jabbed Nick in the shoulder, then flashed the sickening grin. "Just kidding, buckaroo, just kidding. Lighten up. I'll bet you've had your fun with the ladies, huh?"

The reporter didn't respond. He didn't want to engage Gold Chains in locker room, jock-snapping banter. Instead, he headed for the door.

Gold Chains zipped up the suitcase. He helped Nick secure it with bungee cords to the rack on the back of the three-speed bike. The two shook hands and Nick asked if he could call if other questions arose. Meade gave Nick his card and urged him to use the contact info anytime.

Nick rode toward the riding stable, feeling unsettled by the slime dripping from Jerry Meade.

Chapter 4
Tuesday Afternoon
Auburn

Dave Balz agreed to meet Sherry Conaway's boyfriend in Auburn's Machelski Park at 1 p.m. Mark Williams, a Western High School senior, asked for the meeting to take place in a public area and only on the condition that he could record the interview. The young man's parents had already signed off on the meeting, telling Balz over the phone that their son had nothing to hide and had cooperated fully with all efforts to find his sweetheart.

Dave readily agreed to both conditions. He was eager to meet the young man and hear, firsthand, his version of events on the night when Sherry went missing. The reporter had already spoken with the Western High student counselor, a friend and colleague of Tanya's, and Mark's employer, a Bay County landscaper who put the young guy to work whenever he had free time from school and family obligations.

Both raved about Mark's authenticity. Like law enforcement authorities, they said the lad was a straight shooter—honest, trustworthy, dependable, loyal, earnest, and hardworking, a real Boy Scout in so many ways.

When Dave rolled up in his green, hand-painted, barking Ford F-150, Mark was already waiting for him, sitting on a bench in the small city park. A shower of sunshine burst through the heavy cloud cover overhead as the F-150 parked. The bushy-haired and bearded reporter, looking rustic with faded jeans and a tan Carhartt canvas jacket, greeted the Western senior with an outstretched hand.

The lad checked Dave out, focusing his attention on the reporter's shiner, still a veritable rainbow of various shades of blue, purple, and yellow.

"I hate to do this, but could I see some identification?" Mark asked, slowly raising his meaty paw to shake with Dave. "Forgive me, but when I agreed to meet you on the phone, a different vision of a news reporter popped to mind. You look more like my boss—without the black eye."

Dave whipped out his wallet and produced a *Bay City Blade* ID card. "No problem. I get that a lot, I don't mind." He used the tip of his right index finger to lightly tap the side of his bruised eye, dismissing it as "a clumsy accident. They don't call me Grace for nothing."

They both laughed, easing the tension that shrouded the outset of their meeting. Dave studied the high school senior—a potential Eagle Scout, indeed. Short dark hair, chiseled features, tall and slender in tan khaki pants, a blue sweater and a Western High varsity jacket, the W adorned with medals for track, cross-country, and baseball.

The young man held up his recorder so Dave could see it. The reporter nodded, then produced his own recorder. "We match. Let's start them, identify ourselves, and note the time and date."

They did. Dave began by saying that he and Nick Steele, also with *The Blade*, were looking into the disappearance of Sherry Conaway at the request of her parents. This meeting, he continued, was strictly for information-gathering purposes.

"I know you've been through this process—perhaps repeatedly—with law enforcement," Dave said, crossing his legs and stretching one arm out on the back of the park bench. "But we're not cops, we don't represent the authorities, and Nick and I are coming in on this months after Sherry disappeared. So, please bring us up to date and tell us what happened from your point of view."

"Fair enough," Mark said, stretching his long legs out and crossing them at the ankles. He set the recorder between them on the bench and put his hands in the side pockets of the varsity jacket, warming them against a cool, fall breeze. "Sherry and I had been seeing each other for more than a year when she disappeared."

Mark recounted the events of the night, pretty much echoing the police and news accounts that Dave and Nick had reviewed. When the lad started talking about waiting for Sherry at the gas station on Euclid in the early morning hours, he became emotional, stopping several times to collect himself as he recalled the minutes, which, at the time, he maintained felt like hours to him.

"I called her cell, texted, and snap-chatted her several times," the young man said, his voice breaking. He pulled his legs in and pushed his behind to the edge of the bench, holding his face in his hands. His eyes watered. "She didn't respond. I waited and waited. Finally, I got out of my car and walked to the intersection. She was nowhere in sight. I called out her name into the dark, but nothing."

Dave waited for a moment for Mark to recover. He asked why the teen didn't drive to the apartment and check on Sherry before he left.

Mark sucked snot back hard and looked Dave in the eye. "She insisted that I stay away from the house because guys had been there earlier—guys with pot and booze, and the cops had been called. Sherry was thinking of me. She didn't want me walking into something that might hurt my reputation."

Dave asked why the sweethearts were meeting so late. Why not simply wait until the next day to get together?

The young man nodded, his big hands joined under his chin, elbows on knees. He chewed the knuckle on his left index finger. "Really, that's what we should have done, but I was scheduled to leave on a week-long college tour in the morning. At the time, I had several sports scholarships on the table—for track. I needed to make some decisions about school, so I was leaving to visit colleges in Michigan and Ohio."

"O-hi-o?" Dave intoned, arching an eyebrow at the idea of going to rival schools in a neighboring state. "Really?"

Mark snorted a laugh at the comment. "Yeah, well, not really. But I needed to check them out. At least that was the plan. When Sherry disappeared, I called off the college tour to search for her. I got lots of time to run track later. Right now, me and my friends and family, we're all focused on finding her."

Dave returned to the night in question. "When you last talked, what time was it?"

The young guy said their last exchange was a text message just after 1 a.m. He told Dave the message said Sherry was waiting for the last girlfriend in the living room to fall asleep, then she'd slip out of the apartment and let him know when she was on her way.

"It's all right there in my phone, which the cops took," Mark said. "All our back and forth, there's a record. I was worried because she'd been drinking—and maybe smoking. Lord, she's only 15 and she's tiny. Sherry couldn't handle much. She didn't have the tolerance for it, but she was part of a group that was ready to party that night."

Dave was impressed. Mark seemed sincere and genuinely concerned about Sherry.

"You indicated you'd been seeing each other for more than a year and it sounds like you'd bonded. How close were you? Were you in love?"

The lad stared at Dave, pausing to think before answering. He leaned back against the bench. "We weren't intimate, if that's what you're asking. She's too young and I knew I'd be heading off to college, so we didn't go there. But, yeah, we were in love. We both felt it, lived it, and said it to each other. I'd do anything for her."

Mark's eyes watered again, and his sinuses betrayed him. He wiped at his nose with his long hands. Dave reached in his pocket and pulled out a cloth handkerchief that had been used and stuck together at the corners. "No thanks," the high school senior said, recoiling from the soiled rag. "I'm OK."

Dave let the young man collect himself. He shifted on the park bench and then took the interview in another direction. "The police told me you've been active in the community searches for Sherry. After more than three months, what's your theory on what became of her?"

Mark checked his recorder. It continued to roll. He took a deep breath and turned sideways on the bench, clearing his throat from sinus runoff. "Every weekend search teams, mostly students and family members from Central and Western, go out looking for traces of Sherry—any clue at all. We've been all over Bay County, Saginaw, and Midland, too.

"My track and cross-country buddies have posted Missing Person flyers on every utility pole in three counties," he continued, jabbing an index finger in the air like a debater making a point. "And nothing.

We've come up empty at every turn. It's like she vanished. I can't believe nobody saw or heard a thing. Jada's dad said he saw her in the sleeping bag on his living room floor—then poof, gone."

Dave studied him closely. "And now Jada's dad is gone. When you were in contact with Sherry that night, did she say anything about him? What about the boys who crashed the party?"

The lad rubbed his hands up and down the top of his legs like he was trying to scrape off the khaki. A car pulled up alongside the park at the corner of Auburn and Midland roads. The driver, an older man under a gray fedora, watched the two men for a moment. He tooted the horn and waved at Mark, who nodded and waved back.

Fedora man turned his blinker on and pulled around the corner. The history teacher at Western, Mark commented, adding that he was a nice guy who had organized search teams for Sherry in the Midland area.

Mark refocused and went back to the night of the party.

"Sherry was on her cell and said it started out pretty easy going. Each of the girls had brought their own drinks. Jada shared a pint of orange vodka with her," he continued, adding that she noted the girls were listening to music and dancing in the living room.

"Then the party got fast and loud when two boyfriends showed up. They brought a fifth of tequila and a shot glass. Jada's dad joined in, passing out shots during a drinking game. Then somebody lit a joint and passed it, then another. The boys and Mr. Stapleton joined the dancing. Sherry said she caught Jada's dad leering at her.

"That was the last conversation I had with Sherry," Mark said, "it was just text messages after that."

Dave lifted his recorder. Before clicking it off, he asked if the young man had shared all that information with the police. The young man nodded.

"I'm available to help. Sherry is special to me," he said. "Call me if you need anything else, or want to interview anyone else."

Chapter 5

Tuesday Afternoon
Mackinac Island

The Sunny Day Stable, one of several horse and carriage rental businesses on Mackinac Island, bustled with activity when Nick arrived on his three-speed. Groups of tourists, young and old, went through the preparation to take horses in riding parties out into the island's substantial and beautiful state park.

Those who were renting horses had to fill out a questionnaire about their riding experience and knowledge. They were also given a list of stable rules about riding to read and sign, including one that forbade beating or mistreating the animals and another that discouraged dismounting or leaving their steeds once in the park. Stable guides answered a beehive of questions that arose from riders as they readied for their adventures.

Nick waited patiently, not wanting to leave his bike and the suitcase strapped to its back unattended. Soon, a tall, dark-haired woman approached. Her shoulder-length hair framed brown, almond eyes and a sharp nose. She wore blue, knee-length shorts and a red short-sleeved shirt, the same uniform as the guides helping prospective riders. Her name tag designated her as "Sharon, Manager." The reporter greeted her by name and identified himself. They shook hands.

Nick asked where he could leave the bicycle. "The bag on the back isn't mine. I need to protect it while we're out."

Sharon motioned for him to follow her inside the stable. She pointed toward a corner where it could be parked inside her office. Nick used his foot to activate the kickstand and thanked her.

"I appreciate you meeting with me," he said, smiling. "I can see how busy you are around here. I had no idea there was this much interest in riding on the island."

"Glad to help," she replied, walking to a corkboard covered with photographs on her back wall. She pulled one off and handed it to Nick. It showed Eric Stapleton smiling, standing alongside a chestnut mare with a white nose. "Mr. Stapleton was a regular customer. This is him with Lucy, his fav, just this summer. We were all horrified by his accident. We've had riders occasionally fall from their horses, but we've never had one die—especially not someone so experienced and familiar with his ride."

"Was Eric riding Lucy when he fell?"

Sharon nodded, adding that Lucy stayed with Stapleton until he was discovered by other riders.

"Hmmm. Maybe I misunderstood, but I thought Eric's foot was tangled in the stirrup and he was dragged by the horse after he fell," the reporter said. "Did I get that wrong? Dragged 100 feet, according to the police chief."

Sharon looked at Nick blankly, hesitating before answering. "Not exactly. Kinda like that but a little different. I'll take you there and show you the area where the accident happened. Do you ride?"

Nick smiled and shook his head no, the photo still in his right hand. "I grew up on a farm, but we didn't have horses. I know almost nothing about them except what I've seen in Westerns."

Sharon laughed like she'd just heard a side-splitter. "That's funny. But it's OK. I've got a buggy out back. We'll go together, just give me a few minutes to get ready."

The reporter handed the photo back to her, saying, "One more thing. I see Eric is wearing a turtleneck in this summertime photo. Was that always the case with him?"

"I never thought about it, but now that you mention it, yes, he was a turtleneck kind of guy," she said, pinning the photo back on the board. "I'll put him back here in this grouping with his friends."

Sharon left to get the horse and buggy ready. Nick went to the corkboard and studied the grouping of Eric's friends. Right away, Gold Chains smirked out of the crowd. The others looked like a wild mix of women and men with bizarre tattoos and piercings. Long, multicolored hair, blue jeans, and leather vests. Bikers popped into Nick's mind. Only Stapleton wore a turtleneck.

Within minutes, Sharon and Nick were on a paved trail inside the state park. Walkers, hikers, joggers, bicyclists, and horses with riders dotted the landscape, moving along paths that seemed to go in every direction. Towering oaks stood above a smorgasbord of pines, maples, birch, ash, beech, aspen, box elders, and cottonwoods lining the trails. Protected by Lake Huron, the trees were now just starting to transform from lush greenery to fall colors. In a few weeks, bursts of striking hues would paint the horizon in a rainbow of colors.

"Almost a hundred miles of trails in the park, something to suit just about everyone," Sharon said, holding the reins with one hand and using the other to point out park landmarks. Nick could tell she loved the place. It oozed out of her. He was glad to have her as a guide. "We will be coming up on the site of the accident soon. We've had it blocked off since the police and EMS arrived."

As they trotted along in the buggy and rounded a long curve, sawhorses and orange cones came into view, blocking the path ahead. Sharon maneuvered around them and aimed for yellow tape draped around tree trunks on both sides of the paved path. She pulled up just short of the tape, jumping out of the buggy and securing the horse to a tree.

Nick walked in the grass along the path, trying to visualize how the accident occurred and Eric Stapleton died. Sharon caught up to him and pointed to a dark, almost black, spot on the faded gray asphalt.

"This is where the police believe Eric landed when he fell," she said, walking ahead about 50 feet or so. "He and Lucy were found just up the path."

The reporter asked if the island had experienced any rain since Sunday, the day of the accident. "The chief cited a blood trail of about 100 feet, indicating Stapleton had been dragged by his horse. I don't see the trail."

"No rain since Sunday. I wasn't working that day, so I didn't come out here until yesterday," she said, staring at the asphalt. "Frankly, I don't see a blood trail, either."

Nick stood up and faced Sharon. "So, what do you think happened? What caused Eric—an experienced rider on a familiar, friendly horse—to fall?"

The question caused Sharon some angst. Nick could see the distress in her face and her shoulders hunched up. He tried to talk her down from her peaking anxiety.

"I'm not trying to put you on the spot or cause trouble for you on the island," he said in a calm, reassuring voice. "I won't quote you on this. I'm just trying to figure it out. Logically, what happened here? Please, speak freely. I think you know your stuff. What do you think?"

Sharon placed her hands on her hips. She took a deep breath and exhaled, her shoulders falling as she spoke. "Well, something happened on the trail to spook Lucy or Eric, or both of them. That's the only reason I can think of for him to fall. Something or someone came out of the woods, causing the horse to rear, or Eric to lose his balance."

Nick scanned the tree line on both sides, looking for answers. "Like a bear, or a deer, or a fox, or a person? What came out of the woods?"

"Don't know. Could be any of the above," she said, moving ahead from the dark spot on the trail. "But then, the horse and Eric ended up here. Honestly, I don't believe Lucy would have dragged Eric. That's not her nature. She's the meekest animal in our barn. She stayed with him while he was on the ground. She didn't run off."

The police account of what occurred crumbled in Nick's mind. It didn't make sense. Sharon did. "Thanks for being straight with me. I'll simply go back to the chief when we receive the official report and press her on what happened without mentioning you or your comments."

The reporter pulled out his cell and took photos of every scene within the yellow tape. He then recorded his observations of the area, focusing on the asphalt where a blood trail could not be viewed.

Sharon brought the horse and buggy around for Nick to board. "I hope I'm not going to regret meeting and talking to you," she said, watching the reporter settle into his seat. "Believe me, everybody who works on the island wants to be seen as a team player. If you're not part of the team, then it won't be long before you find yourself swimming to the mainland on your own."

Having worked other stories on the island, he was familiar with the all-out effort to put a smiley face on every aspect of island life—even when a frown may have been more fitting. Nick liked her, thought she was solid, and brave for speaking frankly. He assured her he would do his best to protect her and her candor. "You can trust me. This won't fall back on you. I'm used to being viewed as the prick reporter who keeps asking questions and won't let go. I'm good at it. Very, very believable."

They rode back to the stable in silence. He thanked her and said he would keep her apprised of the case, which he now believed, deep down, was no accident.

Hank the horse handler sat in a booth at the Mustang Lounge sipping at the lip of a frosty mug of pale ale. It was near the end of the workday and the popular pub for tourists and local islanders was filled with revelers. When Nick entered through a door off Astor Street, he spotted Hank, his sweat-soiled, sagging Stetson pushed back on a sea of gray curls.

"Howdy, Nick! How the hell is it hangin' you ole short-legged snake! Good to see ya," said the island cowboy, standing to greet the reporter with an open mitt. He wore a faded blue-jean jacket over a "Hang at the Stang" T-shirt and denim jeans with thread-bare holes in the knees worn thin by work—not fashion. "Ain't seen you in a coon's age. What brings you to these parts?"

Sight of his favorite islander brought a smile to Nick's face. They'd worked together on several stories over the years and stayed in contact, meeting for a beer whenever either came within drinking range of the other. Hank had a niece living in Midland, so he connected with Nick at least a few times each year.

"Great to see you, Hank," he said, gripping his long, strong right hand. In his other hand, Nick clutched the handle of the Stapleton bag, not risking leaving it unattended in the street on the bike. "Glad you could slip out of work. I'm here checking on the death of a Bay City resident—the guy who fell from his horse in the state park Sunday."

The horse handler, who had worked for island stables for more than 25 years, said he'd heard about the accident but didn't know the victim was from Bay City. He'd saved a seat for Nick and waved at a waitress, signaling a desire for two cold ones.

They leaned in close so they could hear each other above the rising din of the watering hole. "If you're here, I gotta stinkin' hunch that the death ain't accidental," Hank said, draining the last of his beer from the mug. "That right? Gotta murder on your hands?"

"Well, it's definitely not a suicide and I'm having doubts about it being accidental," Nick said, eager for his beer to quench his rising thirst. "So far, the police report is not adding up. I was out to the scene this afternoon. Lots of questions that need answers. What have you heard through the grapevine?"

Hank shrugged. "Not much. Guy fell off horse, broke neck. Dead."

A waitress named Trixie dropped two frosty beers at the table and winked at the cowboy, clearly flirting. Hank's dancing eyebrows returned the playful gesture. He asked what time her shift ended. "I'm done when happy hour winds down. These two are on me, but don't get shit-faced," she said, smiling and scooting off, only stopping to turn and see if he watched her sashay away.

When finished ogling, he asked Nick to repeat the question, raising the new beer to his lips.

"Does the idea of the dead guy being dragged by the horse sound logical?" Nick asked, wiping condensation from his mug so it wouldn't drip on his shirt.

"It's possible. Depends on what kind of footwear the rider wore. Was he wearing sneakers, sandals, street shoes, boots? Did he know how to ride, how to use his legs to guide the horse, how to use the stirrups? And what disrupted the ride? Did the horse rear or bolt? Lot of factors involved."

Nick took a swig of beer and considered Hank's comments, reaching in his jacket for pen and notebook. He could find out about the footwear, but answers to the other questions remained unknown. "How could you tell if the rider was dragged?"

"Ankle or shin bruising," the horse handler said. "When somebody gets tangled and dragged, it causes severe trauma to the foot, ankle, and shin areas. You'd see heavy bruising, scraping, maybe even broken bones. Think about it. The full weight of a man's body being yanked by a 1,000-pound animal. Bound to be some damage—even while wearing leather boots."

Nick scribbled in his notebook and checked his watch. A ferry would be heading out at 6:30 p.m. and he still needed to return the rented bike. With luck, he could be back in Bay City by midnight. Time enough for one more beer. He hailed Suzie and told Hank he'd buy before heading out.

"Now, that's what I call a good day at the bar," the horse handler said, smiling broadly. "I get three cold beers without spending a nickel and a little filly wants to hook up in about an hour. You gotta come back to visit more often, my friend."

They both laughed, spending the rest of their time catching up with one another with friendly chatter.

Then Nick grabbed the suitcase and headed for the door, hoping to catch the ferry in time to leave the dream island. He wondered if a nightmare awaited.

Chapter 6

Wednesday Morning
Nick and Tanya's apartment, West Side Bay City

Tanya poured orange juice into tall tumblers for herself and Nick as she scurried about, getting ready for work. Her husband had just finished shaving and was getting dressed. They caught up with one another from different rooms, speaking over the Eagles's "Hotel California" playing gently from their apartment living room.

They had not had a chance to talk since Nick rolled in late last night from his run to Mackinac Island. Tanya said she'd been working with senior Central High students eager to land college grants and scholarships. She noted that two students had asked her to confirm a rumor at school that the Conaways had asked Nick to help find Sherry, their missing daughter.

"I was happy to tell them that you'd met with Sherry's folks," Tanya said, buttering toast to accompany the juice. "They were excited about the news. Sherry is missed by her friends and teachers. I'm sure word about your involvement will spread quickly. Tell me about your trip Up North. Was it worthwhile?"

Nick joined his spouse in the kitchen and put his hands around her waist from behind. He pulled her close, nuzzling behind her left ear. "I missed you. Too bad you couldn't have joined me. It's a long drive, but mostly beautiful. Fall colors just starting, and the island is always terrific. It wasn't as crowded as usual. Tourist season is winding down, big time."

He refused to release his hold on her. She munched a piece of toast and enjoyed the hug. "Maybe I can go on your next run up there," Tanya said, turning her head sideways to receive a quick kiss, which transferred breadcrumbs from her lips to his. "Will you need a return trip?"

Nick said he was sure he would need to go back to the island again soon. He gave her a quick summary of his interviews on Tuesday, noting the discrepancies in the police account of how Eric Stapleton died. "Have you noticed the suitcase by the front door?"

"I was going to ask you about that," she said, sipping from her tumbler. "I wondered if Hank the horse handler was moving in with us for the winter months."

Nick laughed. "Nope. Hank's doing well and sends his regards. The bag is Stapleton's stuff. I met one of his work buddies at the cottage they use, and he was packing it. Asked me to deliver it to Eric's mom, here in town."

Tanya asked if he'd looked through the bag. He shook his head no.

"Dave will be here shortly, and we're going to pick through it. I called Louise on the drive home last night to let her know I had the bag. She asked what was in it and encouraged me to look inside. She's been busy with funeral arrangements. Says the body is being transported back here this morning, which also means the police have concluded the investigation."

A knock at the door signaled Dave's arrival. Tanya wiggled from Nick's grasp and turned for a real kiss, then rushed to gather her things for school. Her husband opened the door and greeted Dave, who smiled and nodded, then grimaced as he limped into the living room.

"Oh, no. Did you fall?" Nick asked, watching his friend favor his right leg all the way to the couch. He closed the door and offered his friend coffee.

"Coffee would be good," Dave said, stretching the bum leg out. "It's my mom, again. I visited her last night, and all seemed to be going well. She didn't know my name, but she was nice to me like she kinda had an idea who I was. I tried to help her move some things and—boom—her mood changed. I saw the cane come up in the air, raised my hands to block another blow to my head, and she swung down and clobbered my knee. Took me right to the floor."

Nick was stunned, his mouth hanging open. Tanya entered the room carrying her fall coat and a briefcase. She'd heard Dave's story from another room and shared her husband's dismay, offering sympathy.

"So sorry to hear about your mom," she said, reaching for the apartment door. "First your eye and now your knee. Is it bruised, too? What do your mom's doctors say? Is her decline a temporary lapse, or do they think it will worsen?"

Dave rubbed the knee with both hands on its sides. "My injury is temporary, but the docs say my mom is only going to get worse. They say she has moved into severe dementia because of Alzheimer's. Her caregivers say she's harder to manage every day."

Nick placed a cup of coffee on a table next to Dave. He asked his friend if he had anyone examine the knee. "Sure it's not the knee cap that's hurt? That injury can be bad news."

Dave blew on his coffee and sipped at it gingerly. "I'll be OK. Thanks for caring—both of you. I just gotta figure out how to get through this with my mom. Hurts me to my core to see her like this."

Tanya opened the door and asked if they could talk about it more later. Dave nodded as she whisked away to work. Nick grabbed the suitcase and pulled it close to the couch so the two friends could paw through it. He gave Dave a quick overview of his meetings on Mackinac Island, emphasizing the troubling information he learned about Eric Stapleton.

"The interviews involving Sherry Conaway's boyfriend was a study in All-American lore," Dave said, commenting that he ended up really liking the guy. "I can see why Sherry's family and the police buy his story."

Dave leaned in to look inside the bag. "So, what are we looking for?"

"Don't know," Nick said, lifting the key and hoop that Gold Chains had tossed onto the top of the bag's contents. "Anything and everything that tells us more about the life of the guy who owned this stuff."

The key looked like it fit a standard dead-bolt door lock. It had a plastic cover on its base with the initials S.B. in bold print, and the numbers 6912 underneath.

"This was hanging on a hook by a bunch of cottage keys," Nick said, holding it up to the light. "His work buddy, a real piece of work, said he had no idea what it was for. He figured it belonged to Eric."

Nick showed Dave the framed photo of Stapleton and Gold Chains at the cottage. Folded clothing was stacked neatly in the bag. Three pairs of cargo shorts—tan, blue, gold—four short-sleeved knit turtlenecks, each a bright pastel, and three sets of tattered boxer shorts, multicolored. A reversible black/brown belt, a pair of sneakers, and sandals completed the duds in the bag. A folder filled with papers: receipts, invoices, shopping lists, letters, work time cards, and island tourist flyers.

Dave fished through the pile of letters, mostly notes from Jada about school. A couple showed a return address for Louise. Birthday cards and letters from Underwater Solutions comprised the rest.

The reporters looked through the stack. Dave checked the pockets of the cargo pants and came up empty-handed. The shirts had no pockets. "I didn't know they made short-sleeved turtlenecks for guys," he said, noting that two of the shirts had what looked like dried blood in the collars.

As Nick flipped through the folder of papers, he replied that Gold Chains suggested Stapleton wore the shirts to hide the results of his lusty encounters with women. Then he held up a receipt from the Sand Box, a storage-unit business in Kawkawlin, a small river town just north of Bay City. It showed a six-month cash payment for unit 6912.

"OK now we know what the key is for," Nick said. "That's interesting. I'll ask Louise about it when I let her know what we found in the bag."

Then Nick found a small notebook and a flip cell phone and charger cord in a zipper pocket of the bag's lid. He stuck the notebook in his pocket to review later. The cell flashed to life when he opened it, requiring a four-digit passcode for entry and indicating its battery was low.

The reporter plugged the phone into an outlet and tinkered with the passcode, punching in letters "Mom"—no good. Eric, nothing. Jada, failure. Nick paused, thought for a moment, then tried another: Lucy, jackpot! He was inside. A quick review revealed two dozen voicemail and text messages and a trove of phone contacts. He closed the phone and put it in his pocket with the notebook to examine later.

The reporters decided to split up. Dave planned to check in with the C-Man and the police, hoping for updates in both cases. Nick called

Louise and asked if they could meet at her son's place again. He said he wanted to bring her up to speed on his visit to Mackinac Island and what he'd learned about her son's death, adding that he would bring Eric's bag with him.

Louise agreed, eager to hear what he'd discovered. She said she expected her son's body to arrive at the Rest In Peace Funeral Chapel on Bay City's West Side around noon.

On the way, Nick decided to drive the length of the alley between Stapleton's apartment and Euclid Avenue, just to check it out more thoroughly. When he'd walked the street earlier, the alley seemed like the one place along the route that could hide a lurking kidnapper. Since then, that scenario had nagged at him. What if Sherry had staggered down the alley looking for a shortcut to the gas station where her boyfriend awaited?

He turned to the right and traveled north, idling along as slow as the Firebird would go. To his left, he spotted a picnic table, a rope swing hanging from a willow, and a wooden bench at the edge of a resident's yard. Three trash cans stood at the edge of the alley. The scene was similar all the way down the alley. Minimal yard furniture and landscaping surrounding utility poles with trash cans for easy pickup down the narrow passage. Same to the south.

When the reporter arrived at Stapleton's, the drapes were open and the apartment lit. Nick parked and carried Eric's bag into the living room where Louise had set two cups of coffee and cookies on a small table. She took the bag and set it upright in the entry closet, gesturing for Nick to sit down. He reached in his jacket pocket and produced the key on its hoop, the flip phone, and the small notebook, placing them on the table next to the cookies.

"Thanks, I'm ready for a coffee. You're a mind reader," he said, testing the coffee for its temperature. He blew on it and sipped, making a light slurping noise, which caused Louise to smile as she lifted her cup. "First, let's talk about Mackinac Island. I met with the police chief, and she gave me an overview of their report about Eric's death. We should get the official report today."

"Do you think the police did a thorough job? I can't imagine the island having a big police force. Do they even have detectives?"

Nick nodded. Louise was on the right track.

"I've got some problems with the police report. I made detailed notes from the chief's description of the accident and then visited the scene with the manager of the riding stable," he said, assaulting the chocolate chip cookie and wiping his lips with a paper napkin. "I must say the police report does not seem to sync with what happened out on that horse-riding trail. It doesn't add up. Especially the part about Eric being dragged by the horse.

"One of my longtime buddies on the island, a guy who has worked with horses for decades, says your son's right leg would have telltale signs of bruising and scraping if he was dragged. The chief also said Eric's head had been scraped during the accident."

Louise put down her cup. Her eyes watered as Nick described her son's injuries. She reached for tissue in her purse on the couch. "I'm sorry. Hearing the details—well, they're making me weepy. Eric had his faults, no doubt about it. But he's still my only son."

Nick paused, allowing her time to digest what he'd described. He opened his reporting notebook and reviewed the information he'd gotten from the chief. When he looked up at Louise, she'd regained her composure. She urged him to continue.

He treaded lightly, not quite sure how she would handle his next question. "Not quite sure how to ask this, and I hope you won't be offended or grossed out, but I was hoping you would give me permission to view your son's body at the funeral home before the undertakers start working on him for the funeral."

Louise took a gulp of her coffee. "And you want to do that because … you want to see if his injuries match what the police told you about his accident?"

Nick nodded. "That's it, precisely. What do you think?"

Louise looked down at her hands, folded neatly in her lap. She bit her lower lip. Nick did not want to rush her. She looked out the apartment's front window and took a deep breath.

"If you think it's necessary, Nick," she said, looking him directly in the eye. "I don't want to see him until the funeral home tells me they have him ready to view. I want my last memory to be of him at his best. But I'll call the funeral home and give them permission to show him to you. They should be ready for you by early afternoon. And then, please, let me know if you think there's a problem with the official version of his death."

Nick thanked her for trusting him. He said he'd let her know right away if the viewing raised any concerns. He took a sip of coffee, then held up the flip phone, punching in the pass code before handing it to Louise.

"This phone was in his bag, which was packed by his workmate at the rental on Mackinac Island," Nick said, taking another nibble of cookie. "Perhaps you could take a look at Eric's contacts and his messages—just to see if you recognize the people he's been talking to. His final conversations might be useful to know as we sort out his death."

Louise looked through the contacts and messages, scrolling deep into the phone's storage. After several minutes, she closed the cell. "I only recognize Jada and her mother's numbers. Everything else is a puzzle. I have no idea about most of it."

Nick nodded and took the phone back, sticking it in his jacket pocket. "I didn't look at it closely earlier, but I'd like to if you don't mind. I'd like to do the same with this notebook."

She nodded and sipped from her cup again. The last item on the table was the hoop and key. She used her index finger to turn the key so she could read it.

"Do you recognize it?" Nick asked. "A receipt in Eric's bag indicates it's for a storage locker. Were you aware he had one?"

Louise shook her head. "I have no idea. Maybe he's storing something for work. Could be diving equipment for Underwater Solutions. He's never mentioned it. Like the notebook and the phone, let me know if you discover something I should be aware of."

Nick drained his coffee and thanked her for the hospitality. He checked his watch and headed for The *Blade* newsroom to update with

Dave. But first, he wanted to check out the storage unit in Kawkawlin.

The Firebird responded as he pressed the accelerator, rolling around a sharp curve as he left the city limits. A giant billboard advertised Sand Box Deluxe Storage Condos just a half-mile ahead.

The sign boasted that each unit was designed to provide the ultimate protection for the owner's precious private property—antique cars, unique boats, fancy motorcycles, unique motorhomes, exquisite collections—in unequaled accommodations. Depending upon need, each unit could be temperature controlled, powered by a natural gas generator, fully soundproofed, and decked out with luxurious kitchen, bath, and electronic entertainment systems.

Nick was impressed. He'd never run across deluxe storage before. It made him even more curious about Stapleton's unit. As he turned into the storage condo yard, the huge units—each bigger than a three-car garage—stretched out in three rows as far as he could see. He drove down each black-topped row, checking numbers, looking for 6912.

When it came into view, it was at the end of a row next to a unit with one of its garage doors open. A middle-aged man with dark hair, a ruddy complexion tanned golden bronze, and a heavily muscled physique polished his deep blue '72 Mustang with a soft white cloth. A new black Lincoln rested just off to the side of the classic muscle car. Nick parked his gold Firebird, slightly embarrassed by its less-than-pristine appearance, in front of 6912, the number spaced between a fourteen-foot garage door and a steel entry door—both windowless.

Ruddy Man paused mid-polish stroke as Nick shut the Firebird door. "Nice ride. That a '67 or '68 'Bird? Always liked that little buggy," he said, smiling and walking toward the reporter. "I'll bet she really scoots. How long you had her?"

Both men appreciated each other's hot rod, which meant a long-winded conversation could be building up steam. Nick introduced himself and happily answered the questions, noting the Firebird's big V-8 was original and how badly she needed pampering with a steam bath and fresh coat of wax. He wanted a quick introduction to the Mustang.

Ruddy Man said his name was Charlie Moore, a retired Ford executive who had recently moved into a downtown condo overlooking the Saginaw River. "Store my Carver out here when she's not docked in the water. Got a Harley inside—want to take a look?"

Nick could not resist. Charlie marched ahead through the open garage door. Off to the right side, a gleaming orange, black, and chrome 1968 Harley-Davidson Shovelhead rested quietly. He was drawn to the classic street bike like metal to a magnet.

"Wow, what a beauty!" the reporter exclaimed, resisting the urge to touch, which is a big no-no among all who admire and love classic rides. His new friend basked in the praise as he stood, hands on hips, polish rag in hand, ready to wipe away any noticed blemish. "How long you had her?"

"Twelve years now," he responded, watching Nick check out his baby. "I take her out every Sunday, weather permitting, during the season. She just glides and purrs on the open road. Love getting her out on the nice, paved roads running along the lakeshore."

Nick looked around the massive garage. Plenty of room for the Mustang and the Carver. Lots of workspace and all the best, shiny tools for his toys. The back of the garage looked like a bar, complete with a pool table, pinball machines, and a giant 1948 Wurlitzer 1015 jukebox. Behind the shelf of booze, a scripted, flashing neon sign declared it: Charlie's Place!

"Love your unit," Nick said. "Why would you ever go home?"

Charlie laughed. "Little lady at home gives me a long leash as long as I don't stray. Got a good thing going and want to keep it that way."

Nick marveled at the size of the unit. He told Charlie he was a reporter with the *Blade* and was looking into the death of his unit neighbor, Eric Stapleton, at the request of a relative. He asked how well he knew the deceased.

"Not too much," he said. "The guy kept to himself, quiet. I didn't much care for his friends, either. They referred to me as the Capitalist or Money Bags. Hey, I worked hard for my money and earned every penny of it, unlike them, who looked like they didn't work at all."

The reporter said he had stopped today to take a look inside Stapleton's unit, curious about what he might find. Charlie replied he had no idea. He'd never been inside. Seemed to hold a lot of meetings, he said. Small groups gathered for hours.

Nick thanked Charlie and walked to unit 6912. He tried the key—the door swung open. The unit was dark. He fumbled to find a wall light switch, flicking on fluorescent lights hanging from the ceiling, revealing what looked like a classroom. His first reaction: could it be a training facility for Underwater Solutions?

A large whiteboard and gigantic flat-screen TV stood in front of dozens of metal chairs with an oversized vinyl couch in the back row. Behind the classroom and across the back wall was a double bookcase with storge cabinets on top and across the bottom. The bookcase shelves held a wide assortment of videos, periodicals, books, and knick-knacks. A sturdy workbench, with a variety of fine tools, wiring, and electronics, anchored a wall to the side of the classroom. Two doors, one marked MEN and the other WOMEN, stood next to the bookcase.

Nick studied the scene. It struck him as quiet, interesting, and totally the opposite of **Charlie's Place**. The unit smelled musty to Nick as he stood in the entryway. Was it because the place had been closed up? He was about to venture in for a closer look when his cell pinged a text. It was Dave. His note indicated the police report from Mackinac Island on Eric Stapleton's death had landed at the *Blade* via email. He glanced around the classroom again and flicked off the light. He would come back later for a second, more thorough look.

The reporter waved at Charlie as he hopped into the Firebird and sped away, burning just a tad of rubber. He checked his watch. Noon. Just enough time to review the report with Dave before Stapleton's body would be available to view.

As the Firebird rumbled into Bay City, Nick kept thinking about the two deluxe storage units he'd just seen and how different they were. Something about the Stapleton unit seemed odd but he couldn't quite identify it. The setup? The aroma? The starkness? Perhaps Dave could return with him, and they both could give it a good look. Eric Stapleton largely remained a puzzle, but he was determined to keep digging for a broad picture of the man and his life as he zeroed in on how he died.

When Nick rolled into the newsroom, he joined Dave and the C-Man as they hovered over the report in the managing editor's office. It didn't take long to figure out that the report was no different than the preliminary he'd received verbally from the island police chief. The Stapleton death was ruled accidental. Broken neck, shoulder blade, and head injury as a result of a fall from a horse on a trail in the state park on Sunday.

Clapper said the report seemed straightforward and to the point. Nick told him about visiting the scene of the death with the stable manager, who was befuddled by the idea that the deceased had been dragged by the horse. He mentioned the leg injuries that would result from dragging.

"I have permission to view the body this afternoon," he said, sitting on a corner of Clapper's cluttered desk. A stack of magazines fell to the floor, causing copy editors and reporters to look toward the C-Man's office to see if the chief was throwing shit again. "I'm curious about the head injury as well. The report refers to a blood trail, but we didn't see it at the scene."

Dave mentioned the Stapleton bag, telling Clapper that he and Nick had sifted through it before turning it over to the deceased's mother. Nick gave a quick update on the cell phone, notebook, and key to the storage unit.

"I was blown away by the Sand Box," Nick said, restacking the fallen mags. "No idea little Kawkawlin had such a business. Deluxe condo storage units. Looks like Stapleton used his for training. I was only able to take a quick peek, but would love to give it a hard look. Want to go with me?"

Dave said he'd love to but was scheduled to meet with his mother's caregivers during the afternoon. He indicated he'd given the C-Man an update on her condition.

"You gotta look after your mom," Clapper said, turning to Nick. "Want me to assign another reporter to go with you to the funeral home and the storage unit? Are you sure you're OK with checking out a lifeless body? We're not exactly trained for that, and the guy died on Sunday."

Nick assured them he would be OK. "Both may just turn out to be routine follow-ups. I can check out both and write a story. No problem. Good luck with your mom, Dave. Let me know how it goes."

Both reporters left the newsroom seeking answers from different sources. They had no idea what they were walking into.

The Rest In Peace Funeral Chapel was a second-generation family operation. R.I.P. had been the valued business that took care of final preparations for the burial of Louise Stapleton's deceased husband and her parents some 20 years earlier. She trusted the owners and their services, so it was no wonder that she called on the longtime West Side Bay City company to handle the final services and remembrances for her only son, Eric.

It was considered highly unusual for a news reporter, or any member of the public for that matter, to view and examine the body of the deceased before funeral preparation. But Mrs. Stapleton was a valued, longtime client and her wishes were honored by the company—though she was cautioned about what might occur if the untrained entered the world of mortuary science.

When Nick Steele arrived at R.I.P. he was subjected to a barrage of questions about his experience with the dearly departed by mortician and funeral home manager, Arthur Shields. Had he viewed dead bodies previously? Had he experienced the deceased after they had been involved in violent accidents? Had he seen the dead with missing, or mutilated, body parts? Would he like smelling salts if he were to feel that he was being overcome by the aroma of a corpse?

"Nope," Nick replied. "I'm good. I've been a reporter for 25 years. I've been to horrendous car accidents, train wrecks, plane crashes. I'm a Marine Corps combat veteran. I've seen human carnage at multiple levels. I've even pulled a person out of a house fire who was smoldering with skin melting off his body. I can handle this. I'm ready."

Shields, hands clasped atop his round belly, nodded, and smiled grimly. He was a tall, burly man, with thinning red hair spread across his head in a desperate comb-over, dressed in a traditional black suit, white shirt, gray tie, and black patent leather shoes. He motioned for the reporter to follow.

The two walked to the back of the funeral home, entering a brightly lit, cool, and sterile preparation room. In the center of the space, under a plethora of overhead lights, rested the body of Eric Stapleton, which had been transported in a body bag from the Upper Peninsula, but now rested on a full prep table under a sheet.

The undertaker walked to the head of the table and asked Nick, again, "Are you ready?" The reporter nodded and Shields pulled back the sheet halfway, resting its top at the waistline. The mortician stepped to the side and Nick paused to view the top half of the body from its right side. He pulled out his recorder and clicked it on to establish a record of what he viewed.

Nick stated the time, date, place, and location of the recording, then moved slowly around the body. When he came to the left side, he noted severe bruising under the left arm of the deceased. He stepped closer, recording his thoughts. "It appears as though a circular black spot—about three inches in diameter—highlights the center of the bruising."

Crouched over and bent at the knees, Nick moved toward the top of the deceased's head. Horror spread across his face as he closed in. The whole top portion of the head and hair had been removed. Crusted blood lined the edges of the side hair on both sides. It appeared as though the hairline, starting just above the eyebrows, had been cut and then torn, side to side, all the way past the crown to the back of the head.

Nick stood up straight. "Holy shit, he's been scalped!" Once more, he moved in close, covering his nose with a handkerchief, to examine the cutting and tearing of tissue.

Nick turned to face the undertaker. "Have you ever seen anything like this?"

Shields shook his head. "Not in 30 years. I've never seen a scalping before. Please don't quote me on that. I would only say on the record that your observations are correct."

Nick spoke into the recorder: "This is not a scrape or an abrasion or a contusion to the side or back or front of the head. The scalp has been cut and torn from the skull."

The reporter asked the mortician while the recorder was running if photos would be taken of the deceased's skull from all angles. Shields responded that he would take photos himself for insurance purposes as a safeguard. "Also, Louise has asked for photos of anything significant discovered."

Nick also noted for the recorder that the deceased's neck, over top of the Adam's apple, exhibited extensive bruising in the form of chain links, some lines deep and crusty with what appeared to be dried blood on the edges. "It appeared Eric Stapleton had been leashed like a dog at some point before the incident that took his life," Nick remarked into the recorder.

The reporter then asked for the rest of the sheet to be removed. He said he wanted to see the legs and feet of the deceased. Shields pulled the sheet up from the bottom and doubled it at the waistline.

Nick moved to the end of the table. He spoke into the recorder. "The feet, ankles, and lower leg areas of the deceased are unmarked. No bruising, scraping, or tearing of the skin is visible—injuries that might be expected if the body had been dragged by the lower extremities—the part of the body from the hip to the toes."

After pausing for several minutes to collect his thoughts, the reporter slowly walked around the preparation table once more to make sure he had not missed any signs of injury. He stopped again at the left arm. He asked Shields, who wore plastic gloves, if he would lift the arm so the armpit could be viewed more closely. He did.

Nick clicked on his recorder again and noted that the bruising he'd seen earlier extended through the armpit to the underside of the arm.

When finished, Nick said he was going to suggest to Louise that she commission a full forensic examination of the body. "I'm not an expert, but what I see here does not match the conclusions of the report completed by the Mackinac Island Police Department."

Shields covered the body, head to toe. He snapped off his plastic gloves and then turned to Nick, asking again not to be quoted in the *Blade*. "I don't disagree with you. I will wait to hear from Louise."

As the two men left the prep room, Nick asked if any of the deceased's personal effects came back with him from St. Ignace. Shields said he had a large manila envelope, marked "personals," that was inside the body bag. He said he planned to give it to Mrs. Stapleton when she came to the funeral home.

"That may be a while if she decides to hire an outside firm to conduct an autopsy and testing," Nick said. "I'll call her now. She can decide what she'd like to do."

Louise answered the call on the second ring. "Hello, Nick. Are you at the funeral home now?"

The reporter responded that he had viewed her son's body and thought his head injury was much more serious than described by police. He said Eric also had severe bruising under one arm that was completely unexplained. In addition, his legs did not appear to be injured at all, he said, which makes it hard to believe the body had been dragged.

"You may want to commission a full autopsy and testing," Nick said. "One more thing. Your son had circular markings on his neck, which looked like chain links to me."

"What? Chain links? Like he was tied up?" Louise asked, gasping. She cried out, wailing. "No, no … why? Why would he be chained? Oh, my God."

Nick didn't say anything. He let her vent, listening as she cried. He was her only son and the reporter's words were crushing her.

Shields, who had been listening to the conversation, understood the gravity of it. He held up the bag of personal effects so Nick could see it, arching his bushy eyebrows.

"The funeral director says an envelope of personal effects accompanied Eric," Nick said, pausing to let that sink in. "Do you want me to bring it to you for review?"

Mrs. Stapleton collected herself, clearing her throat, and thought for a moment. "Yes, Nick, that would be wonderful. Is Mr. Shields nearby? Could I talk with him? If he agrees, I think we should have a separate, professional review. And I'll ask him to give you the envelope."

Nick handed the cell phone to the undertaker. "Louise would like to chat with you." He took the phone and spoke with Eric's mother for several minutes. When Shields returned the phone to the reporter, he offered a compliment: "Well done."

Chapter 7
Wednesday Afternoon
Shady Lane Assisted Living Facility

Knots formed in Dave Balz's stomach as he pushed his F-150 until it rattled on the way to meeting the chief caregivers at his mom's nursing home. An emergency meeting had been called because of her recent behavior. From his own experience, he knew she seemed to be getting worse: she didn't recognize him anymore, could not remember his name, and was becoming violent. He worried about what the caregivers had experienced.

The Shady Lane assisted-care facility came into view as Dave entered Essexville, the bedroom community on Bay City's east boundary. The parking lot was full because Wednesday afternoon had traditionally been a prime visitation day for families that had warehoused their elders.

When he signed in at the front desk, Dave was immediately directed to a meeting room off the lobby where they were waiting for him. They consisted of the facility day manager, mom's immediate day-time caregiver, and a floor orderly—each had regular contact with Mrs. Balz.

Manager Della Stephenson, a stern-looking 60-something with hard features and short silver hair, spoke first. Dave had only dealt with her on a few occasions. He thought of her as the warden and cautioned his mom not to cross her.

"Mr. Balz, we asked for this meeting because your mother is becoming increasingly hard to work with," she said, her high-pitched nasally voice striking Dave like fingernails raking a chalkboard. "We've documented increased days of disorientation and more frequent episodes of her becoming hostile and violent."

Dave sat quietly, trying to control his emotions. His right knee, out of view as he sat at the meeting table, bounced up and down. His eyes shifted to the three sitting across from him, trying to read what was on their minds.

Della cleared her throat before continuing. "In fact, Mrs. Balz became unruly last night and refused to take her medicine and retire at the appointed time. Unfortunately, she had to be restrained because her safety and staff safety were threatened."

"What do you mean restrained?" Dave interjected. Both knees bounced now like churning engine pistons. "Like how, and for how long? Who did the restraining?"

"I'm coming to that," Della responded, slowing down a discussion that had suddenly escalated to high-tension status. "A safety belt was employed by a floor orderly to keep Mrs. Balz seated. During the implementation of the safety belt, her lower lip received slight bruising. During the encounter, the orderly received a sprained arm. This was extremely unfortunate."

"You mean you gave my mom a fat lip and she tried to break somebody's arm?" Dave asked, trying to mask his irritation. "Yes, I'd agree. Extremely unfortunate. I don't like the idea of you hurting my mom. That's not your job. You're supposed to care for her, not manhandle her."

The three Shady Lane representatives shifted in their seats, avoiding eye contact with Dave. Della tried to regain control of the meeting.

"Ahem," she started. "This is why we are recommending a re-evaluation by her doctors and a possible change in medication. Her safety is our greatest concern."

Dave listened. He didn't want to overreact, but he was pissed about his mother getting hurt by people being paid to take care of her. He paused for a moment, his mind racing. Then he unloaded.

"Well, I'm glad to hear that," he said. "Because I'd hate to think that your greatest concern was keeping a client on your rolls that pays every month and has good insurance. If I thought that were the case, I'd pull her out of here faster than you can blink.

"Yes, let's have the docs re-evaluate. And I want a full physical examination by her personal doctor to make sure she has no other injuries as a result of so-called belting implementation. Now, I'm going down to visit my mom. Are we done here?"

Della forced a curling of her lips to produce a mini-smile and nodded. "Yes, we will compile a full medical report for your review."

Dave chugged down beige, sterile hallways to his mom's room. He knocked on the door. No answer. He rapped again, his beefy knuckles causing an echo. When there was still no answer, he tried the door handle. It turned and he pushed the door open. His mom sat in her rocker, her chin on her chest, her lip fattened, and she cried when she saw her son. He rushed to her, going down on one knee to hug her.

"David, I hate this place," she whispered. "I hate my life. Please help me. I don't want to live like this anymore."

Her son was shocked. Dave wept on her shoulder. Though she remembered his name and clearly recognized him, it hurt to hear, see, and feel her pain. "I will, Ma. I'll help. We'll get this figured out. Your doctor is coming to visit. We'll make this better, I promise."

Dave stayed with her through dinner time and tucked her into bed before he left. He would speak with her doctor and vowed to do whatever he could to help her. As he left the room, he was approached by a slender, silver-haired woman his mom's age. She wore a pink bathrobe and furry slippers that looked like calico kitties.

"Yoo-hoo, yoo-hoo! Are you Mr. Balz, the reporter with the *Blade?*" she asked, her right hand thrust in the air. Dave noticed she had pink fingernails, the same shade as her robe. "I've been reading your stories in the paper for years. When your mom came here to live, she was so proud of you and talked about your work with your assistant, Nick."

The comment made Dave laugh. His mood lightened. Here was someone who had known his mom since she checked into Shady Lane. Calico Kitty Lady was a woman he wanted to get to know. He stuck out his hand. "Yes, I'm Dave. What's your name?"

"I'm Leona Hayden," she said, smiling. She inserted her tiny, frail hand into the reporter's thick, calloused mitt. He didn't squeeze, afraid it might hurt her. "How's your mom doing tonight?"

They walked to a nearby set of chairs with a small table in the hall. Dave said he was worried about his mother. She seemed to be struggling recently and not sure of herself or her surroundings.

Leona nodded, saying she understood. "Your mom is having a tough time of it. I've noticed the last few months that her memory comes and goes. Lately, it's been mostly gone. Does she recognize you?"

"Sometimes, I'm sad to say," he said quietly. "These days, she doesn't seem to have a clue who I am, or really, who she is. It bothers me, of course, but I'm worried about her safety."

Leona shuffled her feet, making the kitties look like they were playing. She said she checked in on Dave's mom every day. They often had tea and cookies in the early afternoon, then watched a soap opera on TV.

That comforted him. Dave was grateful someone so kind, and sane, was watching out for his mom. He asked Leona about the other residents. Had she discovered unusual characters?

"Define unusual," she responded, a slight smile dancing across her lips. "We've got all levels here and it can be socially … challenging, shall we say. That's why I came down to your mom's room. Just wanted to check on her. Most here are harmless, but some a little off. Have you met Captain America yet?"

Dave sat up straight. No, he said, not yet. He pulled out his wallet and produced a business card. "Thanks, Leona. I'm really glad we met and had this chat. Here's my phone number at work, my cell, and my email. Please, shoot me a note anytime. Call, text, or write if you need anything or if you think my mom does."

She took the card, her eyes lighting up as she held it up in front of her nose to read it. "So nice meeting you, too, Dave. I'll call if necessary. Please stop and say hello when visiting your mom. I'm just down the hall in 32. I'll tell her we chatted."

Dave reached over and touched Leona's arm. "My mom was injured. She's got a fat lip. Sounds like she struggled with an orderly. Are they—the staff—too rough? Have you experienced that, or seen it?"

She responded that staff members were generally professional and responsible. They do not react well to resistance, she said, suggesting that's when problems arise. "I think sometimes they are too quick to use the safety belt. They don't realize how humiliating, how frustrating it is to be bound. Glad that's not happened to me."

Dave thanked her again, asking if he could give her a hug. She smiled and nodded. The burly reporter pulled her close, careful of her fragility. He left glad to have met Leona.

As Nick drove back to the Sand Box storage facility, he called the Mackinac Island police chief to talk about the conclusion of the official report on Eric Stapleton's death. But Debra Westover did not pick up the call; it went to voicemail. The reporter left a short message, imploring her to call him back.

When he pulled up to unit 6912, the black Lincoln had disappeared, the shiny Mustang tucked away, and **Charlie's Place** was closed for the day. Nick opened the Stapleton unit and flicked the overhead lights to life. The musty smell hit him again. He left the door propped open, hoping the place would air out quickly.

Earlier, he had not noticed a work desk off to the side of the big-screen TV and whiteboard. He checked it out, pulling open the desk's lap drawer. Underneath several neatly folded Straits of Mackinac and Lake Huron maps, he found another flip phone and spiral notebook. He stuck them both in the side pocket of his sports jacket to review later. The other desk drawers were locked.

Nick walked to the bookcase, noting several titles about deep diving in fresh-water lakes. He also found several books about the U.S. Constitution and the intent of the founding fathers, which he thought was odd if this was a training facility for Underwater Solutions.

But then he discovered more disturbing material. A row of videos was marked "Patriot Training." The magazines addressed survivalists, guerilla warfare, and weapons and ammo. A dozen worn and frayed copies of *The Turner Diaries*, a white supremacist manual of extremism, and *The Anarchist Cookbook*, a murder manual for terrorists, mass shooters, and other extremists, rounded out the reading material.

Nick used his cell to take photos of the bookcase and its contents, which he found jarring. This was a new side of Eric Stapleton that had not been previously revealed. He'd share it with the C-Man and Dave.

Then he checked out the bathrooms, located on the back wall next to the bookcase. Each contained standard porcelain facilities for lavatories, but also had showers, whirlpool baths, and lockers. Each room was long and narrow, rectangle shaped. They were used but clean.

Nick stood in front of both doors. Suddenly, he wondered what was behind the bookcase. If the bathrooms ran roughly 12 feet in depth, then it looked as though another room of similar depth was behind the bookcase. Storage? Weapons, explosives, ammunition, or survivalist gear to match the theme of the reading material?

Nick looked closer. A center post in the bookcase separated it in 14-foot halves. He pushed on the shelving on the left side. It didn't budge. He did the same to the right side. He felt it give slightly, making a clicking sound. Nick used the flashlight function on his phone to shine inside the edges of the center post. Nothing on the left, but he spotted metal on the right side. Hinges?

Nick explored the far-right side of the bookcase for a lever or some kind of release handle. Removing *The Turner Diaries* uncovered a beige-colored metal latch in the upper corner. He pulled it and the right edge of the bookcase released. As he pulled the bookcase open, an interior light turned on and the musty smell hit him full force.

There, on a bed and chained to the wall, laid a young woman, clad only in a man's long white T-shirt with no undergarments. It was Sherry Conaway. He was sure of it from the Missing Person flyers.

Nick rushed to her and checked her pulse. Weak. She was unconscious, barely breathing. He tried 9-1-1, but the call would not go through from inside the soundproof, hidden room.

Nick ran outside the building and called again. This time he got through to a dispatcher. He asked for an ambulance and police to respond immediately—he'd found a failing young woman who needed emergency care. He told the dispatcher he believed he'd found Sherry Conaway, missing for more than three months.

When he went back inside, Nick checked the workbench. He grabbed a long-handled bolt cutter hanging from a pegboard hook, returning to Sherry's side and cutting the chain that held her to the wall. He spotted an empty bowl and a blanket crumpled on the floor. He covered her cold, shivering body.

Nick looked around her cell. Besides the bed and bowl, the only other object in the room was a toilet. Its bowl overflowed onto the floor, causing the gassy aroma. The toilet tank was empty, which made Nick think she'd been drinking from it—probably for the last week. Stapleton had been on Mackinac Island since at least the previous Friday, maybe longer.

The young woman had been without food and water for at least five days.

Nick didn't know if she could hear him, but he spoke to her quietly. "You are safe now, Sherry. Help is on the way. Your folks love you and have been searching for you every day. Your nightmare is over. Hang on. You're going to be OK."

In the distance, Nick could hear sirens through the opened doors of Sherry's cell growing louder by the minute. They couldn't arrive soon enough. Two Bay County Sheriff's Deputy cruisers roared up, flashers dancing, sirens screaming.

Nick stood outside, flagging the cruisers. He'd carried Sherry in his arms to the meeting room and put her down with the blanket on a vinyl couch, taking her out of the suffocating stench and close to the open front door. He directed the deputies inside just as an ambulance screeched and slid sideways turning into the Sand Box entrance.

Nick took photos of the deputies and EMTs coming to Sherry's rescue. Within minutes, the first responders had Sherry on a stretcher, oxygen over her face and an IV drip in place. They whisked her away, sirens screeching, one deputy leading the ambulance.

The other deputy asked Nick for a statement and a rundown on what had occurred. More police vehicles—Michigan State Troopers, Bay City Public Safety, and Saginaw County deputies—arrived, securing the crime scene. Nick took more photos, slipping back inside unit 6912 to take pictures of Sherry's dungeon.

When they had finished with Nick, he told them he was going to the *Blade* newsroom. "One more thing, one of you should notify the family.

The Conaways will want to know about their daughter right away. In case you don't have it handy, here's how to reach her dad." He opened his cell and gave the sergeant in charge a number to call.

As Nick swerved the Firebird through a maze of police vehicles, he suddenly felt exhausted. He had to sit for a few minutes to catch his breath before pulling back into traffic on Euclid Avenue. He called Tanya, who picked up after the first ring. "We found Sherry Conaway. She's in rough shape, but alive."

Tanya squealed in joy, then started to cry. "Oh, Nick. How wonderful!"

"Tell you all about it when I get home."

Chapter 8

Thursday Morning
Bay City Blade newsroom

At 8:31 a.m., grandmotherly receptionist Helen leaped into a defensive martial arts position while security guard Phil tried to fend off the bulldozing advance of Ben Conaway as he rolled past them both into the newsroom.

"Where's Nick Steele?" he roared. "Gotta see him now!"

The protests of Helen and Phil did not slow him down. His hard-charging march had now captured the attention of all reporters and editors. Alarmed, Nick stood up from his desk and walked toward the giant. The reporter stuck out his hand as a greeting. Conaway, his face beaming a broad smile as warm as rays of morning sunshine, grabbed Nick and pulled him into his sternum, embracing and swallowing him up in a full bear hug.

"We can't thank you enough," he said, rocking Nick sideways. "Cops told us how you saved our baby girl. Thank you, thank you, thank you."

"Kinda hard to breathe in here," Nick responded, his voice muffled by the big guy's massive arms and broad shoulders. "You're welcome. So glad we could help."

The C-Man and Dave stood nearby, soaking up the joy of the moment, as Nick was released.

"How's Sherry doing this morning?" Clapper asked.

"Better," Big Ben said. "It was touch and go last night. She was in horrible shape, but we could see her improving hour by hour—she's fighting back. We stayed with her all night; her mom is there now. We promised we'd never leave her alone again. Can't tell you how thrilled we are. I'm running on adrenaline, still jacked-up happy."

"She endured so much. Is she talking with you? Talking with her docs?"

69

"She's just beginning to speak, mostly sleeping," Ben said, his voice ragged, his breathing labored. "Her rest is broken. She drifts off, then wakes in a panic, still not sure where she is, or that she's safe. That S.O.B. Stapleton put her through absolute hell."

The whole newsroom had quieted. Reporters and editors forgot about the demands of deadline for the moment and listened intently. Dave told Ben his family had the full support of the community.

"Everyone is with you and sharing your happiness," he said. "Our phones started ringing last night as word spread that Sherry had been found. Still going this morning. They all want to know how she's doing and if she needs anything."

"When the time is right, I'm sure she'll talk with Nick," Ben said, still beaming. "She remembers him carrying her out of that shithole. She cried talking about how exhilarating it was to finally be able to breathe, thinking she might finally be safe."

Conaway said he was running errands and picking up supplies before heading back to the hospital. "Me and the wife are going to take breaks and sleep in shifts while Sherry recovers. The docs say it's going to take awhile. She's young, so she'll come back physically pretty quick. Not so much emotionally. We'll have to do that a step at a time."

Big Ben left like he entered—in a charging rush. As he headed for the door, Helen and Phil jumped out of the way. Without looking back, Conaway hollered his thanks again and told Nick to call anytime for an update.

The newsroom shifted back to its usual clatter and morning deadline rhythm. Reporters hustled about, editors huddled to discuss newshole (how much room was available for stories and photos in that day's paper), and the phones continued screaming for attention—especially now with the development of the Sherry Conaway story.

The C-Man asked Nick how his stories for that day's paper were coming along. He and Dave had three news articles in the works: the banner story would be Sherry's discovery, rescue, and condition; a sidebar article on the Sand Box dungeon, how it was found, and its connection to Eric Stapleton; and a third piece on Stapleton's death officially being ruled an accident on Mackinac Island despite discrepancies in the police narrative of how he died.

Photos would play a huge part in telling the story. The images of the Sand Box and Sherry's dungeon were shocking. Pictures of her on a stretcher in the care of EMTs were riveting. Graphics developed from Mackinac Island showed where Stapleton fell from his horse and the location of his company's rental cottage and placed them into relation to the island's popular and familiar tourist traps.

The deadline clock continued to tick. Nick and Dave returned to whirring computers to write their articles while editors peered over their shoulders, gingerly offering advice and tips as the body of work took shape.

As usual, the C-Man paced across the newsroom, hands on hips, loosened necktie dangling over his round belly, and beads of sweat dotting his furrowed brow. From years of practice, he knew when to apply pressure and when to stand down, allowing his handpicked professionals to do their jobs.

All too soon, it seemed, time would expire. As deadline came, the pressure and intensity rose. Lots of cussing and snorting and shouts erupted in alternating bursts. Finally, the news package was complete. It was sent by computer to the composing room where it would be fitted on pages before it received a final edit check and review. The final steps were platemaking for the printing press. At the same time, paginators readied the news package—with even more photos and graphics—for internet publication.

Nick and Dave, who had arrived at the newsroom at 5 a.m. to begin assembling information and evaluating photos, took a break from the hard morning rush. They needed food and coffee to refuel for the day ahead.

Clapper had already alerted them to a strategy session in his office at 11:15 a.m. They munched on protein bars and slurped fresh brew, chatting quietly about what they'd just written and what information did not make it into their articles. Then Dave broke free to check in on his mom and her doctor re-evaluation, and Nick called Tanya, who he had not spoken with since last night.

When they reconvened in the C-Man's office, the chief wanted to discuss the path ahead. "How do we chase these stories from here?"

Nick said he had spent the previous evening evaluating the notebooks and cell phones he'd collected from Stapleton's island suitcase and Sand Box desk. He said he had compiled a list of frequently called numbers and common text and voicemail messages. He suggested that he and Dave divide up the contacts and figure out who they were and what role they played in Stapleton's life.

"We also need to figure out what was happening in the Sand Box," he said. "Besides being used as a dungeon for Sherry Conaway, what else was it being used for? And what about the extremist information found there. How does that all play together?"

"And the Mackinac Island police ..." Dave started, "are they sticking with their 'accidental death' declaration? What is really going on up there? We have so many questions about Stapleton; we still don't really know who he was and what he was doing."

The C-Man agreed, urging the two reporters to work together and continue attacking the story. "I think we're just scratching the surface—keep digging. Was that dungeon built for Sherry Conaway, or was she just its latest occupant? How many others—women and men—had been held there? What became of the others, if there were any?"

The reporters jotted notes as the three discussed possible directions for new stories. They agreed to keep in touch and meet again at the end of the day to assess what they'd learned. Nick left the newsroom to lunch with Tanya. Dave ran to meet with doctors and check in on his mom, whom he continued to fret about.

On his way to the parking lot, Nick stopped in the pressroom to catch one of the first newspapers rolling to life. It was a tradition for him when he had a significant story publishing, so it was no surprise to pressmen when he popped into their domain. Plus, Nick loved the smell of fresh ink hitting newsprint. He drew in a snoot full of the sweet aroma. A pressman at the end of the production line snagged two copies for Nick, who quickly scanned one to see how it came out, how it was reproducing.

"Lookin' good, guys!" he shouted, competing with the roar of the massive presses. He gave a thumbs up as he headed for the back door. "Thanks! You guys do great work!"

Nick agreed to meet Tanya at Grampa Tony's, the popular Italian restaurant located on Columbus Avenue, the gateway to Bay City's South End. The colorful eatery was also just down the street from Bay City Central, making it easy access for Tanya. She would arrive first, get a table, and order an antipasto salad with homemade dressing and garlic bread.

The reporter placed a call to Louise Stapleton as the Firebird rumbled south on Madison, dodging potholes and jaywalkers to keep pace with timed stoplights. She answered on the first ring, sniffling into the phone. Nick could tell she'd been crying.

"Nick, I'm just, just devastated," she said in a halting voice. "I can't believe my Eric would be involved in any way with kidnapping that poor girl."

Louise blew her nose, then continued. "The police contacted me this morning. They want to search his apartment for evidence of the kidnapping. They want his laptop, phone, and car."

"What about Eric's car? Is it still sitting in the ferry parking lot in Mackinaw City? I'm sure Dave and I are going to return to the island. We could bring it back for you but I'm sure the police will seize it for evidence."

"I'm drowning here, Nick. Just overwhelmed," she said, her voice halting between sobs. "I'm still locating a pathologist to review Eric's body, and now it sounds like he was involved in the kidnapping of one of Jada's friends, the Conaway girl. This is like a nightmare I can't wake up from."

"I'm sure this is painful for you, and I'll try to help," Nick said, offering to look through the envelope he received from the R.I.P. mortician. "If it contains vehicle keys and a parking slip, I'll let you know. The police are going to want to see everything that could be evidence. Even though Eric is gone, the cops need to piece this together to make sure of his involvement and possible accomplices—who helped him or knew about it. Let me get back with you."

Grampa Tony's came into view as Nick clicked off his phone. He parked next to Tanya's Chevy SUV and rushed into the restaurant to meet her. A waitress with a name tag that said in all caps she was ANGIE dropped a large salad, bread, and dressing on the table before disappearing. He gave Tanya a kiss on the cheek and slid into the booth seat across from her.

"What a day!" she said. "Actually, you've had two big days. How are you holding up?"

He laughed. "Yup, it's been wild. Sherry Conaway's dad showed up in the newsroom first thing today. He was beside himself happy, and he's as big as a house, so his appearance was quite a display. Says Sherry was in rough shape last night but coming along slow but sure."

Nick handed Tanya a paper, literally hot off the press. She looked at the front page and tucked it in her bag to take back to school.

They dug into the food. Nick was starving. Tanya watched him load his plate, remarking about the atmosphere at Central High as buzz spread across the school about the rescue of Sherry Conaway.

"You'd have thought we won a football championship," she said, taking her turn at scooping salad onto her plate. "It was electric. It's all the kids wanted to talk about all morning long. The principal made a P.A. announcement about 10:15 a.m., saying he had spoken with her parents and was delighted to let schoolmates know she was found, and her health is improving at Bay Med.

"A cheer went up, almost in unison, from every classroom," she continued, breaking off a heel from the bread. "The hall monitors said it could be heard throughout the building. Incredible. Jubilation everywhere."

Nick nodded. He said that the reaction in the newsroom was almost the same. "Happiness and a sense of relief. So often, a young lady goes missing for months and the outcome is not so glorious."

Tanya asked about Sherry's condition. Nick shook his head. Suddenly, the luncheon went sour.

"When I found her, it was shocking," he said, pausing from his salad. "I didn't write everything in today's story. Too horrifying. Eventually, it will all come out, but I didn't want to take away from the main thrust of the story, which is that she was found alive."

Angie returned to refill water glasses and check on the quality of the food. Nick waited until she left to continue.

"Are you sure you want to hear more while eating? It's nasty."

"Spare me the pure grit," she said, focusing on Nick's facial expression. "My guess is that she was thin and frail."

"I carried her. She was well under 100 pounds," he said. "I thought she's been starved. Obviously, she'd been drugged. Needle marks on her arms. Sedatives were probably mixed in with what little food she received to keep her passive.

"The bed I found her on was absolutely filthy, as you can imagine, after repeated sexual abuse. I'm sure they're testing her for STDs and pregnancy. Just awful. Carrying her out almost made me cry."

Tanya sat quietly, not eating, or talking. She excused herself to use the restroom. Nick watched her walk away, hoping she wasn't going to become ill. He wished he'd not told her details until later. He flagged Angie, asking for a check. They both had to hustle back to work.

When Tanya returned, he asked if she was OK.

"Yes, I'm a big girl," she said, sitting back down. "It's just so sickening, especially since I know Sherry. She's been in my office often; I've worked with her. She's got a big heart and a good head on her shoulders, is mature for her age…. I just hope she can come back from this. She's 15—what a horrible thing to have to overcome. I'm going to reach out to the Conaways. Sherry may want to talk with someone she knows, and I want to be there for her."

Nick nodded. "She's going to need a lot of support. It's important for the school to rally around her."

Angie brought the check to the table. Nick paid with cash and left a nice tip. They left without finishing their lunches. Sherry's plight was too much to stomach.

Dave raced to his mother's room after meeting with her doctors. They confirmed what he knew. Mrs. Balz was in serious decline. They adjusted her medication, hoping to find a medium where she could continue with normal activities but do so with relative calm. It was a difficult balancing act, but her son did not want to see her drugged into a stupor.

He knocked on her door, which was not closed all the way. Dave could hear her talking with someone, a voice he didn't recognize. He entered. An elderly man, thin and balding, sat in a chair next to her.

"Hi, Ma," he beamed at the two. "Just thought I'd pop in to visit for a bit."

"Are you a salesman?" Mrs. Balz asked, her eyes wide but blank. Right away he knew she didn't recognize him.

"Whatever you're selling, I don't want any," she said, laughing. "My son doesn't give me any money, so I can't buy anything. My son is very stingy with me."

The comment caused Frail Man to join in the laughter.

"Mom, it's me, Dave," he said, ignoring the old guy. "I'm your son. I was just here last night with you. Remember?"

She shook her head and picked up a cup of tea from the table beside her. "No, my son is named David and he's much more handsome than you. You can just leave your sales brochure on the table by the door."

Dave smiled, deciding it was better not to argue with her. She was calm and seemed to be enjoying herself with this stranger. He walked closer to the two and offered his hand to Frail Man. "Hi, I'm Dave, her son. I don't believe we've met."

The stranger didn't stand. He sat, his mouth opened slightly, watching Dave carefully, like he didn't believe him. Dave used his left hand to pick the stranger's right arm out of his lap. He shook the dangling hand and asked for his name.

Frail Man smiled. "Why, I'm Captain America. Everybody in these parts knows that. I have special powers. It's my job to save everyone and bring peace and justice to all."

Mrs. Balz smiled at this assertion and sipped her tea.

Ah, Dave thought. Finally, here is the captain. He decided to go with the flow. "Nice to meet you, Captain America. Glad my mom has found a good friend."

"You're not her son," the captain said. "She said so."

Mrs. Balz smiled and nodded. "That's right. My David is so much more handsome."

Dave was stunned, but thought the correct course was just to accept them and move on. He would come back later. At least she seemed at ease, and nobody was fattening her lip today. He backed his way out of the room, smiled, and waved, leaving the door just as he'd found it.

Room 32 was just down the hall, he'd been told. Dave decided to say hello to Mrs. Hayden. The door was open; he rapped on the frame.

"Yoo-hoo, yoo-hoo! Mr. Balz! I'm over here," Leona called from further down the hall. "I'm on my way."

Dave turned to see the Calico Kitty Lady moving toward him, arms churning. She was smiling, knees pumping. A navy-blue, soft sweat suit had replaced her pink bathrobe. Her silver hair was wrapped in a rainbow-colored scarf. Her kitty slippers scuffed the floor. "Hold on. Going as fast as I can."

"No rush," Dave replied, the sight forcing a smile. He turned to meet her just as she pulled up, slightly out of breath. "Just thought I'd stop to say hello."

Leona asked about Dave's mom. "I haven't popped in on her yet. I know she was going to meet with her doctor. Doing better?"

Dave said she seemed content, though not all there. "By the way, I met Captain America. You were right, very odd. But they seemed to be entertaining each other. Would you happen to know his real name?"

"If I remember correctly, I think it's Thomas Redding, but everyone refers to him by his nickname. Claims he has special powers," she said, her thin eyebrows dancing up and down.

Leona invited him into her room for tea, but Dave declined. She put her hand on his arm. "I've heard from some of the other ladies that your mom is sliding, doesn't know where she is more and more. Physically, she seems strong but she's struggling mentally."

Dave nodded. He thanked her for checking on his mom. "I've got to run, but I'll be back. Let me know if she gets in trouble."

Leona smiled and patted his arm. Dave left, not knowing what to think.

Chapter 9

Late Thursday Afternoon
Bay City Blade newsroom

As Nick hustled into the newsroom, the sight of reporters and editors gathered around the office's biggest computer screen grabbed his attention. Drayton Clapper spotted Nick and motioned him over to join the group.

"Nick, you gotta see this," the C-Man said, turning back to the screen. "It's a YouTube video from Mackinac Island, shot this morning. Shocking." Those gawking at the screen guffawed, hooted, and howled, not knowing how to take it.

The reporter wasn't sure he could take any more "shocking" than he'd experienced in the past 24 hours. But his sensibilities were about to be rattled again. There, on the screen, was a giant image of the front door of the Mackinac Island Community Hall Building, the two-story, nondescript home to local government, on Market Street.

A large poster was attached to the front door. The printed declaration was stunning. It said: "You can't COVER this up. WE ARE AT WAR! SHUT DOWN LINE 5 NOW. Stapleton is the first to die. MANY MORE WILL FOLLOW. Stay tuned." Attached to the bottom of the poster was Eric Stapleton's scalp, a large rectangle of bushy black hair with blood-crusted edges.

"Ho-ly shit!" Nick declared. Having just seen the condition of the top of Stapleton's head in the prep room of the R.I.P. Funeral Chapel, he knew the scalp was real. "What now?"

The Community Hall declaration was unsigned, but it alluded to the growing discord between those who want to keep the oil pipelines, known as Line 5, and the environmentalists, including Native American tribes who view the Straits of Mackinac and Mackinac Island as sacred, holy grounds. Until now, the dispute had been largely civil—public protests, marches, meetings, rallies, videos, and prominent billboards the only sign of unrest.

But now, it appeared as though an employee of a company contracted to help monitor and maintain the controversial pipeline had been murdered despite the claim, which Nick thought was lame, by island police that the death of Eric Stapleton was accidental. The Bay City man's obvious injuries simply did not match the manner of death described in the official report, which had just been released.

Dave Balz joined the newsroom banter, which had become boisterous. He quickly absorbed the stunning Mackinac Island video, which was now capturing national and international attention. Copy editor Steve had flipped on the newsroom TV. News channel surfing showed clips of the island murder and scalping highlighting CNN, Fox, Reuters, NPR, ProPublica, BBC, and C-SPAN, among others.

The C-Man called for Nick and Dave to meet in his office. The Stapleton story had taken yet another neck-breaking turn. They needed to map out a plan to continue chasing the Stapleton murder, the Stapleton kidnapping, the Stapleton Sand Box unit and dungeon, and the recovery of Sherry Conaway.

"OK, guys, where do we go with this?" the chief asked, sitting in his chair and folding his hands across the top of his belly. "First big question: Who killed Eric Stapleton and why? Is it tied to the pipeline controversy or the kidnapping? How—if at all—are they connected?"

Nick reminded the two that he still had two of Stapleton's cell phones and two of his personal notebooks. He noted that Stapleton's vehicle, and perhaps his laptop computer, were still in a Mackinaw City parking lot.

"Now that there's international implications, the police—most likely the Michigan State Police—will take this over, and they'll want to see everything," Nick said. "I should turn over what I have to the cops today. I figured out Stapelton's pass code and I was able to get a look at his phone calls, email, and text messages. I noted most frequent callers and contacts and subject matter. That should give us some leads."

Dave shook his head. "Despite everything we know about Eric

Stapleton, the man is still a complete enigma. Who was he, and what was he up to? How weird and kinky was he? And what got him killed?"

"We're going to need updated stories every day," the C-Man noted. "Let's go back to the island authorities. What's the reaction to the Community Hall declaration of war, the admission of murder, and the scalping? Is the death still an accident? And we need reaction and comment from the environmentalists, the oil company, and the Native Americans. Let's keep digging."

The reporters left Clapper's office and divided up the assignment. Nick would call island police, Louise Stapleton, and the oil company. Dave would connect with the environmentalists and the Native American tribes involved. They'd gather as much information as possible and write a story together.

Nick returned to his desk and tried calling the island's Chief Westover. Not surprisingly, her line was busy. The whole world, at least many of its news agencies, had placed calls to the location of a very public murder, a grisly mutilation, and a potential environmental time bomb that ticked with every passing minute. He kept trying the chief's number; he had to get through somehow. In the meantime, he called around to get reactions to the events on the island. While he waited to connect, he looked through the information he'd gleaned from Eric Stapleton's cell phones and notebooks.

The three names and numbers that came up repeatedly were Leon, Travis, and Randy. No last names. He shot them text messages from Stapleton's phones, hoping the recipients had not been paying attention to the news since Sunday and were unaware of his demise. No response. He tried calling the numbers, but no one picked up.

After several minutes, a text flashed on the screen from Randy. "Who is this? Thought you were dead?"

Nick thought about how to respond. He texted back: "Friend of the family. Checking in with Eric's old amigos. Want to get together, catch a beer?"

Randy paused before answering. "Friend, huh? OK, you get the friend rate. It's a hundred bucks an hour at my place, like usual."

Nick paused, wondering who he was chatting with. "First time, I'd like to meet in public. Bar or restaurant. Just talk."

Randy: "Talk is still one hundred bucks. One hour. A nice tip always gets you extras. Spinning Wheel on Broadway. See you in 30 minutes."

Nick: "How will I know you?"

"Raven red hair, black jumpsuit, nose ring, tatted boobs."

The reporter grabbed his jacket and told Dave he had to run to meet one of Stapleton's friends. On the way to the parking lot, he checked his wallet to see if he had a hundred bucks. He did, with a couple of twenties to spare.

Nick had stopped at the Spinning Wheel many times over the years. It was an old-school South End neighborhood bar where many of the patrons could simply stumble home after drinking and eating their fill. Live, head-banging music on the weekends. Friendly waitstaff. Shaundra commanded the bar as its chief, he recalled, and offered inexpensive, oddball drinks. His favorite: dill pickle double vodka—four bucks.

The reporter looked for a safe place to park the Firebird, which would attract a lot of envious South End eyeballs. But it was broad daylight on Broadway, and Nick hoped his hot rod would be OK. It was 3:30 p.m. and he was glad to get to the Wheel before happy hour, usually noisy and sometimes a little crazy, depending upon how freely the booze was flowing. As he walked to the front, he noticed two women standing outside a side door, passing a joint. He couldn't tell if they were customers or employees.

Inside, the Wheel came into focus as Nick's eyes adjusted from natural light to dim, neon-highlighted bar view. It was just as he remembered, though he hadn't visited in a few years. Neighborhood bars in Bay City thrive on their familiarity and predictability to the neighbors.

Off to the side, next to the pool tables, he spotted a woman in a booth. Their eyes locked. Nick approached. "Randy? Hi, I'm Nick. We talked on the phone a half hour ago." Raven Hair was a big woman: wide shoulders and hips, pleasingly plump with lightning blue eyes, jumpsuit with plunging neckline, and revealing tatted boobs, as she had described. Late 20s.

The reporter sat across from her, took a deep breath, and identified himself. She stared at him without saying a word. Then she stood, placing her left hand on the table: "I don't talk to cops or reporters."

Nick cupped her hand with one of his. "Your friend is dead. I simply want to find out why. I'm only here to talk. You won't be mentioned in the newspaper. I'm just after information, not here to harm you or get you in trouble."

Raven Hair relaxed slightly. "No quotes in the paper and you have to promise not to rat me out to the cops."

He nodded. "I promise. You will be protected."

She sat back down. Her eyes danced to see if anyone watched, then focused on Nick.

"It's still a hundred bucks and the clock started ticking when you walked in the door." A smile erupted across her face, revealing sparkling white teeth with a dimple dotting each end like a period ending a sentence. She motioned for a waiter. "And you buy the drinks."

Tony appeared out of nowhere. He sported a bullseye tattoo on his face with its center dot on his nose. Nick hoped it was a temporary tat. Hardware dangled up and down his ear lobes like flashy fishing tackle. "What can I get yous?"

Raven Hair said she'd take the dill pickle double vodka special. Since it was nearly 4 p.m., Nick asked for a draft of Labatt Blue. He would figure out how to explain having a drink with a strange woman and the loss of a hundred bucks to Tanya later.

First question: "Is your name really Randy?" Nick asked.

"Yes, but I'm not giving you my last name, at least not right now," she said with a half-smile. "My dad wanted a boy, so he stuck me with that name. I get the next question, and clock keeps ticking. Did you write the story about the young girl chained to a wall in Eric's place?"

"Were you shocked to read Eric would treat a young woman that way?"

"Nope," she said flatly, spinning a thin gold bracelet on her wrist. "Eric was kinky like that. He was into chains and bondage. And it also explains why I haven't seen much of him recently."

Nick asked Randy to describe her relationship to Eric Stapleton and how long she had known him.

"Strictly business. He wanted sex and I wanted money. Purely transactional. We connected about three years ago," she said, pausing while Bullseye Face set two drinks and a small cup of trail mix on the table. Tony dashed toward another table, saying over his shoulder: "Yous want anything else, holla'."

Nick took a sip of beer and licked the foam from his graying moustache. "How did you two meet?"

Randy said Stapleton answered one of her Craigslist ads. "We met during the day at my mom's place while she was at work. For my safety, I always meet clients—especially until I know them well—with another girl. So, he had to pay for the company of me and Brandi."

Hmmm. Randy and Brandi? He wondered if Raven Hair was playing him. He decided to ask her something about Stapleton that would tell him whether she really knew the guy or had simply read the newspaper and was trying to capitalize on Nick's text to her.

"You mentioned earlier that Eric was into chains and bondage," he said, watching her closely. "Did he wear clothing to hide markings?"

She laughed. "You mean the turtlenecks? Hell ya! He loved wearing a choker chain dog collar. He'd have me get naked on the bed and hook a leash to the choker and tie it off to my bedroom door. Then he'd drop to his knees and lean ahead toward me against the chain while I strummed my banjo."

"Strummed your banjo?"

"Yeah, you know. Used my fingers down there."

"Oh, OK, got it," Nick said, blushing once the full impact of the activity registered. "And that would make Eric excited?"

"Hell ya! He'd start snorting, and slobbering, and gagging all at once—turning beet red. Then, he usually either reached full orgasm or passed out, sometimes both. Couple times I had to loosen the choker and kick him in the chest to get him going again."

Well, that certainly would explain the bloody chain-link marks on Stapleton's neck that he'd witnessed in the R.I.P. prep room. And it solves the summertime turtlenecks puzzle. Randy seemed to be a legit source, despite being a call girl who had catered to a kidnapper and rapist. What else did she know about him?

Randy hailed Tony, signaling another round. She said they had time for one more. "Before we continue," she added, "slip me a hundred bucks under the table." Nick dug out his wallet.

"Don't paw through your billfold out here," she said, glancing around the bar. "Go to the can, get your money out, fold it so you can palm it, then give it to me under the table when you come back. Damn, what a rookie! Gotta tell you everything."

Nick blushed again at his naivete. "OK, sorry." He tried to walk casually to the men's room to take care of his financial obligation but was aware that his one hour was quickly evaporating.

When he returned, he checked his watch, then passed the palmed cash to Randy. **Smooth**, he thought.

"Do Travis and Leon mean anything to you?" he asked. "I found their names and numbers in the same way I discovered you, but they didn't respond to my messages."

Bullseye Face swooped in with two drinks on a tray. "I see yous lookin' at your watch. Ready for a check?" Nick nodded.

Randy said she and Brandi had connected with Travis and Leon via Eric only twice. She indicated the two were disgusting and filthy and refused further meetings. "Pretty low down if you got good money and you get turned down by hookers, right? Well, that should tell you about those two. Violent with mean streaks. Real Neanderthals, low-brow, cave-man types. We used to joke that their granddads were probably chimpanzees."

Nick asked how they were connected to Stapleton. "Are they Bay City guys? Did they work with Eric at Underwater Solutions?" Tony flashed by, flipping a check on the table. The reporter dropped a twenty on top of the check.

"Not from around here, I'm proud to declare," she said, pulling the pickle and hitting the vodka drink hard. "They were from way out, deep in the backwoods of the Thumb. Argyle, Decker are the towns

I remember. They wore camo gear and thick, black boots. Took them more time to get undressed and dressed than it did for service. Fast and hard, like dogs—if you know what I mean."

Regrettably, Nick understood exactly what she meant, but the visual imagery of her words made him laugh, nonetheless. He took a long pull on his draft beer, erasing foam from his upper lip with a quick flick of his tongue.

"Argyle and Decker. That's extremist country. Hardcore. Sounds like militia types. Did they talk in conspiracy lingo? Hate for the government? That kind of thing?"

Randy said they didn't talk much, just did a lot of grunting. "Definitely racists. They kept asking if we'd ever been with Africans, Mexicans, or Jews. Course, that's none of their damn business. One thing they kept referring to is 'The Plan,' and how it was going to change everything. We thought it was just more bravado bullshit. Me and Brandi got our fill of those two real fast. We cut ties."

She spun the bracelet on her wrist for the last time and polished her drink in two quick gulps. "Times up, gotta go. Thanks for the drinks, and remember, no quotes in the paper. I don't want a visit from those two Neanderthals. Got it?"

Nick assured her again that he would honor her wishes. He thanked her and asked for a call if she thought of anything else that might be related to their discussion. He asked if he could snap a photo of her, just to prove to his boss that she was an unnamed source of information. "Hey, I want to turn this in on my expense account as a legitimate business expenditure. You provided a lot of useful and interesting information. Like I said, I'll protect your name and photo."

Randy didn't like it, but he could tell she was flattered that she'd been helpful. Plus, it was obvious that she liked and trusted Nick. She agreed to one photo alongside the Spinning Wheel logo—like she worked there.

Before they parted, she asked a final question. "How's that girl doing? Sherry. Sounds like Eric hurt her pretty bad."

Nick was pleased she asked. "Sherry is having a tough go of it, but the docs think she'll be OK in time. It's going to take a while, but she's getting support from everyone; all across the community people want to know how they can help."

Randy smiled, flashing the pearlies and dimples again. "I'm glad to hear that. Add me to the list. Me and Brandi will help, too. Believe me, I know Eric could be a real monster."

When Nick jumped back into the Firebird, he hoped to leverage a nugget of information that he panned from Randy. He picked one of Eric's cells and sent new messages to Travis and Leon, the Argyle Neanderthals: "I know all about 'The Plan.' It's not going to work. You're already busted. Eric would be pissed that you screwed this up. Contact me to fix it."

The reporter took a deep breath and wondered aloud: "Hope that riles them up enough to get them to respond." He fired up his ride and headed toward home.

Tanya pulled into the packed Bay Med visitor's parking lot. It was end-of-the-day visiting hours and men and women of all ages hustled from their vehicles into the huge hospital on Columbus Avenue to see loved ones who were ill or injured. When Tanya had reached out to the Conaway family, Ben said his daughter had asked to see her friend from school.

The message thrilled Tanya, who wrapped up her school counseling duties as quick as she could to visit the injured Central student. She left a voice message on Nick's recorder that she was rushing to the hospital, and she might not be home for dinner.

Danielle Conaway waited for Tanya in the hallway outside her daughter's room. Big Ben was inside comforting Sherry. They had decided it was best for Danielle to meet Tanya first and prepare her for the shock of seeing their daughter. The two women hugged, and Danielle pulled Tanya to a couple of chairs out of earshot from Sherry's room.

"I can't thank you enough for coming," said Danielle, who clutched a wet handkerchief in her right hand. Dark circles ringed her red, tired eyes. "You're Sherry's first visitor outside of family and our priest. She's responding well considering what she's been through, but she's not the young girl in your memory from school. I want to prepare you for meeting her. She's so skinny and frail and hurt—it may shock you.

"One more thing," Danielle continued, leaning in closer. "Her tests came back today. No STDs, but she is pregnant. My girl is still processing that. She's shocked and trying to figure it out."

Tanya held Danielle's hands in hers with a firm grip. Stunned by the revelation, Tanya fought the urge to cry. It would be overwhelming for any woman. She was determined to be strong, comforting, and helpful to Sherry and her folks. "Thanks for the heads up. I'm here for you all. Glad to help in any way I can."

They hugged while sitting. "Are you ready?" Danielle asked. "Sherry knows you're here. She perked up when I told her you'd called and were coming to visit."

Tanya smiled and took a deep breath. "Let's go," she said. Danielle took her by the hand, and they walked to the door. She knocked on it lightly, then stuck her head inside. "Sherry, look who's here. Tanya."

The two stepped inside the room. Its lights were dim, and it felt toasty. Ben, smiling and holding Sherry's hand, stood up from the chair next to his daughter's bed, which was propped up in a three-quarters sitting position. Sherry let go of his hand, leaned forward with her arms outstretched for Tanya, and smiled.

Tanya had steeled herself to keep the look of shock off her face, but her first view of Sherry fully tested that resolve. Danielle was right. This was not the confident, beaming young woman she remembered from school. This tiny waif barely resembled the bubbly teen she knew: deep-set eyes, all skin and bones, once silky hair now stiff as straw with clumps missing, revealing knot-size bald spots.

Nevertheless, smiling Tanya rushed to the girl's outstretched arms and the two embraced, holding onto each other tightly, rocking slightly. They didn't speak for minutes. Danielle and Ben watched quietly, tears streaming down the big guy's cheeks.

"Lord, I am so happy to see you, Sherry," she gushed in the teen's ear. "Everyone at school is so happy. They all send their best and can hardly wait for you to return."

Ben scooted his chair forward so Tanya could slide into it, but Sherry would not let her school counselor and friend go. She ended up sitting on the side of the bed where the embrace continued. Tears perked from Danielle's eyes as she watched her daughter receive support and love from a woman she trusted completely.

The mother dabbed at her eyes, then whispered, "Your dad and I are going to step outside so you two can talk. We'll be right outside if you need us." She grabbed her husband's paw and dragged him to the exit.

The door had barely clicked shut when the dam broke and Sherry burst into tears, sobbing to Tanya: "Did they tell you I'm pregnant? I've got a monster's baby inside me—a brutal, ugly, perverted son of a bitch growing inside me. Did they tell you?"

"Oh, Sherry. Yes, your mom told me about your pregnancy. You've got an innocent baby growing inside you—a baby who needs your love," Tanya said in a calm, reassuring voice.

"No, no, no! I want it out of me," the girl gushed, sobbing. "I'm not going to give birth to another rapist, a sodomizer, an evil, cruel demon. My God. I want to get rid of it. I'd be doing the world a favor."

Tanya hung onto the girl, who she felt shudder in her arms. Counselor and friend Tanya had to step forward because the woman Tanya found it hard to disagree with Sherry. She was familiar with research that had showed evidence of violent traits and tendencies being passed generation to generation.

"I hear you, Sherry. I understand your fear," she said, quietly. "I can't imagine being in your position. This is so much for any woman to deal with. This is really, really hard. What you are thinking and saying—it's understandable, it's not wrong.

"But what I also hope you will think about is that your baby is part you—and you're not a monster. Far from it. Your baby is also part your dad and he's a wonderful man, a great dad. Your baby is also part your mom—and think how terrific she is."

Sherry continued crying, but the convulsiveness of her sobs eased as she held on to Tanya, listening intently. Counselor and friend Tanya continued. "Your baby deserves a chance to be you, and your dad, and your mom. As a mother, you can guide and shape your baby. Your family and friends will help you on this journey. I will help you."

The teenager calmed. She hadn't thought of her pregnancy this way. Until now, her condition, which she did not choose and had no control of, had only given her rage and anger. Eric Stapleton had stepped into her life and changed it with violence, degradation, humiliation, and a baby. She had not been able to see through the red to find the full pallet of what her life could look like in the future.

Sherry shifted their discussion away from the pregnancy. She feared that time would erase the jubilant goodwill her friends had for her right now. Eventually, the joy of her rescue and recovery would fade and she would be left to deal with the bottom line.

"I'll always be damaged goods," she said, lightening her hold on Tanya. "There's no getting away from that. People will look at me and they'll think: she's the girl who was kept in a dungeon and raped. She's the girl who was violated in every way imaginable. She was the girl who had her hair pulled out by a bastard while he raped and sodomized her."

The flood of anger hit Tanya like a tidal wave. This poor girl had suffered and experienced so much abuse. It was heartbreaking. The counselor wept quietly, then stiffened to offer solace.

"Yes, yes. People may think that Sherry," Tanya said, renewing her firm embrace of the girl. "But remember, they'll also know you overcame the abuse. They'll also admire your strength for rising above the horror you endured. They will marvel at your resolve to rise from the devastating hand you were dealt to build a big life for you and your baby.

"You've got that kind of strength, Sherry. You can do it," she continued. "You're bigger than anything Eric Stapleton did to you. You had no control of what he did, but you do have control of what lies ahead. You can make your own path forward."

Sherry leaned ahead, falling into Tanya's lap. The crying had stopped. The teen sighed heavily, sniffling hard. The counselor kept one arm fully around the girl and used her free hand to stroke Sherry's forehead, gently caressing with her fingertips.

"What about Mark?" the teen asked. "You probably don't know him. He goes to Western. He was my boyfriend before all this happened. We never had sex because he thought I was too young. Now, he knows I've been used and abused. Soiled. Treated like a waste bucket. When he hears about the baby, he'll freak out."

"Don't sell him short. He may surprise you. Lots of people love and respect you. Give them a chance to continue with that. You've got lots of people in your corner. Trust me. Lots of love coming your way."

The girl settled and Tanya continued to soothe. They fell into small talk, the woman giving the girl updates from among her friends and classmates at school. Sherry had missed plenty in the past three months. Soon they were giggling about school happenings, the highs and lows of life in the halls of Central.

Tanya stayed with Sherry until hospital visiting hours ended. The visit also gave her parents a much-needed respite. The counselor left, giving Sherry a hug, promising to return soon.

Danielle walked Tanya to the elevator while Ben returned to his bedside chair. Sherry's mom took Tanya's hand. "We heard everything standing in the hall. Thank you so much, you were great."

Tanya smiled, nodded, and squeezed her hand back. "That poor girl is going through so much. She's going to need professional help and lots of love. I know you and Ben will stick with her. So will I. It's going to be a tough road ahead."

They hugged as the elevator door dinged open. Tanya left, worried sick about Sherry, her unborn baby, and their future. She was determined to find a way she and Nick could help.

Dave scurried down the halls of Shady Lane to his mom's room. The door was partially opened. He knocked. A stranger's voice answered, "Yes?" He pushed it open with his forearm, revealing a shocking scene: Mrs. Balz strapped to a chair, a bruise on her forehead, and her chin resting on her chest. A young orderly, dressed in white, stood next to the chair. On the other side, a nurse appeared as though she was administering a shot into his mom's arm.

"What's going on here?" Dave asked, rushing forward. The orderly turned to face him and held up his hands. The move stopped Dave; he focused on his mom, who was babbling. The nurse finished her task and turned. "Again, what's going on with my mom?"

"Mrs. Balz had another violent episode," the nurse, who he didn't recognize, responded. "She lashed out physically with staff, refusing to take meds, and remaining highly agitated. We decided to sedate her—we were afraid she was going to hurt herself."

Dave moved to his mom's side and went down on one knee. "And how did she get this bruise on her forehead? Was she hurt in any other way?"

"She fought us and resisted the safety belt," she said. The orderly said nothing, allowing the older, more experienced health professional to explain. "Of course, we're sorry whenever there's an injury. But it couldn't be avoided. I was here. I observed. We did our best."

The response softened Dave's edge. He was both saddened and hurt to see his mom battered and drugged into submission, incoherent. Mrs. Balz still had not looked up or acknowledged her son's presence. He pressed in closer to her side. "Are you OK, mom? Can you hear me? It's Dave."

The sedative was taking hold. Mrs. Balz blinked and drooled slightly but did not answer her son. She wore a turquoise sleeping gown and hairnet. Soft slippers covered her feet. He snagged a tissue from the desk beside her bed and dabbed at the liquid, now dripping from the end of her chin. He spoke to her in whispers, trying to soothe her.

The Shady Lane staffers moved toward the door. The nurse said Mrs. Balz would be ready for bed soon and they would return shortly to check on her. Dave nodded, grimly. He did not thank them because he was not sure they deserved it.

When they left, Dave loosened the safety strap holding her snug to the chair. She sagged and slid slightly forward. Deciding to put her into bed, he pulled back her covers and gently slid the chair sideways so he could lift her up and steer her into bed in one motion. He leaned into her and felt her warm breath on his neck. When he lifted her, he felt her hug back. The embrace was glorious.

"I've got you mom," he whispered. "I'm going to get you tucked in so you can rest. You're OK now. You're safe. I've got you."

He lowered her into the bed and straightened her legs and feet, pulling the sheet and comforter over her outstretched body. He savored the tender moment with his mom. As he rolled back the top of the comforter away from her chin, she grabbed his arm firmly.

"Are you really my son?" she asked, her blue eyes open and blinking at him, searching for something recognizable.

"Yes, this is Dave."

"Then, you've got to help me. I hate this. I can't go on. Please, help me die. I beg you. I've got pills. You can use a pillow. Just put me to sleep. I'm ready to meet Jesus. This world is not for me anymore."

Mrs. Balz's plea broke Dave's heart. He didn't want her to die, and he sure had no intention of helping her take her life. "Mom, please don't say that. We're going to get this fixed. We're going to find a way for you to be happy."

Tears welled in her eyes as she drifted toward sleep, Dave's heart sinking further as she rolled to her side away from him. He kissed her on the cheek and moved to the chair she'd just occupied. He watched her breathing, the comforter rising and falling into an easy rhythm. Finally, he relaxed and hoped she would have a restful night.

Dave cleaned up the top of her desk, discarding used tissues and water cups and plastic wrappers. He opened the desk drawer to put away her notepad and pen and noticed several small mint and candy tins, her favs. He shook each to check if full or empty. They sounded full except for one, which rattled. He opened it and discovered the box nearly full of pills. More than a dozen, all shapes, sizes, and colors.

She'd been saving her meds instead of taking them. No wonder she'd gotten out of sorts, he thought. Dave studied them but had no idea what they were. He thought about her declaration: "I've got pills." He did not want her to become despondent and use them. He closed the tin and stuck it in his pocket, deciding to call her doctor in the morning to alert him and ask what to do with the drugs.

As he quietly pulled the chair away from the bed, the nurse and orderly returned to the room. Dave whispered to them that she seemed to be resting, perhaps even sleeping, quietly. The nurse nodded and motioned for him to join her in the hallway.

"I've made a notation in her chart about the incident tonight," she said quietly. "You can discuss the situation with my floor manager tomorrow if you like. And we'll check on her tonight, like usual."

Dave nodded, said OK, and walked down the hall, not feeling well at all about what had transpired in his mom's room. He felt horrible that he couldn't help her more, help ease what pained her. His stomach turned as he recalled her wish to die and her request for his assistance in making that happen. A feeling of gloom drooped his shoulders as he reached the F-150 in the parking lot. He dreaded facing his mom's future.

Chapter 10

Friday Morning
Bay City Blade newsroom

Chief Westover from the Mackinac Island Police Department returned Nick's call at 7:30 a.m. She told Nick she had been up all night answering media inquiries from across the world. The public declaration of war, the admission of murder, and the posted scalp of Eric Stapleton had captured the attention of millions.

In addition to media, hundreds of tourists on the island had captured the early morning Community Hall visual on their cell phones and hurled it across the internet, creating an extraordinary viral event.

"Sorry it took me so long to get back to you," the chief said. "This whole thing with Eric Stapleton has turned into a pure shitstorm. Never seen anything like it. Of course, we're sitting on a powder keg up here."

Nick asked her to explain. She said environmentalists, Native Americans, the oil company that owns Line 5, and Underwater Solutions were all in an uproar, declaring they had nothing to do with the posting at Community Hall.

"Tensions are at an all-time high," she continued, "and, of course, they all blame me for how this whole thing was handled. I'll probably get handed my walking papers, and, frankly, I don't give a shit. We tried to tamp the murder down, call it an accident, ignore the scalping, and quietly move on. I thought we could keep a lid on it, but it's all blown up on us."

Nick asked if the chief was acknowledging that she had knowingly falsified the police report and investigation into Eric Stapleton's death.

"I'm saying that this whole case is now in the hands of the Michigan State Police, which will conduct its own investigation and issue a report," the chief said. "All future inquiries should go to MSP. I did the best I could given my restrictions and limitations."

The reporter asked the cop if she had a theory about who killed Stapleton. Nick said he understood that she could not comment on the record for publication, but did the chief have a hunch about what happened out on the Mackinac Island horse trail?

After a long pause, she said: "I've got my suspicions. If you quote me on this, I'll deny it. But I think it was an inside murder. I think Stapleton knew the killer. Somebody came out of the woods, knocked him off the horse with a walking stick or pole, watched him die from a broken neck—or maybe gave his head a quick twist to make sure—then scalped the man after he'd died."

Finally, an honest assessment from this police officer, Nick thought. "Care to share your suspicion about the identity of the killer?"

"Nope. Got my ideas, but no hard evidence," she said. "It was very well planned out. The killer knew Stapleton's riding routine, waited to make sure there were no witnesses, then attacked. And lack of blood on the trail indicated that Stapleton had been dead for a while before the scalping happened. His heart had quit pumping, no big bleed out."

Hmmm, interesting, the reporter thought. "So, the scalping was an afterthought?"

Westover laughed. "I think the killer was hoping to throw suspicion on the Indians, which is ridiculous because Michigan Native American Tribes have never been known for taking scalps. Culturally, that's mostly a Western thing. Local tribes called what happened to Stapleton a sickening cliché aimed at maligning them, which ticked them off. They found it insulting."

Nick said he had one more question. Why not face it head-on? Why was it declared accidental?

The chief chuckled. "Come on, Nick, you're a smart guy. Mackinac Island is a dreamland for visitors. Tourist la-la land. And, honestly, we don't have much crime here, so a murder doesn't fit the picture. Not a good look, and not one the Chamber of Commerce wants pushed out there."

The reporter thanked the chief and wished her good luck. He

looked at the stack of official statements from the oil company, the environmentalists, and the Native Americans that had been emailed overnight. Westover was right. They each expressed outrage and pointed fingers in other directions. He still needed to talk with Louise Stapleton about her son's murder, too.

Nick checked the big newsroom deadline clock. He thought Dave would be in to help write the main update story about the murder inquiry by now.

Clapper had also asked for an update story on the recovery of Sherry Conaway as well as the multiple fundraising efforts to help the young woman. Tanya had told him about her emotional meeting with the teen last night, and Big Ben Conaway had already touched base with Nick on his daughter's condition that morning: stable and improving.

As Nick started writing the main news story, a text pinged on Stapleton's cell. "'The Plan' is already in place. You got information—come to Argyle Roadhouse at 2 this afternoon. No cops."

Nick signaled back: "Got it."

The C-Man roared up to Nick's desk like a chugging freight train. "Nick, just got some bad news. Dave called. His mom passed away last night. He's pretty busted up about it. Needless to say, he won't be in today. Let me know if you need help pulling those stories together."

"Damn, sorry to hear that," Nick said, surprised that he'd not heard the news from his friend. "I'll get these pieces together right now."

He picked up his cell. A call from Dave went to voicemail while Nick was talking to Chief Westover. He hit callback to his friend; the line was busy. He'd try again later. Nick shot a text to Tanya, who was now at school. "Dave's mom died last night. Still trying to reach him." She responded, "So sad, give him hugs from me."

Distracted by Dave's disheartening news, Nick turned his focus to the top story of the day. He decided to peg his main story on the announcement from the Michigan State Police that its regional posts in the Tri-Cities (Freeland) and St. Ignace (including Mackinac Island) would handle the investigation into the death of Eric Stapleton. A desk sergeant told Nick that troopers, who happened to be testifying in Bay

City federal court that morning, would stop by the *Blade* newsroom to pick up Stapleton's cell phones and notebooks.

The unforgiving deadline clock continued to tick, and Nick worked feverishly against it. He knew today was going to be another wild ride.

Dave paced in front of the administration office at Shady Lane. He was awakened at 6:30 a.m. at home when the facility's overnight floor manager alerted him that his mother had been unresponsive when a nurse tried to wake her for morning meds and breakfast. Mrs. Balz's son jumped out of bed and into clothes as if he'd been hit by lightning. It was a phone call he'd worried about receiving for the past five years—the amount of time she'd been in assisted living.

When the F-150 roared up to the rest home's front door, an ambulance blocked the entryway. He parked, illegally, next to the rescue vehicle and ran inside where he found two paramedics and the county medical examiner hovering over his mom. An orderly blocked him from entering the room, saying professionals were doing their jobs and shouldn't be interrupted. That didn't sit well with Dave, but there was nothing he could do to help them. Police were stationed in the parking lot and outside the room.

The floor manager, her face twisted with grief, approached Dave. He pleaded with her for information and peppered her with questions. "What happened? When did you find her? Did anyone try to revive her? What did the paramedics say?"

"Hold on, hold on," she responded, steering him away from his mother's room. She led him to a bend in the hallway where they could talk without others hearing. "We could not wake her up this morning for meds. 9-1-1 was called immediately. Paramedics and police showed up immediately, then the medical examiner."

"When I left last night, you were going to look in on her."

"We saw her when you left, then did a visual at midnight and 3 a.m.," she said. "Each check, she was on her back and did not appear to be in distress. I'm so sorry."

The manager suggested that Dave take a seat in her office where he could find fresh coffee. He thanked her but could not sit down. Instead, he walked back and forth in the hall, his head swiveling from the floor to the doorway of his mom's room. He watched the police speak in muffled tones into the microphones attached to their shoulders.

When the medical examiner came out of Mrs. Balz's room, he motioned for Dave to follow him. "I need to talk with you. I'm going to recommend a full autopsy. I see signs of asphyxiation."

Dave was stunned. "You think she was smothered? Oh, my God. Somebody killed her?"

"Preliminary. But I see bruising and bloodshot eyes," he said. "She has no history of serious heart issues. We'll know more after testing. Doesn't look like natural causes to me."

Dave turned just in time to see paramedics wheel her covered body out to the ambulance. He put his head in his hands and cried. The floor manager joined them and the medical examiner spoke to her quietly.

His final words to them both: "The police will want to talk with you."

Two officers approached. Separately, they took statements from the floor manager and from Dave. They asked each for their view of events involving Mrs. Balz from the previous evening until she was discovered this morning.

Dave revealed everything he recalled except for her final whispers, the ones where she asked him to take her life. He believed those words were too personal and irrelevant, since he believed she was out of her mind at the time, not even knowing for sure if she was talking to her son.

However, Dave did tell the officer about discovering his mother's candy tin of hoarded meds. He pulled the small box out of his pocket and handed it over. "I didn't know why she was saving these, but I was afraid they might harm her, so I took them out of her desk."

By the time he finished his statement, Nick walked in the front door of Shady Lane. The two friends embraced. Nick expressed his condolences and said he was sorry he missed Dave's call earlier in the morning.

"Do they know what happened to your mom? Was it a heart attack?" Nick asked quietly.

Dave fought back tears. "The M.E. thinks she might have been smothered. Can you believe it? He thinks she might have been killed."

Shocked, Nick didn't know how to respond. He studied his friend. "Holy shit! How long before they find out for sure?"

Dave shook his head, staring at the floor. "Testing. They've got to run some tests. I'm just sick about it…. I can't believe this is happening."

Nick said he had interviews scheduled for the day. One in Bay City before noon, and then one out in the Thumb in the afternoon. "Please, keep me updated on what's going on. Tanya sends her best. We are hurting for you, buddy. Let me know what we can do, how we can help."

The friends hugged. Dave said he'd be in touch and wished Nick luck.

The morning rush to deadline had prevented Nick from reaching Louise Stapleton for her comments regarding the news that her son had been murdered and mutilated on Mackinac Island. When she did return his call, she was distraught and reeling from the shocking turn of events involving her son. She agreed to meet with him at her son's duplex apartment off Euclid Avenue.

He also wanted to find out more about Eric Stapleton, who was still largely a mystery. The emerging picture of him was that of a monster. He'd kidnapped a teenager, held her captive in a dark dungeon, and brutalized her in unimaginable ways. Was he a psychopath? A sociopath? A combination of both? And now he'd been murdered, perhaps by someone who had known and stalked him.

Police records for Stapleton were thin and revealed very little. His work life was not impressive. Before Underwater Solutions, Stapleton had held several different sales-rep jobs in the Saginaw and Bay City areas. Nick called three of them seeking a reference for future employment. Managers would only say that their companies would never rehire the military veteran—at any level. After high school, he served a hitch in the U.S. Army where he displayed antisocial behavior and received an Other Than Honorable Discharge. An OTH usually means the service member got fired or kicked out. It's not a Dishonorable Discharge, but close. A military recruiter Nick knew took a look at Stapleton's private file and said he got booted for fighting, disobeying orders, abuse of authority, and suspected drug use. Not a pretty picture.

What was Stapleton's life like growing up? What were the forces that had shaped him? Nick hoped Louise would help fill in the blanks.

The Firebird zipped in and out of the traffic on Euclid as a light, cold rain shower made the six-lane highway slippery and unforgiving. Nick had just under an hour to spend with Louise before heading out to the Thumb for his 2 p.m. meeting in Argyle. He also hoped that Bea McDonald, the pie baker who lived across the street from the duplex, was home and available for a quick visit.

The lights in Eric's place were on and the front door ajar as Nick pulled up and parked. He dashed through the rain to the porch, ducking under its awning. Louise opened the door for him, telling Nick not to worry about wet shoes. The living room, lit only by a single floor lamp, was dim and cool with a musty smell.

"Want coffee, Nick?" she asked, heading toward the kitchen. Nick wiped his shoes on the entry mat and sat down in a wooden rocking chair. He didn't respond because Louise was already out of range. When she reappeared, she carried two steaming cups. "I figured you'd want some—it's so damp out."

"Thanks Louise—for the coffee and for meeting me," he said. "This must be a terrible time for you. The news about your son must be unsettling."

She set one cup on the small table next to Nick and the other on the table in front of the couch. Louise's dark hair was bunched into a ponytail. She looked tired; puffy pouches, the size of tea bags, hung under her eyes. She'd dressed casually—blue jeans and a yellow, knit sweater, long sleeves pulled down to just above her wrists.

"I haven't been able to sleep much. The last several days have been absolutely crazy," she said, lifting her cup to her lips. "You've been a great help, Nick. I'm being shunned by friends, even family members are not reaching out. Can't tell you how much I appreciate it."

When she set the cup down, Nick noticed that the right sleeve of the yellow sweater had pulled back to reveal the first word of a blue and red tattoo: "Born." Louise glanced at Nick and quickly pulled the sleeve down.

The reporter asked if the state police had talked with her about the investigation into Eric's death. She nodded.

"I told them I'd already ordered an independent forensic autopsy by a reputable pathologist," she said, noting the unprofessional way Mackinac Island authorities had handled her son's death. "The sergeant I talked with said he understood—the MSP would do its own forensic examination and investigation."

Louise asked how Sherry Conaway was doing. "I still can't believe Eric took that poor girl and hurt her. It's just sickening."

Nick repeated the information he'd reported in that day's edition of the *Blade*, highlighting the official health update from Ben Conaway. He also mentioned the outpouring of support Sherry was getting from across the community. But Nick did not reveal the personal details he'd learned about Sherry from her confidential discussion with Tanya as a counselor. He was here to solve the enigma of Eric Stapleton.

"Besides traffic tickets and a driving-while-impaired conviction at 19, your son had no record of run-ins with the police. What was he like growing up?"

"He was wild, out of control at times when he was a youngster," she said, focusing on her hands in her lap. "At school, they wanted to drug him—ADHD. I resisted until they threatened to kick him out. I gave in, but only to half the dosage. Believe me, he was a handful."

"Violence? Did he hurt other kids, pets?"

"No. Rough-housing, yes—but I never saw him get to the point where I thought he enjoyed hurting others," she continued, sipping at her coffee. "He was always the toughest kid, bumps and bruises. Shiners. I raised him by myself—did the best I could. His dad and I split up when Eric was seven. I had to break away from his dad for both our sakes."

Nick's earlier interview with Stapleton's ex-wife echoed in his mind. She, too, said she had to break from Eric in Jada's best interests. Sounded like the apple really didn't fall far from the tree.

Her head dropped into her open hands. She rubbed her eyes and forehead with her fingertips. Nick thought he saw a profound sadness suddenly come over her. He didn't push or pry, deciding to give Louise time to collect herself. He sipped his coffee.

After a few moments, he picked up where she had left off. "Was Eric's dad difficult to live with? Did he have problems?"

She grunted a laugh "Yeah, you could say that. He was a biker. Belonged to a gang. In fact, we both did. I couldn't continue to live that life. When Eric came along, things had to change. I didn't want Eric to grow up around it."

Nick was stunned. "You both were bikers? You mean like motorcycle-gang biker?"

Louise nodded and pulled up her right sleeve, revealing the whole tattoo on her forearm: "Born to Raise Holy Hell."

The reporter could not take his eyes off the body art. It was hard for Nick to think of Louise as a member of a motorcycle gang, especially since the initiation rituals he'd read about for biker chicks were so brutal.

"Really, you both were gang members?" he asked. "Was that here in Michigan or somewhere else?"

Louise blushed, then answered. "Road Kingsmen—out of Detroit. We were badasses. Young, stupid, reckless."

Nick shook his head. "I just can't picture you as a biker chick, you're so sweet."

More blushing, then a nervous smile. Louise stood up and turned around, her back now facing Nick. She unbuttoned her blue jeans, then used her thumbs to push them down over her hips, stopping just above her butt crack. Another tattoo: The word "PROPERTY" on the top line just above the crack, then "OF THE" on top of one cheek, then "KINGSMEN" on top of the other cheek. She bent over slightly and all four words got bigger.

Enough said. "OK, then. I got it!" Nick exclaimed. Louise hiked her jeans and undies up with a short hop, fastened them, and turned to face Nick.

"So, I decided Eric and I had to run. That was no life for either of us—the drugs, the alcohol, the violence, the car thefts—too much," she said, sitting back down and drinking her coffee. "His dad really didn't care when we left. He had a mean streak. Got physically aroused by the sound of bones cracking. Eric and I were a hindrance. I read later in the *Free Press* that he died in a shoot-out with the feds—the DEA, I think."

Nick took a minute or two to process that. "You never remarried?"

"Nope, the right situation never came up," she said, finishing her coffee. "I was happy to just get Eric to the age of 17, then he joined the Army and became Uncle Sam's problem."

Nick drained his coffee, glad to have it. "Well, very interesting discussion. Learned a lot. Thanks for the coffee. I'll be in touch. Don't hesitate to call me if you need to talk. I've got to get going to another appointment. Later, I'm going to meet some of Eric's friends out in the Thumb."

Louise said she'd never met his Thumb friends, but she had heard him talk about them. "True patriots. That's what he called them. The kind of men who could change history."

Nick nodded. More interesting information. Certainly not the way Randy described the same men. He thanked her and left.

The sky had cleared, and rain gave way to soggy sunshine as Nick dashed across the street. Bea McDonald had been watching since the reporter pulled up; he waved as he bounded up her front steps. The door opened and he was slapped in the nostrils with the warm aroma of peach pie.

"Hello, Bea," he said, grabbing the door handle. She stood back, wiping her hands on her apricot bib apron. "Have you got a minute? Wanted to show you something."

Mrs. McDonald invited Nick into the kitchen, offering pie and coffee. He was very tempted but running out of time. He begged for a rain check on both, pulling his cell phone out of his sports jacket side pocket.

"Got a photo here I want to show you," he said, thumbing through images on his device. When he found the picture of Randy, he enlarged it and showed it to Bea. "Do you recognize this woman? Was she one of the people visiting Eric across the street?"

A set of horned-rimmed glasses were snagged from an apron pocket. She perched them on the bridge of her nose, then bobbed her head up and down until the cell phone image came into focus. "Yes, that's her," she said. "The one Eric handed money to out there in the street. I'm sure of it."

Nick thanked her. It was a confirmation that Randy was the woman she claimed to be and had met Eric at his place.

"I'll be back for the pie and coffee," Nick said as he hustled out the door. "Thanks again, Bea. Gotta fly."

On his hour-long drive out into the Thumb to meet Travis and Leon, the Argyle Neanderthals, Nick thought about Stapleton's history. Son of bikers, troubled through school, ugly military service, and poor job performance until he landed at Underwater Solutions, where he seemed to thrive.

The guy had been promoted to a supervisory position, monitoring the performance of employees and the maintenance and protection of an international oil pipeline. It was an impressive-sounding position. He wondered if Stapleton had suddenly matured professionally and found his calling. Why the change of trajectory in his life?

As he drove through miles of flat sugar beet, field corn, and bean fields, the reporter hoped to find out more about what Stapleton was up to with this run out to Argyle, but he knew it was chancy. All he had to work with was one nugget of information that he'd picked up from Randy, a Bay City call girl.

The nugget had been enough to get him a meeting with Stapleton's cohorts, but doubtful it would get him much more—a bluff would only carry him so far. Even the Neanderthals would quickly see he was on an information fishing expedition.

Suddenly, the reporter had to slow down. Two multi-ton sugar beet trucks pulled from a field onto the highway. It was fall harvest for the vegetable that was sliced, boiled, and processed into high-grade sugar. Trucks and harvesters crisscrossed the Thumb and mid-Michigan moving the crop before winter took hold and froze the ground.

As he passed the lumbering, giant trucks, Nick refocused on the task at hand. He knew he was heading into unfriendly, and possibly unsafe territory. The northern Sanilac and southern Huron county areas were hotbeds of distrust for established institutions—institutions like the mainstream media. Hatred for the so-called "Deep State"—agencies, red tape, and bureaucrats—coursed through the veins of area residents like red-hot fever.

It was dangerous for Nick to waltz into the region, and he was fearful of getting burned on the dance floor. As a precaution, he decided to call his old friend J.D. Ratchett, a Huron County Sheriff's Department deputy. He and Booger had worked together on a number of previous cases that ended up being big stories for Nick and feathers in Ratchett's cop cap. He turned down his radio to just below the hum of the Firebird's powerful V-8 and placed the call. Ratchett answered as only he could.

"Howdy, you got Booger, now don't try to flick me off," he said, ending with a long chuckle. "Now, what can I do ya for?"

"Hey, Boog, it's Nick Steele. You got a minute?"

"Why, Nick, you ol' son of a rabid bird dog, how you doin'? For you, I got two minutes."

The reporter laughed, then explained his undertaking and its purpose. He asked if the deputy happened to be patrolling in the southern Huron County area that afternoon.

"Not on my immediate radar," he said, "but we are looking for a dude down that way who's got an arrest warrant out for theft—hotwired a truck loaded with construction tools. Got to be a little careful with jurisdiction, but I can give my buds in Sanilac County a heads up that I'm moseyin' through the area in pursuit."

"Sounds great, Boog," Nick said. "Meeting a couple of guys at the Argyle Roadhouse that I don't know much about. I'd feel a whole lot more comfortable if you're in that neck of the woods."

Ratchett suggested Nick shoot him a text alert just before his meeting. "Be careful with them boys, Nick. A lot of them got quick tempers and slow wits. Don't meet up with them alone; the more folks around the better."

"Thanks, J.D. And who knows, maybe they will think better of it and not show up. I'll keep you posted."

Mackinac Murder   107

The Argyle Roadhouse was located near Ubly and Argyle Roads in northern Sanilac County, roughly 60 miles south and east of Bay City. A village of about 700 people, the area is mostly middle-class farm country with multiple pockets of dirt-poor poverty. It's fiercely conservative, with some elements so anti-government that Michigan militia groups find it to be a fertile meeting, recruiting, and training ground.

Argyle is just a dozen miles north of Decker, the rural area that was home to a couple of infamous domestic terrorists—Terry Nichols and Timothy McVeigh, bombers of the Oklahoma City federal building in 1995. The bombers used a yellow Ryder moving van, loaded with fuel oil and farm fertilizer, to blast the building apart, killing 168 people and injuring hundreds more.

The attack shocked the nation and reverberated around the world. McVeigh and Nichols hatched the Oklahoma City bombing plan while learning how to create explosives on farms in northern Sanilac County. McVeigh, a disgruntled U.S. Army veteran who used *The Turner Diaries* as his terrorist handbook, was executed for his role in the plot. Nichols got a life prison sentence.

Nick entered Argyle, rolling past a hardware store, a machine shop, a U.S. Post Office, Catholic and Methodist churches, and a convenience store. The town wasn't big enough for a traffic light or a decent restaurant, but visitors could find beer and whiskey at the local watering hole.

The Roadhouse was an old-school farmer's bar. Garlic bologna, hard-boiled eggs, or spicy dill pickles were available for a dollar each on the oak bar. Pabst Blue Ribbon or Busch were on tap behind the bar or Kessler and Smirnoff could be found in the liquor well underneath it. Daily special: shot and shell chaser—three bucks.

The lighting in the place was cranked up for the sitting games: euchre and rummy; pool, shuffleboard, or darts for those standing. An ax-throwing game had been the local rage but it was quickly discarded when a ricochet caught a guy named Homer in the side of his head. Needless to say, Homer no longer patronized the Roadhouse.

Nick parked the Firebird at the end of a row of pickup trucks out front and shot a text to Booger. "Here, going in. If you don't hear from me in twenty minutes, come and get me."

The lunch-and-beer crowd had petered out when Nick entered the place just after 2 o'clock. He wore work jeans, a Spartan-green sweatshirt, and hiking boots, easily making him the Roadhouse fashion plate. But following the dress code wouldn't cover up the fact that he was a stone-cold stranger. The place went dead silent when he stood in the entry and surveyed a dozen or so customers clustered in small groups.

His eyes settled on two guys at the bar in their early 30s, unshaven under dusty, red ballcaps and clad in worn denim with cowboy boots, their pointed leather toes scuffed and kicked raw. **Had to be Travis and Leon,** Nick thought. He stood just down from them, propping his right foot on the bar's beaten metal floor rail. He said "PBR" when the aging bartender limped up to him, then checked out the Neanderthals' reflection in the smoke-clouded mirror behind the bar.

The old guy, his knuckles knobby and stiff from toil, set the draft in front of Nick and picked up his five spot, returning four ones in one smooth move with his right hand. The reporter couldn't help but notice the battered and worn gold ring with a scuffed blue stone. Its center piece was unmistakable: the Eagle, Globe, and Anchor.

"Semper Fi," Nick said quietly. The weathered bartender nodded, "Semper Fi." They fist bumped.

"Looking for Travis and Leon," the reporter said, lifting the shell for a sip of Pabst. Foam hung on the edge of his silver moustache before an index finger cleaned it like a windshield wiper doing its job.

One of the guys to Nick's right answered for the barkeep. "Over here. We took bets on whether you'd show up or not," said the taller, lankier of the two. Both men nursed bottles of Bud. "I'm Leon, this here's Travis. You said you knew all about "The Plan." Talk. We want to hear what you know."

Nick studied the two while taking another sip. **Here goes,** he thought, **let's see how far I can string this out.** "Well, I know it's not going to work. Too complicated, too many people involved. Word is already leaking out."

The short guy, Travis, grunted. "Right off, you exposed yourself to be full of shit. Beauty of 'The Plan' is its simplicity. Your crap is showing, and it stinks!"

Nick laughed, trying to exude confidence. "Shows how little you know, my friend."

That comment sparked fire from Leon. Tall Man leaned over top of his buddy, pushing his chin out toward Nick. "We ain't your friends. You ain't shit to us. As far as we know, you ain't shit to Eric, either. We know he's dead, got what was coming to him for getting cold feet. Now, what's your connection to him?"

Another slow, casual sip of beer, then he set his shell down and turned to face the Neanderthals. "I wrote his obituary, and I've been all through his files and papers. Also got his cell, that's how I found you two clowns. So, I probably know more about 'The Plan' than either of you."

Now, Shorty got ticked. "Who you callin' clowns? And what do you mean you wrote his obit? You work at the funeral parlor?"

Nick shook his head and grinned. "Nope, I'm a reporter with the *Blade*. I was up at Eric's place on the island," he said, becoming assertive. "I went to the trail where your buddy was killed, and I discovered the Sand Box and its dungeon where he assaulted that teenager. My guess is you two had a hand in that girl's kidnapping and rape. How's life in prison sound?"

Shorty shot back. "Wait just a damn minute."

Leon interrupted his friend, grabbing his shoulder. "Don't say no more. He's got nothin' and we ain't talking to no reporter."

Tall man, his face locked in a tight grimace, nodded at Travis, punching him in the shoulder in a sign of affirmation. Nick watched, thinking Randy had summed up these two perfectly. And, she was right, they were filthy and smelled bad. He pushed ahead, leveraging more information against the two.

"I know Eric connected you two with Randy and Brandi and you paid for it until the hookers wouldn't have you anymore," Nick said. "Pretty disgusting if you ask me."

"Nobody's asking you," shouted Leon, getting agitated again.

"Damn straight," Shorty barked, then added: "You see them whores, tell them I want my jacket back."

Nick studied the two and let them bleet. He made a mental note to ask Randy about the jacket. He checked his watch, pretending to listen to their rants. He hoped J.D. was nearby because this interview had hit the wall.

Leon held up two fingers. "Tommy, couple of Buds over here."

The bartender asked Nick if he wanted another draft. Before he could respond, Leon said, "No. He's all done here."

When the three men started talking, a good six feet separated Nick from the Neanderthals at the bar. Now, they were on top of him. He looked around and others in the bar had closed in, too. They had been listening. Too close. Feeling surrounded, he was afraid he could suddenly be jumped and overwhelmed.

Leon seemed to know it as well. "You gotta lot of balls coming in here and talking to us like that. You're just another one of those smart-ass elites, thinking you got all the brain power, thinking you can tell us what to do. I got news for you, buddy. I think you're gonna leave here on a stretcher."

As if on cue, the front door of the bar opened and Booger walked in, stopping to put his hands on his holstered hips. The deputy scanned the bar. "Whose got the gold Firebird out front? You're double parked. I want to see your license, registration, and insurance papers—right now."

Nick finished his beer in one gulp, left two singles on the bar for Tommy, and nodded at the Neanderthals. "I'm not your buddy, boys. I'm your nightmare. Gotta go."

The reporter pulled his wallet, fishing out his license, registration, and insurance as he walked toward the door. He handed them to Booger and asked: "Am I really double parked?" The deputy grinned, glanced at the legals, and handed them back. He urged a quick exit.

In the parking lot, Ratchett said he would follow Nick out of the region. "Let's get back to civilization."

Chapter 11

Late Friday Afternoon
Bay City

Tanya left Central High early to visit Sherry Conaway at Bay Med. This time, she lugged a large, black plastic bag, hauling it over her shoulder, the top bunched in her left fist like Santa bearing gifts on Christmas Eve.

The high school counselor greeted Danielle Conaway in the hallway outside her daughter's room with a firm, sustained hug. She asked about the big bag.

"Gifts, of sorts," said Tanya, smiling as she planted a kiss on the mom's cheek. She switched hands to carry the heavy bag into the battered teen's room. "I've got something for our girl."

Sherry couldn't take her eyes off the bag. She leaned forward to hug her friend from school. "Back already? I'm so glad to see you—thanks for coming. What's in the bag?"

Tanya opened it and let its contents spill onto Sherry's bed. "Love. I brought you love from your schoolmates. Handmade cards. More than 700 before I quit counting. When they heard I was visiting you, they went to work. Each one original, from the heart. Your friends."

Sherry grabbed a dozen in one hand, using the other to hold them up one at a time to read. She smiled, laughed, squealed. Tears welled in her eyes and began slow treks down her cheeks. She sniffled and grinned, and laughed some more, wiggling in her bed. Tanya helped her stack the cards so she could take her time going through them the rest of the night.

"Wow! A–maz–ing. So nice," Sherry said, savoring the moment and its warm and fuzzy glow. "Tell everyone thanks so much. In fact, I'll make a card and you can post it for all to see."

In the room's attached bath, Danielle's hair stylist packed up her gear. Suzie had been asked to take a look at Sherry's shattered hair and develop a plan to give it some vitality. The beautician brought special shampoos and conditioners, giving the teen a slow, warm wash, massaging the treatments into her scalp. She'd just finished before Tanya arrived.

Sherry thanked Suzie for visiting. She stopped at the teen's bed and gave her a hug, whispering in her ear, "We'll get you fixed up. A couple more treatments, then a nice trim that will help cover the bald spots. You'll look great, Sherry."

Big Ben Conaway pulled out his checkbook to compensate Suzie. The petite, dark-haired woman held up her hand. "Absolutely not. It's my pleasure to help our girl. I'm so glad and honored you called me."

Everyone, it seemed, wanted to help the teen in their community who had been captured, brutalized for months, and finally rescued after many had given up hope that she'd ever be found.

Donations continued to flow in to help Sherry Conaway. Even Charlie Moore, creator of **Charlie's Place** in the Sand Box, was so overwhelmed by what had occurred in the storage unit next to his that he mounted a high-pressure, fundraising campaign.

The former Ford exec went to work and managed to squeeze donations of $3,000 out of each of the 30 skinflint owners of Sand Box units to establish a college fund for the Conaways' daughter. Ninety grand was a good start and Charlie vowed to keep going until her education was fully funded.

Tanya took off her jacket and began to settle in for her visit. Danielle grabbed Ben's hand and pulled him toward the door. "We're going to the cafeteria. We'll be back in a bit. You two can talk."

A nurse steamrolled into the room to check Sherry's vitals: blood pressure, temperature, heart rate. Friendly and efficient, she asked if the teen needed anything. "How's your water bottle? Need a refill? Warm enough? Gets chilly in here if you're not moving every minute."

"I'm good," Sherry assured her. "But could you ask if I can have something to help me sleep? I'm dead tired but I can't fall into a good sleep."

"I'm changing shifts soon, but I'll get the question in for you right away and try for an answer before I leave." She smiled and left the room with the same bustle that accompanied her entry.

"Is it too busy in here for you to sleep?" Tanya asked. "Too many people?"

Sherry shrugged and turned glum. "I hate feeling this way. Everyone has been terrific, helping in so many ways. It's kind of staggering. People I don't even know and will probably never meet are coming forward in big, big ways. Can you believe I've got a college fund?"

The school counselor smiled and took Sherry's hand. "The support you're getting is wonderful. I'm so happy for you. And yet, you still feel badly. Am I getting that right?"

Sherry nodded, looking down at her hands. "I should be happy, jumping up and down, right? But I just feel so broken, so low, so worthless, I don't know how to get past it. I can't get my juice back."

Tanya patted her hands. "You've been through horrors that most people can't even imagine. You cannot simply erase them from your mind. You can't close your eyes and wish them away. It's going to take a while."

Sherry said she couldn't find sleep because she feared waking and finding herself back inside the dark, stinking cell. "Closing my eyes—even for a little while—takes me back to the hours I laid there in the dark, waiting, hoping to die. I had no sense of time. I had given up on the idea of surviving. In fact, I figured when he got tired of raping me, he'd just kill me or let me starve to death."

Tanya sat on the side of her bed and pulled her close, the girl's head resting against her shoulder. "And yet, through all of the horrors, you did survive. It shows how strong you are, Sherry. You're going to get stronger and better every day."

The teenager sighed heavily and seemed to slump harder, her full weight leaning into Tanya.

"I hate myself for what happened—for allowing it to happen," Sherry said just above a whisper. "I can't believe how stupid I was. Here I am, getting drunk with a bunch of other young girls, smoking pot, and opening myself up to this. I should have known better when Jada's dad kept staring at me, kept trying to get me to sit on his lap. I should have called my dad to come and get me the hell out of there. But no, I was flattered by the attention, by the flirtation. I started dancing. Unbelievable."

Tanya asked her if she recalled how Eric Stapleton moved her from the apartment to the dungeon. "The other girls said you were planning to meet Mark at a gas station. Did you leave the apartment on your own? Do you remember that part of the night?"

Sherry said she did. She recalled waiting until she thought everyone was asleep, then sliding out the front door as quietly as she could.

"I wanted to meet Mark because he was heading off to school. I started walking toward Euclid, but I was so drunk and high I kept tripping and falling. I sat down on a bench in the alley because my head was spinning," she said, pausing to sniffle. "Then I was about half awake when Eric shook me and put me in the back seat of his car. When I woke up, I was chained to a wall in a dark room. I screamed. I cried. I yelled. No one answered for what seemed like forever. Then I heard the lock click, the light came on, and Jada's dad turned into a monster. He tore my clothes off and beat me with his belt, laughing and calling me a whore."

Sherry went quiet. Tanya stroked her forehead with her fingertips. "You can't blame yourself. We all take missteps in life. You didn't ask for any of this to happen. What happened is not your fault. Jada's dad did this, brought this on you. You didn't want this. Don't you dare blame yourself."

The two rocked on the bed, leaning against each other. Tanya felt weepy. She fought the urge to cry, believing she had to stay strong for Sherry.

The teen said she had one request to make before her folks returned. "I need to find out about abortion. Mom and dad won't discuss it. We're Catholic. They keep trotting Father Don in here three times a day—morning, afternoon, and night. I can't talk with him about any of this. He has no clue and I'm already sick of his B.S. I'm sorry. Prayer is not the answer to everything. And he isn't the one who was knocked up by the devil. I was."

"What do you want to know? The mechanics of it? How it's done? That kind of thing?"

Sherry nodded. "How much time do I have to decide? They say I'm six weeks along. I know it gets harder the longer I wait, but I want to know it all—as much as I can."

Tanya promised to come back with more information. She urged her to talk with her doctor about the procedure and its ramifications. "If you decide to go this way, it will affect you physically, emotionally, and mentally—perhaps for years to come. This is a life and death decision."

Sherry buried her face in her hands and wept softly. "All these things keep crashing around in my head. I'm trying to sort it out."

"Here's one more thing I hope you will think about. Adoption," Tanya said. "There are plenty of childless couples out there who would be happy to have a baby. May I also provide you with some of that information? Someone you can talk with?"

Sherry nodded and wiped her tears away with the top of her blanket. The two could hear the Conaways in the hall. The door opened and Danielle returned to the room, announcing that Ben was running some errands.

She asked her daughter if she could look at some of the cards she received. The two did it together, thumbing through a pile of colorful, creative cards, most covered with hand-drawn hearts and symbols from school. Tanya watched, delighted to see the two enjoying the missives and the moment together.

Time to go, Tanya thought. She gave Sherry and Danielle quick hugs, grabbed her jacket, and said she planned to meet Nick for dinner. Tanya left with a heavy heart. She knew Sherry was struggling to come to terms with what had happened to her. She was more determined than ever to help the teen through the turbulent days ahead.

As Nick entered Bay County on the way back from the Thumb, he placed a call to Randy, the South End call girl who had told him about

Eric Stapleton's deviant past. She had met him for years, exchanging sex for money. In the process, she'd picked up substantial information from him during pillow talk. Now, Nick wanted to ask her about the jacket one of the Neanderthals claimed he had left with Brandi.

He also planned to reveal the bits and pieces of information that Travis and Leon had revealed while refusing to talk with Nick. He hoped Randy might remember more after hearing tidbits from the Neanderthals.

The call went to Randy's voicemail. He left a message, urging a return call regardless of the time. Nick checked his watch. Tanya said she would get them a table at Paddy's Green Hut, an Irish pub on Columbus Avenue. It was a fun place that offered to-die-for corned beef and cabbage dinners.

Nick decided to call his buddy Dave. He'd felt bad all afternoon about not being with his friend during his time of grief over the sudden passing of his mother, which now sounded like it might be murder. Again, his call went to voicemail. He left a message, urging a return call.

The Green Hut, another classic Bay City neighborhood bar, which teetered on the edge of the East Side and South End communities, was boisterous at the end of a workday. Revelers stood shoulder to shoulder at the L-shaped bar. Tables overflowed with gleeful drinkers.

Tanya had been overjoyed to snag the last two-seater table and she guarded the empty chair next to her like a pit bull. Nick entered from the North Sheridan side door, sliding past the bar crowd without being stopped for a quick shot and shell before meeting the Mrs.

He pecked her on the cheek and she squeezed his hand before he sat down. He scooted his chair close so they could talk above the bar din. A young waitress with no name tag swung by, carrying a tray of draft beers in one hand over her shoulder. The reporter, who was always amazed how anybody, including acrobats and magicians, could do that, ordered a draft of Labatt's and a double daiquiri. She nodded and whirled away.

Nick asked about Sherry. All day, he'd wondered how the teen was doing. Discovering her, and carrying her out of the dungeon, had hung with him since he found her in Eric Stapleton's private hellhole.

During his career as a reporter, he'd been to countless crime scenes, but nothing had affected him quite like the condition in which he'd found the Conaways' daughter. He simply could not shake the image of her weak and battered body from his mind. Condition updates about her steady improvement had become the highlights of his day. He was eager to hear the latest.

Tanya began with the highlight, telling Nick about the sack full of cards from school. She also told him about the beautician's visit. She paused while No Name Tag rolled up with two drinks, napkins, and menus, dropping each on the table before pirouetting away to handle another order.

"Physically, she seems to be bouncing back incredibly well," said Tanya, sipping her drink. She leaned toward Nick's ear. "Emotionally, struggling. Not a surprise, considering what she went through. I'm worried about her."

Nick nodded. "How are Ben and Danielle holding up?"

"They seem to be OK, still euphoric about getting Sherry back," Tanya said. "But they need family counseling. They're sorting through a lot of issues. Sherry's pregnancy is causing super stress for each of them."

Tanya asked about Nick's trip to the Thumb. He gave her a quick summary: unpleasant, except for connecting with Booger, and only mildly productive.

"Picked up bits and pieces of information with Eric Stapleton's cohorts. They're a couple of slugs up to no good. I've got to figure out what 'The Plan' is with only a handful of clues. Also met a fellow Marine tending the bar. I'm going to call him at the Roadhouse, see if he will help."

"How do you know he's got any information to share?" she asked, sipping her mixed drink. "And what makes you think he'll share it? Those people out there are pretty tight."

"One thing I know from being a reporter for 25 years—bartenders, barbers, beauticians, and secretaries hear everything. And the good ones are selective about what they repeat and who they whisper to. Tommy's an old leatherneck. I want to see if I can appeal to his corps pride."

"Are you going to hum the 'Marine's Hymn' while talking to him?"

"That might be a little over the top, but I'd whistle 'Dixie' through my butt if I thought it would help me figure this story out."

Nick and Tanya toasted, polished their drinks, and hailed No Name Tag for two more. He said he felt like he was spinning his wheels on this story and missed working with Dave, who always seemed to help him think through the angles when they worked together.

Tanya nodded and snuggled as close to Nick as she could without sliding onto his chair with him. She decided it was a good time to bring up another subject, an idea that she had not been able to shake from her mind since learning of Sherry Conaway's pregnancy.

"I've been thinking about Sherry's situation a lot and I need to ask you something. What would you think about adopting her baby? We could build a good life together with that child."

The question almost caused Nick to fall off his chair. They'd had the adoption discussion before when it was determined that Tanya could not have children. Nick had an adult son, named Joe, from an earlier marriage. Joe lived on the West Coast and left Bay City and his dad behind years ago. They talked regularly and usually got together once a year. Parenting was not Nick's strong suit, and he was not eager to become a 60-something dad—especially with a child who might be coming into this world with issues.

"Tanya, we're too old for a baby—ours or anybody else's. Are you serious? Have you really thought this out?"

She gripped his hand harder. "We are not too old. You would be a great dad. This is why I'm bringing it up now. We have lots of time to consider it. Will you at least give it serious thought?"

Nick struggled to answer. "Think about this: when this kid turns 20, I'll be in my 80s and you'll be 70. That's OK to be a U.S. Senator, but not for helping a kid reach adulthood."

Tanya released his hand. "We could make a difference in the child's life; we could give this baby a chance. And it might be our last chance to be parents. Will you think about it?"

Nick nodded. Though he did not like the idea, he would consider it simply because Tanya asked him to. He loved her dearly and would do almost anything she asked. But he also asked Tanya to give thorough thought to what this baby might bring into the world. He said he had learned from Louise Stapleton that Eric's father also had a violent history.

"She told me they were members of a motorcycle gang," Nick said. "She said he was into drugs and alcohol big time. She thinks he was killed in a shoot-out with the feds. Both the dad and the grandfather of this baby had mean streaks. I'm just saying there is a lot to consider with this adoption."

No Name Tag returned to take their food orders. The couple, their hands laced, agreed to talk about the adoption idea again.

Nick's phone rang. It was Dave. He took the call, eager to talk with his friend. Tanya approved. She wanted to know how their friend was doing.

"Hi Dave. Missed you today," he said. "What's happening? How are you doing?"

There was a long pause before Dave spoke. "The police want me to come into the cop shop for a formal interview. I'm a suspect. They think I killed my mom."

Chapter 12

Saturday Morning
Bay City Public Safety Department

Dave Balz sat in the parking lot outside the police and fire headquarters with both hands gripping the steering wheel of his hand-painted, green Ford F-150 pickup. He was treading into unfamiliar territory. Instead of being the hunter, he was the hunted. Police had asked him to voluntarily come in for questioning in his mother's death. It was a possible homicide and Dave was a suspect.

His buddy, Nick, had urged Dave to talk with an attorney before meeting with the police. But he'd declined, saying he had nothing to hide and wanted to help find his mother's killer. Still, his predicament made him nervous. He also was eager to hear what police had discovered in their investigation so far.

Dave checked his watch. He was supposed to meet with Detective John Ripley, a 30-year member of the force who'd worked himself up from beat cop to one of the most respected officers in the department. Dave and Nick had worked with Ripley on numerous cases over the years. But now it was different. The reporter would be sitting on the opposite side of the table from him.

Though it was the weekend, Dave decided to wear a necktie and a clean, mostly wrinkle-free shirt to the interview. But he still wore yesterday's jeans because they appeared unsoiled, and no clean pants hung in his closet.

Ripley, whipcord lean, poked the tip of his fat, black tie into the top of his black pants and guided Dave to an interview room, not the detective's office at the cop shop. That's when the gravity of the situation hit Dave. He'd met with Ripley dozens of times previously, always in his office—never in the perp sweatbox.

The room was the size of a big closet. Its walls were as white as Ripley's shirt. The tiny space felt warm to Dave as soon as he entered. Sparse. Small table, two chairs. Close.

"Thanks for coming in, Dave," Ripley said, pointing to a hard steel chair with a straight back. Dave used his right foot to push it back away from the table that would separate the two men. "As I'm sure you're aware, this conversation will be recorded."

As they took their seats, the detective set a thick file on the table and gave the speech, reading the reporter his Miranda rights and asking if he understood them. Dave nodded, and Ripley asked him to verbally affirm that he'd heard and understood his rights.

Dave did, then launched into the interview, agitated. "I did not kill my mother. You are going to hear that a lot from me today. Let me repeat for the record: I did not kill my mom."

Ripley smiled. "According to nursing home records, you were the last person to speak with your mother and possibly the last to see her alive. I have some questions for you."

"Fire away."

"She had another night of conflict and required sedation. What was your last discussion with her about?"

"She was down, depressed. She said she hated the place and her life. She wished she were dead."

"Did she ask you to take her life?" Ripley asked, watching the reporter closely, studying his body language and facial expression. "Did she want you to end her life?"

Dave considered the question, shifting in his seat. His hands rested flat on top of his thighs. "Yes, but she was down, confused. I asked her not to talk that way. I told her we would try to fix things so she could be happy. It pained me to no end to see her so unhappy at this stage of her life. I repeat, I did not kill my mom."

Ripley flipped through the file on the table. "But, during your initial statement to officers, you didn't mention that she asked you to take her life. Your story is different now. Why is that?"

Dave rubbed his hand up and down his thighs. "At the time, I didn't think she was in her right mind. Sometimes she was tuned in, and others out. I didn't believe she really meant it. I thought she was frustrated and angry because of the conflict she'd had. I also viewed her remarks as personal—just talk between mother and son, not something I would ever repeat."

The detective pulled a sheet of paper out of the file and turned it around for Dave to read. It was a list of books that had been found in his mom's room. He looked over the titles:

The Day I Die: The Untold Story of Assisted Dying in America
Knocking on Heaven's Door
Choosing to Die: A Personal Story by Phyllis Schacter
The Inevitable: Dispatches on the Right to Die

Ripley asked if he knew about the books. "Were you aware of this? Looks like research, like she was very serious about it. Did she discuss these books, these ideas with you?"

"No. I never saw these books in her room. If I had, I would have asked her about them. Where did you find them?"

"They were among her possessions," the detective said, shifting to a new line of questioning. "You didn't become the primary caregiver for your mother until your siblings passed away. Is that correct?"

Dave crossed his arms and leaned back against the steel chair. "That's right. My sister looked after mom until she died, but I helped. I visited regularly, did what I could for her. Then I became more involved recently."

Ripley flipped through his file. "Was your mom a burden to you? From the reports, it seems she was getting harder and more difficult to handle. More incidents of violence and hostility. Was she becoming a problem for you? Were you hoping she would die?"

The reporter didn't like the question or where the interview was going. "No, I did not find her to be a burden, and I have never had one minute in my life where I wished she would die. I also must say, for the record, that I resent the question. Again, I didn't kill my mom."

The detective focused on Dave's face. "You've still got the remnants of a shiner. Lots of purple, yellow, and blue around your upper cheek.

Did your mom give you that black eye?"

"She didn't mean it," Dave said, rubbing his thighs again. "She was confused. She didn't recognize me. She thought she was under attack and lashed out."

"How did that make you feel? Did it make you angry that she didn't recognize you or know your name? Did you want to hurt her for that?"

"Absolutely not. I've never, for a minute in my life, wanted to hurt my mom. And, again, I object to the question. You have no reason to even suggest that."

Ripley thumbed through the file and pulled a page to the top of the stack. "I have a financial statement from the nursing home about the monthly costs of your mom's care. Very expensive, especially on a reporter's salary. Was your mom a financial burden? How were you going to keep paying for her care?"

Dave responded that his mom had insurance, savings, investments. "My brother and sister both left money, they had dough stashed aside to continue my mom's care. Money was not an issue. She was not a burden financially. I repeat. I didn't kill my mom."

The detective did not let up on the line of questioning. "But her care was burning up your inheritance every day, every week, every month. Were you fed up with all that money getting swallowed up by the nursing home and her doctor bills?"

Dave shook his head, crossing his arms again. "Nope, not at all. Money doesn't mean much to me. I live pretty lean. I'm driving a used F-150, and you can see I'm not a clotheshorse. The financial part was no burden. Money for her care was set aside."

The reporter placed one hand on the table and leaned toward the cop. "I've got some questions for you. First off, do you have conclusive proof that my mom was killed?"

Ripley replied that test results were pending. But he noted that traces of blood had been found on Mrs. Balz's pillow. He said she also exhibited facial bruising consistent with suffocation.

Dave asked if the detective saw the incident report where his mother received a fat lip while scuffling with an orderly earlier in the week.

"Yes, I did. But fresh bruising was found inside her mouth, the result of pressure being applied to her face," he said, crossing his arms. "The medical examiner also noted that she had bloodshot eyes."

Ripley closed the file. Dave wondered if that meant the interview was over. He asked if nursing home personnel or other patients were being interviewed.

"Of course," the detective said. "You are one of several. We may want to talk with you again. Thanks for your cooperation, and for coming in for this interview."

The men stood, shook hands, and Dave left, glad it was over. He had a stress headache, and his chest was tight. Outside, he pulled in a deep breath of cool, fall air, and took a moment to bask in the warm rays of the sun. Refreshed and energized, he jumped into the F-150, determined to find out who killed his mom.

Nick had not heard back from Randy, which was a little concerning to him. It was just after lunchtime, and he decided to swing by the Spinning Wheel to ask if she'd been around Friday night or that morning for the Saturday Eye-Opener: a tall Bloody Mary with scrambled eggs and toast.

Bullseye Face hustled tables and asked Nick if he was drinking. "What can I get yous?"

"Coffee, black," Nick shouted above a U-M football game on the big-screen TV. The order caused several patrons to turn and check out who was sober at the Wheel during a college football game.

Almost embarrassed, the reporter took a seat just to the side of the bar and as far away from the game as he could get. The place was not crowded. The weather was too nice outside, and the game was expected to be a snoozer with a second-rate opponent opposing the Wolverines.

Tony pushed a tall cup of hot coffee in front of Nick with one hand, then landed a cup of pretzels next to him with the other. The waiter was about to run off when Nick stopped him.

"I was in here the other day meeting a woman at a table over there," he said, pointing toward the back of the bar. "Do you happen to remember?"

"Yup, yous met up with Randy," he said, smiling. "She's a regular. Tips me good to serve her and her friends and mind my own business."

Nick nodded. "That's her. She been around at all? Last night, this morning?"

"Here last night with Brandi, partying hard until a couple of 'friends' came in," Bullseye Face said. "Left about 10, didn't come back. Shoot her a text, she should be up and movin' by now."

Nick asked about the friends. "One tall and lanky, the other one short. Hard, rough looking dudes."

"That's them," he laughed, "and they smelled bad. Surprised Brandi left with the little guy, really."

The reporter gave the waiter a ten spot and told him to keep the change. He pulled out his cell and knocked out a message to Randy. "I'm at the Wheel having a coffee. Buy you one, or help with some hair of the dog that bit you."

Several minutes passed, then a Randy text pinged: "WTF? What does that mean?"

Generational gap, Nick thought. "Expression for hangover cure, meaning will give you some of what knocked you off your feet to help you get back on your feet."

"Oh, OK. Order me a White Russian. Should be there in a half hour or so. Don't forget it's 100 bucks. I don't do freebies."

Nick sipped his coffee. It was strong and dark as lacquer. He reached over the bar to the ice bin and snagged a few cubes to water it down. He checked his wallet to make sure he had enough cash to meet Randy again. He did. The Wheel crowd roared, with guys standing and cheering, hands raised. Michigan interception and return for a pick-six.

At just past 2 o'clock, Nick called the Argyle Roadhouse, hoping Tommy was working the same shift as he did on Friday. The old Marine answered the bar phone.

"Roadhouse, special today is a burger and beer—six bucks," he announced, a bit breathless.

"Tommy, this is Nick Steele. We met yesterday."

"Yup, I remember. I watched, heard the whole thing with you at the bar. Thought you were going to get your clock cleaned. Would have enjoyed watching you scrap with Leon and Travis. Those boys need a good ass whooping."

His words encouraged Nick. "Did you hear me tell them I'm a reporter?"

"Yup, what you after?"

"Trying to figure out what Travis and Leon—and their Patriot friends—are up to. You're a sharp guy with your ear to the ground. What have they got in the works?"

"No love lost with them two," he said, pausing. Nick guessed he was checking his surroundings. "They figure the best way to change things is to burn it all down. I don't believe that. Too many good military men and women have sacrificed their lives to build this country to throw it all away."

Relief rushed through Nick, from head to toe. "I hear you and agree completely. What are they planning and when?"

Tommy hesitated again, then responded in a hushed tone. "Don't know too much, but what I've picked up is that it's some kind of bombing and scary as hell—involves two locations and blackmail. Gonna really turn things upside down. They're tight-lipped about it, but I think it's in the works, happening now."

"What makes you think that?"

"Big dog, the new boss, was here last night. I heard him say the weather had cleared and boats were on the way."

"Who is the big dog?"

"Jerry Meade. You heard of him?"

Tommy said he had to go, guys with empty mugs were standing at the bar. Nick thanked him and clicked off his phone.

A sense of dread hit Nick. Tommy's words gave him a chill. Bombings? What boats were on the way? Meade in Argyle as the new boss?

The reporter decided to send Tanya a message while he had a chance. She had planned to go shopping in metro Detroit with some friends. Her goal: pick up some new outfits for Sherry Conaway, hoping new duds would brighten the teen's spirits. In his note, Nick mentioned he was meeting a source at the Wheel, and that the Wolverines appeared to be crushing an inferior opponent.

A few minutes later, Tanya replied. "GO BLUE! Don't drink too much. It's early and you're driving." Nick chuckled. She knew him too well.

The Wheel's front door on Broadway swung open and Randy marched in. Heads turned, catching her raven red hair and electric lavender jumpsuit, which hugged her considerable curves as tight as a stock car sparking against a wall at Daytona. The getup included what Nick now figured was her signature look: plunging neckline and eye-popping tats.

Randy's eyes adjusted to the Wheel's shadows, she nodded at Nick, and then continued rolling toward the booth where they'd met the last time. The reporter waited for bar heads to swivel back to the football game before picking up his coffee and joining her. On the way, he caught Tony and ordered the White Russian.

"Hey, Randy. Thanks for coming," Nick said as he slid into the booth across from her. His coffee had cooled, but he finished it. "Wanted to let you know I met Travis and Leon in Argyle yesterday. You described them perfectly."

She nodded, a frown saddening her face. "I know. They came to Bay City last night looking for a jacket Travis had left at Brandi's. They talked about you. Said you were a smart-ass who didn't know his butt from a hole in the ground. I didn't tell them we'd met. I just nodded while they yakked."

Nick told her they said 'The Plan' was in place and could not be stopped, and that only a handful of patriots knew about it. He asked if she had any clue what they were talking about.

"Nope. Hard to say with those two," she said. The drink arrived and Tony filled the coffee cup, then whisked away. "But it must be big if it was worth killing Eric over. I've got something for you."

Randy scanned the Wheel then pulled a small plastic case out of her handbag. She slid it toward Nick, saying she'd already checked it out. He looked at it quickly then stuck it in his jacket pocket. It was a thumb drive.

She took a long sip of the Russian, then leaned toward Nick. "Patriot membership list—names, addresses, and cell numbers. Nothing about

'The Plan' that I could see except for one name that jumped out at me: Reggie Thorpe, a diver from Eric's company. Met him one time at my mom's place. A pig, and he's a sloppy drunk."

Nick laughed. Randy didn't hold back. He liked her bluntness. "How did you get the thumb drive? Was it in the jacket?"

Randy said Brandi had left with Travis. She took another sip of her drink, then continued.

"They left to get the jacket, and he wanted to get down with her. Brandi told me later that he was disgusting—dirty and smelly—that she kicked him out of her place. She said she threw his jeans out the front door. He left with his jacket wrapped around his behind, swearing at her. Brandi found the plastic case in her yard this morning. Must have fallen out of the jeans."

Nick tried the coffee. New pot, much better. "Thanks for giving it to me. I won't use your name, but I think I have to go to the state police, give them an update. I think they'll be interested in the patriot list, and I feel like I should sound the alarm about what I've heard about 'The Plan,' though I have no details."

Randy said she understood. "Just keep me out of it. I don't need the cops sniffing around my business and I just want to be done with the whole Eric thing, including his creepy friends."

Nick excused himself to use the restroom. She nodded, knowing he would most likely return with a hundred bucks in his palm. She finished the Russian and signaled Bullseye Face to bring one more.

In the men's room, Nick's phone pinged. It was Dave. A text asked if he would be available to meet in an hour or so. Nick replied with a thumbs-up.

When the reporter returned to the booth, Randy was sipping from a nearly full rocks glass. He slid into the bench seat, reaching under the table. She took the hundred from his palm.

The football crowd jumped to its collective feet again, screaming and shouting. Nick could not see the TV, but the racket indicated another decisive Wolverines play.

When the crowd settled, Randy asked about Sherry Conaway's

condition. "She still improving, doing better?"

Nick nodded. "Yes, I'm getting daily updates. She's coming along well. I wouldn't be surprised if they let her go home soon, maybe even yet this weekend."

Randy leaned in again. "Curious about something. Is Sherry pregnant?"

The question surprised Nick. He knew that Sherry's pregnancy hadn't been publicly announced, but word was leaking out about the teen's condition. In a town like Bay City, folks swing freely from the grapevine. Rumors and gossip flow across the community like fall leaves in a strong wind.

The reporter did not want to lie to Randy, but he didn't feel comfortable confirming private information for her. He hesitated, studying the bottom of his coffee cup.

Randy continued. "Reason I ask is because Eric had a thing for pregnant women. What's the word? A fascination, or fixation?"

"Fetish?"

"That's it. I knew you, the word jockey, would know it," she said. "He was a dog when it came to pregnant women. One of my girls, Lyndsay, had four kids in four years. She was pregnant all the time and the guys used to line up to get with her. Eric was always at the front of the line."

Her comments hit Nick with a thud. "You think he wanted, or tried, to get Sherry pregnant? That would mean he intended to keep her captive a long time. And then what happens after she gives birth?"

"Knock her up again is where I'd put my money," Randy said. "I told you he was El Kinko when it came to sex. I'll bet he planned to keep her as his own private toy, like a pet. That's how sick he was."

Nick shook his head at the depravity of it all. Her thoughts were sinking in with him and they made his stomach roll. A young woman and child held captive like pets.

Randy finished her Russian and stood. "Now, think about that for a while. I gotta go. Meeting a client in a half hour. Text me if you want to talk again and you've got cash."

Nick thanked her and watched her hustle out the front door of the

Wheel. He sighed, hitting his coffee again. This story weighed on him heavily. Eric, kinky sex, the underage drinking party, the dungeon, Sherry's plight, biker Louise, patriots, the Argyle Neanderthals, 'The Plan,' the Mackinac Island Police. Where was it all going? Where would it end? He checked his watch. Time to meet Dave, hopefully over a stiff drink.

Tanya and her friends split up at the Twelve Oaks Mall in Novi, a trendy, middle-class community northwest of Detroit. They each had their own shopping goals and navigating the sprawling 200-shop monster was no small feat—especially with limited time before they had to head back to Bay City.

Tanya scooted toward the maternity shop within Nordstrom. It had a huge selection of clothing for women in all stages of pregnancy. In no time, she'd found three colorful tops: powder blue, fire-engine red, and canary yellow, Sherry's favorite color according to Danielle, who had offered to pay for the garments.

Tanya insisted on making the purchases, telling Sherry's mom she looked forward to the shopping excursion and the opportunity to hunt for maternity wear. The casual, loose-fitting blouses would work well for the teen's early stage of pregnancy. Two pairs of dark slacks with elastic expandable panels in the front would be functional for at least a few months.

Feeling triumphant, Tanya checked her watch and hustled toward the mall's food court where her friends had agreed to meet. But a giant neon sign on a store just down from Nordstrom stopped her cold. She stood, staring at it, and thinking. Her spirits soared. Then, without hesitancy, she marched inside The Baby Depot, a retail outlet devoted completely to all things related to babies.

Inside, her eyes dashed from one display to another. Each seemed more exhilarating to her than the last. Her walk slowed to a crawl. She could feel her breathing pick up as her heart pounded. Nursery items, baby shoes and socks, pajamas and snuggies, bibs and wipes, body suits, padded cribs and bedding, strollers, car seats, backpacks, toys, and games. She grabbed free brochures at every station and stopped to snap photos. Her heart raced, filling with joy.

So many departments. So many cool things. Everything designed solely for babies and parents. *I've got to get Nick to come here with me*, she thought, as she continued to scan the store. One of her friends happened by and spotted a slow-walking, mesmerized Tanya, joining her.

"Hey Tanya, this is quite the place, isn't it?" the friend said, smiling. "Do you know someone who is expecting?"

Before responding, she hesitated, wondering if she should confide in her friend that she hoped and prayed for adoption. Tanya was about to tell all when her phone pinged, causing her to refrain. It was a text from their group: "We're ordering a bite to eat before heading home. Want a salad or sandwich? Join us."

The two women left The Baby Depot. Tanya would wait to share her dream another time.

Chapter 13

Saturday Afternoon
Blade newsroom

When Nick barreled up the stairs to the second floor of the *Bay City Blade*, he discovered a nearly empty newsroom. A sports reporter sat in a corner actively working the phone, conducting an interview with a football coach from a Friday night game. The TV in sports broadcast the Wolverines' game live, now in the second quarter, with the volume down to a whisper.

With no sign of Dave, Nick headed for his desk, eager to fire up his computer and take a look at the thumb drive from Randy. So far, she had turned out to be a reliable, though expensive, source of information. He wondered how the C-Man would react to two one-hundred-dollar entries on his expense account marked under the category of "entertainment" and with only a first name: Randy.

The computer came to life, started to whir, and his desktop popped onto the screen. Just then, Dave rolled in, stopping to chat with the sports reporter. Dave kept track of all the local high school teams and their top players. The athletes who remained in the area after graduation often made great sources of information when they entered the workforce, started families, and became citizens. They loved it when a news reporter could instantly recall their teams and statistics. Sudden friends for life.

Nick inserted the thumb drive and waited for it to spill its guts. Dave slapped him on the back and asked for an update on the Eric Stapleton story, apologizing for becoming sidetracked with family and personal issues. Nick gave him a very quick summary, noting that he was eager to get a look at the thumb drive's contents.

"I'm making slow, but steady progress," he said, turning to face his friend. "Glad you're here to help me sort it out. But I know you're dealing with a lot yourself. Again, so sorry about your mom. How did your interview go with Ripley?"

"Turns out I'm a so-called 'person of interest' in the case, maybe even the prime suspect in my mom's murder. Mom's murder ..." he said, pausing. "Just seems so odd to be saying that. Never, in my wildest dreams or nightmares, did I ever think of her in those terms."

He outlined the evidence Ripley said they'd discovered: inner-mouth bruising, blood flecks on her pillow, condition of her eyes. "And I was supposedly the last one to talk with her or see her alive. That's their theory and why they're aiming at me."

"Have you started digging into the case yet?"

"I've got some interviews set up through one of my mother's friends. Leona Hayden is sharp as a tack. She's got her ear to the ground inside the nursing home, and has some people lined up to talk with me. I'm going to meet her in an hour."

"Sounds good. Let me know how it goes. Glad to help if I can," said Nick, turning back to his computer. "Take a look at this. Here's a membership list of patriots—the people Stapleton was meeting and working with at the Sand Box storage unit."

A list of more than 150 people, from across Michigan and northern Ohio, Indiana, Illinois, Wisconsin, and Pennsylvania. Interestingly, four names listed Hamilton, Ontario, Canada, as their homes. Nick highlighted two names in Argyle, Michigan.

"Here are the two guys I've had contact with. I couldn't get much out of them," he said. "But they say Stapleton and a handful of other patriots had developed 'The Plan,' it was in place, couldn't be stopped, and Eric was murdered because he got cold feet."

Dave grunted. "Argyle? Isn't that way out in the Thumb by Decker, home to McVeigh and Nichols?"

Nick nodded. "Good memory. That's extremist territory. I felt totally naked and alone inside the Roadhouse bar. Good thing I called on Booger to back me up. Deputy Ratchett showed up just when I needed him, and I was able to get the hell out of there. But it was a little scary."

"OK, let's think about the worst-case scenario," Dave said. "These boys like to play with explosives, and they were working with Stapleton. Are they planning to blow up Line 5 and create an environmental disaster? Why? To create havoc? Is it a distraction for something else? Is it blackmail? Are they planning to take down the Mackinac Bridge?"

"Good questions," Nick said. "Could be any of those things. One of my sources suggested I should focus on this guy—he's a diver and worked at Underwater Solutions with Stapleton."

Nick highlighted Reggie Thorpe on the list. It showed an East Side Bay City home address for him. The reporter copied the address and phone number and saved them to his cell phone.

The drive also contained an employee list, including personal information, for Underwater Solutions. The thirty-three names showed home addresses from all over Michigan. Some had the letter P in parenthesis next to the names, including Jerry Meade. He highlighted the name for Dave.

"This is Gold Chains, one of Eric's co-workers," Nick said. "He showed me the cottage their company rented on Mackinac Island for employees working on the pipeline."

Nick cross-checked the employee list with the letter P next to their names with the patriot list. They matched. "So, Meade and Stapleton were more than co-workers."

"Maybe co-conspirators, too?" Dave wondered aloud. "If Stapleton was killed for getting cold feet on 'The Plan,' maybe Meade was in on his murder."

"Or, maybe he did the killing," Nick said. "Meade knew about Stapleton's penchant for horse riding, and I'll bet he knew about the trails he used on the island."

Nick made a note of the patriot connection between Gold Chains and Stapleton. He underlined it and jotted "KILLER?" next to it. He'd bring it, and the thumb drive, to the attention of the state police.

Dave asked about Sherry Conaway. "Is she still on the rebound?"

Nick said Sherry was doing well physically but struggling emotionally. "I'm not sure if you know this, but she's pregnant and angry about it.

She does not want to have this child, but her folks are against abortion."

"Wow, that's a heavy load for a 15-year-old kid," Dave said. "Is it generally known that she's pregnant? Peer pressure could be immense."

"No formal announcement, but word is leaking out," Nick said, looking down at his hands. "I gotta tell you something else. But please don't breathe a word of it to anyone else. Tanya wants to see if we can adopt the baby if Sherry decides to go full term."

Dave did not respond. He sat, staring at his friend, with his mouth agape. Nick looked up at him and nodded. "Yeah, I know. I'm sure that's how I looked when she sprung it on me."

"A baby, at your age? Wow! How did she take it when you said 'absolutely not?'" Dave asked. "You did say no, right?"

Nick looked down again. "I told her I was against the idea because of our ages, but she didn't give much on it. Made me promise to think about it."

"It's a long shot," Nick added. "Others in the Conaway family may want the baby. Louise Stapleton, or one of her relatives, may want the child. There's a lot of people better positioned to take a baby than we are. Just thought I'd mention it in case it comes up when you see Tanya the next time."

Dave slapped his friend on the back again. "Good luck with that, and the story you're working on. Gotta go meet Leona to see if I can pull myself out of hot water."

Nick said he would catch up with him later. As Dave left the newsroom, he thought about how helpful his buddy had been in hashing out the Stapleton story. "It's like I can't think without Dave around," he thought, smiling.

Nick unplugged the thumb drive and locked it in his desk. He headed out to find Reggie Thorpe and find out what he could about "The Plan."

As Dave arrived at Shady Lane, he could see Leona Hayden pacing in the assisted living facility's open entryway. Since his mother had been killed and her body moved to a funeral home, he was sure he would not be allowed back into the place unless invited by a current resident. Leona had agreed to provide that invitation and introduce him to friends.

Mrs. Balz's friend pushed the front door open for Dave. A cool fall breeze and feathery snow flurries rushed in with him. He extended his hand to Leona, but she brushed it aside and moved in for a hug from the burly, bearded reporter.

"I'm so sorry about your mother," she said, extending on her tiptoes to whisper her condolences. "I'm sure this is painful for you. I enjoyed her so much and we had become good friends. I'm praying for you. In fact, you're now at the center of our circle of prayer warriors."

Dave thanked her and gave her a gentle squeeze. Quietly, he acknowledged that his heart was broken with the passing of his mom. "My whole family is gone now—dad, mom, bro, and sis. All dead. That's just settling in on me. I'm suddenly feeling very alone."

Leona stepped back as Dave caught a tear on his cheek with a knuckle. She squeezed his hand and pulled him into the lobby. "You have friends, here, Dave. We feel for you and we're here for you. Come with me."

He followed the slight petite woman with frosty hair. Dave could feel the eyes of a security guard and orderlies on him as they made their way to a common area where two women waited, smiling, on a sturdy, green couch. The area looked like a giant living room, complete with a roaring fireplace, pastoral paintings on the wall, and soft carpet underfoot.

Leona introduced Dave to Harriet and Penny. The grandmothers could have been sisters. Harriet, thin as a knitting needle, wore a long, colorful flowered dress. Her silver locks were thick and trimmed short above her ears, easy to comb and style. Penny's frame was similar. She sported a light lavender pantsuit with an eggshell white blouse. Gray streaks made her shoulder-length brown hair look two-toned. Bobby pins held her tresses over her ears and tight to her head.

Dave towered over the women as he shook their thin, veiny hands. They each said they were delighted to meet him and were sorry about the passing of his mother.

Penny smiled while recalling Mrs. Balz. "When she was on her game, she was our puzzle master. No crossword too tough for her."

Dave nodded. "I know that's how I developed a love for the written word. She was a stickler with the meaning and use of words. I'm so glad you enjoyed that with her, too."

Harriet noted his mom's organizing skills. "She knew how to put a party together, let me tell you. That girl made every birthday, every holiday, a festive event. Right up until the last several months when we noticed that she wasn't doing well, she was the life of our parties."

"Well, I've always enjoyed a good party, even when I had to start them for myself," Dave replied, chuckling. "But mom always said I got that, and my affinity for beer, from dad."

All three women laughed at his remark, slapping their legs, or clapping their hands, breaking the moment's tranquility. Their joy caught the attention of other small groups of visitors and residents in the giant toasty living room. Amused, they watched Dave and the ladies become comfortable with one another.

Dave pulled a rocking chair close to the couch so they could speak in confidence. He thanked them for meeting with him. He quickly outlined his mom's final days and how it was determined that she'd been killed. He also mentioned that he was being wrongly accused in her death.

"Mom had books in her room about assisted suicide—some she'd purchased, others she'd checked out of Sage Library," he said, quietly, scanning the room to see if others had returned to their conversations. "Do you recall her talking about that? Did that come up in group or individual discussions?"

Leona said the subject of assisted suicide is too dark for most residents to discuss openly, but she had heard it come up among those who were consistently ill. Penny nodded in agreement.

Harriet added that Dave's mom had not been herself in recent months. "I remember her talking about not being happy and wanting out of this life. I took it to mean she wanted out of Shady Lane."

Penny said she heard it discussed in hushed tones the last time Shady Lane experienced a resident dying overnight during sleep. "We had two other cases like your mom's in the last year or so. They were eventually declared natural cause passings, but initially we heard whispers of them being helped into the hereafter."

Interesting, Dave thought, pulling out his notebook to jot down Penny's comment. He would bring it up with Ripley to check out. "What about the orderlies? Would any of them be capable of either assisting suicide, or taking it upon themselves to give an early exit out of here?"

Leona said they had noticed staff becoming more aggressive with his mother as she became more hostile. "The fat lip she received last week shocked a lot of people. She didn't deserve that. Too rough."

Penny said staff members were supposed to be the only ones who had keys to get into rooms after hours. She said that's why she believed Dave's mom had been smothered by a staff member.

Harriet nodded, agreeing. "And those keys are only to be used to check on residents for medical reasons. However, we do hear of items coming up missing from rooms every so often. I think the keys get used inappropriately."

"What about right now?" Leona asked. "We three are here meeting with you. Staff members know we are occupied away from our rooms. How do we know somebody isn't snooping around our rooms this moment?"

The ladies looked at each other, thinking about Leona's statement. Dave watched them. He could see the mistrust, the doubt, in their faces. He listened as they told stories about residents mysteriously losing small pieces of jewelry or money left out in view.

"When we bring up small thefts, we get told that we must be mistaken or our memories are slipping," Leona said. "Of course, nobody wants to hear that or be accused of losing their minds, so we shut up about it."

"How come there are no cameras in the hallways?" Dave asked. "I was kind of surprised to see that. Cameras are everywhere today."

Penny responded that residents objected to the idea of cameras in the halls because of a desire for privacy.

Harriet agreed, adding: "Some of us like to have nighttime visitors. Nobody wants a record of that. The single women here far outnumber the single men. I, for one, want a visitor from time to time. I was married for 50 years and rarely slept alone. No hanky-panky, just someone to cuddle up to."

Dave studied the ladies. They did not disagree with Harriet's assertion. He thought they looked coy, demure, almost bashful in that moment. It made sense to him, he thought. A desire for some level of intimacy would only be natural.

"A girl must be mindful of her reputation," Penny added quickly. Eyes closed; heads nodded.

Leona broke the silence with an idea. "If we believe someone is going into rooms without authorization after hours, how about if we go fishing? Set out bait—rings, bracelets, brooches, change—where it can be seen during the day, and then set the hook by quietly patrolling the hallways at night to see who is slipping into rooms."

The ladies looked at each other while the idea settled on them. Then, one by one, smiles lit up their faces.

"Brilliant," said Harriet, grabbing Leona's hand.

"Love it," added Penny. "Let's put out bait this afternoon and start trolling tonight—see what we catch."

Dave wasn't sure the action would actually help catch his mom's killer, but it could answer a question the ladies obviously wanted an answer to. He urged them to try it and see what they learned. The three huddled on the couch, working out a plan for an after-hours patrol. They'd each carry their cell phones and snap off photos of any suspicious behavior by staff members or residents.

The ladies buzzed over their plan. They discussed the bait they planned to use to not duplicate items. They discussed where the bait would be placed in their small studio-style flats. And then they pledged to each other not to talk about their plan because it would quickly spread among residents and eventually to staff members.

Dave thanked them for meeting with him. He appreciated the information they shared and wished them good luck and happy fishing. He headed out the front door and toward the F-150, happy he'd spent time with these delightful ladies who were eager to help him find his mom's killer.

Chapter 14

Saturday Afternoon
East Side Bay City

Reggie Thorpe rented an apartment in one of the old lumber baron's mansions on Fourth Avenue not far from Johnson Street on Bay City's East Side. His one-bedroom, one-bath efficiency was carved out of the ancient mansion's main floor. His front entry door stood ajar, marijuana smoke wafting out onto the covered front porch.

Nick had tried calling the cell number listed next to his name on the thumb drive. No one answered, and he didn't leave a message. The reporter could smell pungent, skunk-like fumes as he approached the dark apartment. Through the entry, he could hear the TV blaring the Wolverines' football game, now in the fourth quarter. He knocked on the screen door, causing it to bang and rattle against the wood frame.

"Just a damn minute," a voice shouted from the back of the apartment. "Making some munchies, be right with you."

Nick waited, eyeing the living room through the screen. The old mansion's ornate oak trim looked as though it wore a dozen layers of paint. He could see a big, blue corduroy couch, a tall wooden bureau with a desktop computer on it, and a rocking chair. All the furniture was aimed at the front corner of the room where it sounded like the TV was mounted. Soon, he heard someone approaching in hard-soled shoes.

"What you want?" said a man with black curly hair, clad in a stained Ozzy Osbourne T-shirt, faded tight jeans, and black, steel-toed work boots. The reporter guessed his age at 25 or 26. He carried a bowl of popcorn in his left hand.

"I'm looking for Reggie Thorpe," Nick said, smiling through the screen. "Have I found him?"

"Depends," he said, belching loud enough to block out a Wolverines' score. "Again, what you want?"

Nick responded that he was a reporter with the *Blade* and wanted to do a follow-up story on Eric Stapleton after his surprising death. "I heard you were a friend and co-worker. I thought you could tell me about him and your work together at Underwater Solutions."

Thorpe pushed open the screen door, wobbling and leaning on the inside of the door frame. He invited the reporter in and shoved a handful of popcorn in his mouth, kernels flying sideways out of his fist like they were coming out of the popper.

"Yeah, too bad about Eric," he said, his voice trailing off. "Got himself sideways and took the fall for it. I liked him. Taught me a lot."

Steel Toes walked to the couch where he had a forty-ounce beer open and sitting on a side table next to a fifth of Jack Daniels whiskey, also open. A wet shot glass separated the ale and the whiskey.

"Want a drink? Beer in the fridge, shots right here," he said, tossing his head sideways toward the kitchen. He then turned back toward the game, settling his slender, six-foot frame onto the couch with a head pillow supporting the black boots. He shoved the fifth toward Nick, who said nothing.

The reporter pulled out his notebook and pen and took the rocker. He watched Thorpe, who, judging by the heavy aroma of drink and smoke in the air, was absolutely bombed. Nick decided it would be dangerous and stupid to participate in the one-person party.

"Why do the Wolverines even play these flunkies this far into the season?" he asked, taking a long slug from the tall, fat bottle of beer. He wiped his lips and poured a shot of Jack. "It's a joke. Sure you don't want one?"

He dumped the shot down his throat and smacked the glass back down on the table. "Now, what are you here for? Tell me again."

Nick repeated his earlier statement and asked how long he'd worked with Stapleton. Thorpe attempted to focus on the reporter, sitting up on the couch and trying to steady himself with one hand on the work desk with the computer. The reporter noticed that the computer was up and running, unlocked, a dozen or so files visible on its desktop.

"Yeah, too bad about Eric," he said, as if he hadn't just spoken those words to Nick. "Got himself sideways and took the fall for it. I liked him. Taught me a lot."

"Yes, you mentioned that," Nick said. "What did he teach you? How long did you work together?"

Steel Toes considered the question for a second time, then tried to answer. "Well, Eric, you know, he was an original organizer. He built the Underwater Solutions team, refined my skills as a diver. Not everybody is cut out to be a frogman."

Thorpe poured another shot, attempted to toast Nick, and dropped the small glass on the floor, whiskey spilling everywhere, including on the reporter's shoes.

"Oops, that one got away from me," he said, laughing hard at his joke. "Don't worry. Plenty more where that came from." He picked up the shot glass, poured another, and then quickly tossed it back before it, too, could escape.

Nick watched, waited for him to swallow, then asked another question. "How was Underwater Solutions connected to the patriot organization? Were you a member of the patriots before you went to work for them?"

Steel Toes chased the shot with another long drink of beer, nearly finishing the ale. "Got hired first, then became a member of the Proud Patriots of Michigan."

Nick pressed him. "Did Stapleton recruit you to the patriots?"

Thorpe stood up, then fell back into the couch. "Gotta go to the can. 'Scuse me." He jumped up and headed toward the back of the apartment, crashing into the wall of the hallway and then sliding along it as he trudged.

Nick stood and watched the man, expecting him to fall and pass out at any moment. When Steel Toes ducked into the bathroom, the reporter turned his attention back to the computer screen.

He scanned the files on the desktop. He used the mouse to click on a file marked Underwater Solutions. More than a dozen sub files emerged. His eyes darted across the labels: Hamilton, Ontario. Owen Sound. Fishing trawlers. Bay Port. Argyle. Sugar Beet trucks. Midland tankers. Three Rivers. Saginaw Bay. Lake Huron. Mackinaw City. Line 5. Mackinac Bridge. Whitmer. Publicity.

Nick heard Steel Toes snort and crash into the bathtub. He decided to check on him before doing more with the desktop files. The reporter followed the sound of deep snoring. He peeked into the bathroom, discovering Thorpe passed out in the bathtub, a lit joint burning a hole in the shower curtain that had fallen beneath his crashing weight.

Figuring that Reggie was resting uncomfortably and unlikely to hurt himself further or burn the house down, Nick hustled back to the computer. He used the mouse to copy the files he'd discovered and save them to a new file, attaching it to an email and then forwarded it to his personal and work emails.

The reporter then deleted the file he sent to himself, eliminating the record. He checked on Steel Toes once more and found the man still snoring in his tub. Nick returned to the living room, grabbed his notebook and pen, then headed for the front door, just as the Wolverines scored again, completing the thorough trouncing of an inferior foe.

Nick left, certain Reggie Thorpe would awaken with no memory or record of his visit. He checked his watch, wondering if Tanya had returned from her shopping trip. They had planned to meet for dinner, but he was eager to check the files he'd just copied. He headed for the *Blade* newsroom.

Tanya carried her Nordstrom's shopping bags into Bay Med eager to see Sherry Conaway and show her the great finds she discovered during a shopping trip to metro Detroit. The teen continued to ride an emotional roller coaster, from yesterday's high of receiving a sack full of kind words and best wishes from Central High schoolmates to the low of another visit and lecture from the parish priest about the sanctity of life. Tanya wanted to help bolster the girl.

Danielle Conaway met Tanya in the hallway outside Sherry's room. The two embraced, and Tanya asked about the condition of her favorite hospital patient. Sherry's mom hugged her tight, holding her close. "Our girl is having some physical problems. Wanted you to know she's spotting, and it's increasing."

The news stung Tanya. "Oh no. I didn't realize she was having a problem. Did she just start spotting?"

Danielle released the counselor from their embrace. "When she was first admitted, it was very light. The doc thought it might have been the result of injury from the physical abuse she suffered. They've been monitoring more closely since the pregnancy was discovered. Now, the severity of spotting is increasing."

Tanya was afraid to ask but felt she must. "Is she at risk? Do they think she could lose the baby?"

The mom said Sherry was being tested for diabetes and thyroid conditions, either of which could trigger a miscarriage. "They already checked her for infections when they tested for STDs. Both negative. Wanted you to be aware on your way in. Sherry has been asking if you were going to stop by. She's very moody today—we're glad you're here."

Danielle took Tanya's hand and pulled her toward Sherry's room where Ben was doing his best to entertain his daughter with his verbal highlights from an afternoon of college football. They walked into the room. Tanya wore her happy face and gushed at the teen.

"How are you, Sweetie?" Tanya asked, rushing to Sherry's bedside while dropping her bags in a chair. They hugged. Sherry thanked her for coming to the hospital.

Ben shuffled toward the door, saying he planned to run errands and make some calls. Danielle followed, urging Sherry and Tanya to catch up with one another.

When they'd left, Sherry started to weep. "I'm bleeding and they don't know how to stop it, or if it will stop. I don't want to die."

Tanya put her arm around the teen and tried to comfort the troubled young woman. Just yesterday, the head floor nurse had suggested that Sherry might be going home soon. Suddenly, her condition had worsened.

"I'm sure you're getting the best care possible. They'll do everything they can for you," she said, patting Sherry's back gently. "Tell me, are you worried about losing the baby?"

The teen didn't respond immediately. She snuggled into Tanya. "I'm worried about everything. I can't seem to make sense of anything. This whole week has been spinning out of control. I'm just rolling from one crazy nightmare to the next."

Sherry volunteered that her old boyfriend, Mark, had asked the Conaways if he could visit her in the hospital. The thought of seeing him, she continued, caused her to panic.

"What could I possibly say to him? 'Hi Mark, I was chained up in a cell and raped every day for three months, but things are going well now. Oh, and by the way, I've been impregnated by the sadistic monster who kidnapped me. How's your life? Everything cool at Western?' How's that gonna fly? I had my folks tell Mark I wasn't up to it."

Tanya responded that she'd not heard about Mark's request, but it shows how much he cares about her. "I'm sure he simply wanted to check on you and offer support. The details of what happened to you—that's going to be up to you on what and how much you want to reveal over time. Right now, all we want you to do is heal and get better."

Sherry crawled out from Tanya's cocoon to look her in the eye. "I haven't said this to Mom and Dad, but I hope I miscarry. They would freak if they heard me say it out loud. You know I don't want this child. I've made it pretty clear. I do not want to bring another monster into this world."

Her words hit Tanya like a dagger cutting through her heart to her soul. She didn't want to see Sherry miscarry or abort the fetus she carried. All week, she'd harbored the notion that she and Nick could take and accept a child that very few might want. Like Sherry, Tanya had held her true feelings close, only revealing them to Nick as a way of sowing the seed of an idea she hoped he would embrace.

The two sat on Sherry's bed without speaking. Quietly, Tanya asked her how she was feeling. She wanted to know if the teen had a fever, or chills, or nausea. Vomiting?

"Nope, just generally crappy and weak," she said. "I had Jell-O for breakfast and a piece of toast for dinner. I can't eat. Nothing sounds good."

The door opened and a nurse charged into the room, declaring it was time for a vitals check. Blood pressure. Temperature. Heart rate. "Sorry to interrupt, but this will just take a minute or two. Need to update the chart," the young man said.

He was right and efficient, dashing about on both sides of the bed. Tanya stood by the chair with her gifts in it. His final act was a fill up of the water jug before hustling out of the room with a wish for a good night, carrying a note of finality to it.

As the nurse left, Danielle returned by herself. She looked refreshed and relaxed, Tanya thought.

"I'm surprised you two haven't dug into those Nordstrom's bags," Danielle said, smiling broadly and eyeing the prizes. Tanya had called Danielle on her way home from Novi and gave her a preview of her gifts for Sherry. The mom thought they would highlight a day that had been disheartening—Ben's football recap notwithstanding. "What do you think? Shall we see what Tanya brought?"

Sherry's eyes shot to the chair with the bags. She smiled and nodded, squeezing Tanya's hand again. The three ladies spent the next hour poring through the bags. Sherry was so pleased with the colorful tops that she had to pull each one on to see how she looked in them.

Tanya left Bay Med delighted that she'd brought the teen some joy, but also troubled by news that Sherry was having difficulty with her pregnancy. The next six weeks would be critical to the development of her unborn child.

Nick charged up the stairway in the *Blade* building, taking steps two at a time, to the newsroom. Usually, Saturday afternoons were relatively subdued with a skeleton crew of staff members putting the final touches on a newspaper that had largely been put together on Thursday and Friday in advance pages. Nick figured the quiet nature of the newsroom would be ideal for him to dig into the files he'd copied from Reggie Thorpe's desktop.

However, on this Saturday afternoon the newsroom felt alive and kicking as he entered through the front door. Two reporters, two photographers, and a graphic artist huddled around Steve, the veteran weekend news editor. Nick quickened his pace to join them.

"What's happening?" he asked, maneuvering between bodies bent over like human question marks to study images on Steve's computer screen. Raging fire roared out of an apartment building, blue-hot flames licking through the frames of blown-out windows. "Where's that?"

"Hampton Township," Steve said without looking away from the screen. "This is the first building, two more have since erupted in flames. Big wind off Saginaw Bay is pushing the fire."

About three hundred people lived in five Harbor View apartment buildings, a complex located just east and south of Bay City in Hampton Township. Three of the buildings were ablaze and fire officials were trying to keep the other two hosed down and safe. Authorities had called for each building to be evacuated, but an unknown number of residents had been trapped by the fast-moving fire storm.

Sadie Edwards, a fresh young reporter who'd rushed back from the scene to the newsroom to rough in an initial story for Steve, said fire departments and rescue crews from throughout the region were responding to the emergency.

"People are jumping off balconies to escape the flames," Sadie said, her voice breaking as she relayed the horror of what she'd seen. "Bound to be some fatalities, lotta folks hurt. I gotta get back there."

Nick volunteered to help. "I'll go, too. I can pitch in with the interviews—residents and rescuers. Let's get moving."

Steve urged the three reporters and two photographers present to chase the story. He said he would alert the managing editor and complete as much of the Sunday newspaper as possible. "I'll save as much space as I can for breaking news and photos," he said. "Check in with me every 30 minutes."

The five grabbed their gear and scattered toward Hampton Township. Nick shot Tanya a text that he was working on a developing story. The files from Reggie Thorpe would have to wait.

Tanya poured a glass of wine and stretched out in front of the television, just in time to watch a 90-second news clip of the apartment-building fire in Hampton Township. She worried about Nick, who she thought she caught a glimpse of while he interviewed a firefighter in the report. He'd just texted at 10:30 p.m. and said he'd be home shortly after finishing up in the newsroom.

Stinking of smoke and grimy, Nick burst through their front door with a cold six pack of beer under his arm. He'd been thirsty for a beer since early in the afternoon, but now he was finally in position and ready to pop open a cold one. He kicked off his shoes and kissed Tanya, who had risen to greet him at the door. They embraced for a moment. He said he'd missed her all day. They kissed again.

"Oh, you reek of smoke. Let's get your clothes off and get you in the shower before you settle in," she said, leading him by his necktie to their bathroom. She took the six pack and set it on top of the toilet tank, opening a beer for him. Then she stripped him while he sipped the cold brew. "I worried about you. So glad you're home OK."

Nick told her it was a hot, horrible fire that destroyed three buildings. "Hard to believe, but no one died. The firefighters and rescue people were fantastic. Lots of injuries and homeless, but nobody killed. Unbelievable. Heroes—that's the story I wrote. So many selfless rescuers stepped up to save people they'd never met. Touched my heart."

Tanya tossed his soiled, smoky clothes in a pile near the door. She pulled the shower curtain back and ran water for him, testing to make sure it wasn't too hot. He finished the beer and licked his foamy moustache, handing the bottle to Tanya who nudged him toward the steamy shower. He stepped in and pulled the curtain halfway.

"Are you coming in?" he asked, doing his best not to beg. "Room for two in here. I guarantee you'd love it, too."

She laughed. "I know, but if I do, we won't spend any time talking today."

"Talking is way overrated."

Steam filled the bathroom. Nick lathered up and rinsed off. Standing directly under the hot spray of water, he took a deep breath and finally relaxed. When he stepped out, Tanya held a soft, fluffy towel and another cold beer for him. He kissed her again and said he'd be right out to join her on the couch.

Tanya loaded his clothes in the hamper and then hunted for the place where she'd set down her glass of wine. She scooped it off the dining room table and stopped in the kitchen to pull out the cheese and cracker tray she'd put together in anticipation of Nick's return home.

"Tell me about your day. How was the big city?" he asked, carrying beer number two, and wearing only a bathrobe while joining Tanya on the couch. She'd shut off the television and put on music. "Did you find stuff for Sherry?"

"Yes, some cute outfits and she loved them," Tanya said, sipping chardonnay. "Twelve Oaks is so huge, shops of all kinds. Found the outfits at Nordstrom's maternity shop. Then, I found these at a shop next door."

Tanya reached into the handbag on the floor and produced a half dozen brochures from The Baby Depot. She spread them on the coffee table in front of Nick. She smiled. "It's got ev-er-y-th-ing you can imagine for babies. You have to see it."

Nick leaned forward and flipped through the slick pamphlets on the coffee table. "Impressive. I didn't know they had such a place—a whole store devoted to just babies. We'll have to check it out next time we're down that way."

Tanya squeezed his hand and shimmied up to him. "Glad you're at least thinking about it. You know how I feel."

He asked about Sherry. "She still doing OK? Ready to go home yet?"

"She's had a bit of a setback physically," Tanya said, pausing to sip her wine. She nudged the snack tray toward Nick. "Danielle told me she's spotting. I could tell she's more worried about it than Sherry, who says she's OK with a miscarriage. That poor girl has gone through so much. Her head is spinning trying to figure it all out."

Nick made a cracker and cheese sandwich and scarfed it down. "To survive what Stapleton put her through tells me she's stronger than we think. When I carried her out of that cell, I honestly didn't know if she was going to live. And now, in less than a week's time, she's bouncing back. She needs more time."

Tanya nodded. "You're probably right; this has all happened so fast. I'm praying for her and her baby. The docs are running tests to see if she's got underlying problems that may affect her pregnancy—I think she's getting good care."

Nick took a sip of beer and made another sandwich. He hadn't realized he was hungry. He wanted to jump on his computer and check the Thorpe files, but he was dog-tired and enjoying the time with Tanya. He decided to mention that he would have to dig into the files in the morning, wedging them in between breakfast and church.

"I met another of Stapleton's friends this afternoon, a guy who was a co-worker," he began, stopping to take a bite of cheese and cracker. "The guy was so bombed mid-afternoon, he passed out in his bathroom. I noticed his computer was open so I nosed around it and found some files that may be pretty revealing about what he and Stapleton were up to. Tomorrow's Sunday, but I'm going to need to paw through that info."

Tanya was not shocked. She knew he often worked on Sunday, especially when chasing a big story. She asked about Dave, wondering how their friend was working through the loss of his mother and the police investigation into her murder.

"Being a suspect has rattled him, but he seems to be handling it as well as could be expected. Last I saw him, he was heading out to meet with some of his mom's friends about her death. He's a resourceful guy. I gotta tell you it was great for me to brainstorm with him on the Stapleton story. I'll have to check in on him tomorrow."

Nick wanted to tell Tanya about meeting Randy at the Wheel but wasn't quite sure how to bring up the idea he had been meeting with a call girl. Finally, he decided to just blurt it out. He and Tanya did not keep secrets from each other, and he didn't want to start now.

"I wanted to tell you about another meeting I had today," he began, finishing the last swallow of beer and setting the empty bottle on the table. "Also a friend of Stapleton's, but a different kind of associate."

Tanya listened without interrupting. She reached around the empty bottle to pick up a slice of cheese and a cracker while he continued.

"She's a call girl and I met her at the Spinning Wheel in the South End," he said, pausing to watch her reaction.

"A call girl? You mean a whore?" she said, spitting out the last word and putting the cracker back on the tray. Nick sensed tension building. "You met a whore at a bar? Is that what you're saying?"

Nick nodded. "Yes, but the meeting was informational only. We talked, that's all. She was very helpful and pointed me to the guy I mentioned earlier, the guy who passed out in his bathtub."

His spouse seemed to relax slightly. "Well, OK. If you didn't give her any money and it was just talk, I guess it's all right."

Uh-oh, he thought. Time to clarify. "Well, I did have to pay for her time. A hundred bucks for an hour of her time. Talk only, not service."

"Service? You mean sex, right" she responded. He sensed a rise in the tension meter. "Talk only, no sex. Is that correct?"

"Correct, no sex," he said quickly. "Just talk, and very helpful. Solid information."

Tanya asked about Nick getting reimbursed. "Did you clear that with Drayton Clapper? Did the managing editor authorize payment of cash to a hooker? What kind of receipt did you get? Herpes?"

Nick held up his hands. "No receipt, paper or otherwise. I'm sure the C-Man will cover it. That's a legitimate expense. Information only."

"Yeah? When was the last time you paid for an interview?" she asked, taking a long drink from her glass of wine. "When you pay for talk, are you paying by the word? How does that work? I'm trying to sort this out. How often do you pay for someone to talk with you?"

The reporter/spouse was stumped. He could not, immediately, recall paying for an interview. He tried to skirt the question.

"I'll talk to Drayton on Monday," he said quietly, hoping to de-escalate the discussion. "When I explain, I'm sure he'll authorize it as legitimate expense."

Tanya finished her glass of wine. "I hope so. We're not paying for hookers, talk or otherwise, from our budget."

Her spouse pushed back, gently. "You know I take sources out to lunch, out for drinks, out for golf. I get reimbursed for those purchases.

I do it to curry favor with sources to obtain information. Same with fundraisers. I buy raffle tickets; I buy drink tickets at functions. I buy Girl Scout cookies from sources."

Tanya considered his words. "Hmm. So, are you saying giving money to the Girl Scouts is the same as giving money to hookers?"

He rolled his eyes, and then stared at the ceiling for minutes.

Nick let it go, preferring not to respond. He wanted to move on. Tanya picked up her empty glass and went to bed. "Could you take care of the empty bottle and tray? I'm tired. I'm crashing."

Not a good sign, he thought, flipping on the TV to catch the sports report. The lead sports highlight was the Wolverines, a game Nick thought he'd seen that day without actually watching it. The intro for Saturday Night Live shot across the screen. Before the opening monologue finished, he fell asleep on the couch, toppling sideways and snoring like a diesel roaring down the highway.

Chapter 15

Sunday Morning
Shady Lane

It was still dark outside when the cell phone on Dave Balz's bedside table screamed for his attention, yanking him from a drop-dead sleep. He fumbled to grab the blaring device without rising from bed. It didn't work. He dropped it, forcing him to sit up. He could see Leona's name pop up on the cell screen.

"Hi Leona," he croaked into the phone, covering his mouth to cough and clear the early-morning obstruction. "What is it? Are you OK?"

"Someone was in my room," she gasped. "I awoke and he was standing over me with a pillow. I screamed and kicked. He ran out. Dave, I'm so afraid."

The reporter jumped from bed. "I'll be right there."

On the way to Shady Lane, Dave called the direct line to the Bay City Public Safety Department to report the incident and leave a message for Detective Ripley. The duty officer took the message but urged Dave to call 9-1-1 to report the incident. An emergency dispatcher, he said, would send an officer to the scene. The reporter followed orders.

It was 5:30 a.m. and the Shady Lane early risers were just starting to stir as Dave pulled into the parking lot, the F-150 huffing and puffing. Penny, fully dressed in a soft, comfy blue sweat suit and walking shoes, waited for him in the facility's entryway. She pushed the door open for him.

"Hi Penny, how's Leona doing?" Dave asked. Cool, night air slapped her in the face as she held the door. Dave had not bothered to comb his hair and his brown, wooly locks shot out in an unruly, untamed fashion.

"Leona is pretty shook up," Penny reported, stepping out of the big guy's way. "Harriet is with her. She and I were taking turns patrolling the halls through the night. We saw nothing out of the ordinary. I was at the other end of the building when the intruder went into her room."

An orderly stood outside Leona's room as the two friends approached. "Why were you called?" the orderly asked.

"I'm a friend," Dave replied, brushing past the young man, who he figured was probably in his mid-20s. Inside, a security guard stood in front of Leona and Harriet, who were seated at a small table.

The guard jotted notes into his phone but stopped when Dave and Penny entered. He asked them to please wait outside until he finished. Leona nodded at Dave. He took that to mean it was OK.

"Just so you know, I called 9-1-1," Dave said. The security guard frowned. "I was told an officer will stop by."

Dave did not want Shady Lane administrators to simply note, then dismiss, Leona's complaint. He wanted to make sure there was a public record of it, and he also wanted to make sure Ripley received a full report from a trained officer, not simply the notes of a company rent-a-cop.

When Penny and Dave retreated to the hall, it had come alive with residents who milled about, sipping coffee and rubbernecking to discover the source of the ruckus. Penny recognized several Shady Laners, smiling and nodding at them. They wanted to know if Leona was OK. Some said they worried about her having a medical issue.

Penny talked with them quietly, assuring them Leona was OK and saying more information would be coming out later.

Soon, word spread that a police officer was at the front door. Dave suggested to Penny that it would be better for a resident to open the door for the officer. "I'm probably skating on thin ice around here." She nodded and shot for the entry.

Dave listened at Leona's doorway. The security guard was finishing. He heard the guard offer Leona assurance that a representative of Shady Lane would be keeping an eye on her door for her as long as she wanted someone watching. **He said all the right things**, Dave thought, well-schooled in resident relations.

Patrolman Bob Larson, who was also a trained firefighter, approached. Dave recognized him immediately and smiled, happy the veteran officer had been on duty and caught the call to check on Leona's incident. The two shook hands.

Larson volunteered that he'd heard about Dave's mom and offered his condolences. The reporter nodded, saying he appreciated the sentiment. Dave explained that Leona had been a friend of his mother's, and he called in the incident after she reached out to him around 5 a.m.

The security guard emerged from Leona's room and motioned for Larson to follow him. The two walked down the hall to confer, and Dave shot in to visit with Leona and Harriet. The women said they were glad to see him.

Leona apologized for calling him so early, but said she was frightened. "It just stunned me to see a man standing over me in the dark with a pillow in his hands. I yelled and kicked at him. He left right away, but I was shaking."

Dave asked if she could describe the intruder. "Did you have a night light on?"

"No, it was dark except for light from the parking lot through my blinds," she said, using her chin to point them out. "I only saw a silhouette. Nothing I really recognized."

Larson entered the room and identified himself. He looked at Dave, who took the hint and excused himself to wait in the hall.

Outside, the security guard waited for Dave. His name tag said WAYNE in all caps with the name of the facility underneath. He was aggressive with the reporter.

"You may think you are helping, but you're not," he snapped. "It is not your place to call in the police. That's our responsibility after we've made an initial assessment of the situation."

Dave did not back down. "Hey, Leona called me. A friend reached out and said she found a stranger in her room. In light of what happened with my mom, and the other deaths you've had here in the last year, I believed a call to the police was warranted."

Wayne shook his head, his eyes dancing around the hallway where residents still gathered, whispering to each other. "And what you did has caused unnecessary panic. Your actions scared these people. They don't need that, it helps no one."

"If you don't want residents frightened, then how about doing your job and giving them the security and peace of mind they're paying you for?" he suggested. "All I did is report the incident to authorities. I'm not apologizing for that."

Wayne stuck his cell phone in his jacket pocket and walked away, saying, "We'll see about that."

After several minutes, the officer came out of Leona's room. He stopped to chat with Dave.

"I got her version of events and I talked with the guard. I'll write an incident report and file it," the cop said. "She didn't have much in the way of a description, but I'll make sure Ripley sees everything I got. Thanks for the call."

Dave thanked him for coming, then asked him about the security guard. "What did you get from the guard? Does he seem like he's got his shit together?"

Larson paused, considering the question. "Guard says there were no reports of anyone wandering the halls overnight. He says he makes the rounds—every hallway—every 90 minutes. Keeps a written log."

"So, what did the guard make of Leona's story?" Dave asked.

Again, another long pause. "Thinks she may have been dreaming. Not lying, just mistaken. Had a bad dream after what happened to your mom and woke up thinking someone had been in her room. Guard says there's no physical evidence of anyone else being inside. The room lock is secure and doesn't appear to have been tampered with. I checked it out."

Dave nodded. He hadn't had much of a chance to talk with Leona, so he didn't feel like he had enough to contradict the assessment. He thanked the officer again for coming.

Larson left and the reporter returned to Leona's room. The orderly, who had been posted at her door, was gone now. He walked in and sat beside her at the table. Harriet was using the restroom.

"How are you doing?" he asked, taking her tiny hands in his paws. "We had the guard and the police in here. Do you feel better now?"

Leona looked at Dave. He could see frustration in her face. "They didn't believe me, I could tell. They just think I'm a crazy old fool. They were humoring me. The guard suggested I'd simply woken up from a bad dream."

"I know that's what they think," Dave said, trying to comfort her. "I hadn't talked to you so I couldn't argue, but I believe you. The police were here and this incident will become part of the record when a report is filed. Don't worry, you are not going to be dismissed."

"It wasn't a dream—it was real. I could smell him when he hovered over me. His breathing picked up, got fast as he moved in. You don't dream smells. It was a stale smell, like cheap aftershave trying to cover body odor. Old-man stink."

That's pretty specific, Dave thought. "Do you think you'd recognize the odor if you smelled it again?"

"Damn right I would," Leona said. "Never forget it."

Dave squeezed her hands gently. "I hear you. Don't worry, we'll get this figured out. We'll get with Harriet and Penny and come up with a new plan. Don't worry."

Nick cracked eggs into a bowl suitable for scrambling. He woke up early, thanks to a crick in his neck from the couch and noise from the TV. He hadn't planned to sleep in the living room, but it may have been best given Tanya's mood at bedtime. After reflection, he understood her disappointment.

Fresh coffee brewed while he tossed two slices of whole wheat into the toaster. Nick had already peeled an orange and sliced an apple. They chilled in the fridge. He counted on the aroma of the percolating java to wake Tanya, which did the job. Yawning, she entered the kitchen. Her blonde hair hung damp and tangled from a quick shower. A light pink bathrobe clung to her shoulders, tied in the front. He kissed her on the cheek before she'd finished her wake-up rituals. The aroma of Irish Mist hit him as he pulled away from her.

"Good morning," she said, peering past him to the skillet warming on the stove. "Hmmm, you've been busy."

Nick pulled out the fresh fruit for her to pick at. "Sorry about last night. I could have handled that whole thing better. I just hate disappointing you."

Tanya nibbled at the corner of an apple slice. "I overreacted. I trust you and believe in what you're doing, the hooker interview just hit me the wrong way. You didn't have to sleep on the couch. You're always welcome in my bed." She grabbed his hand and slid up behind him as he worked the spatula against the frying eggs.

"Doesn't happen often, but SNL put me out," he said, reaching over and punching the toaster lever to start crisping the brown bread. "Plus, the two beers, the nice treat you made, and a 10-hour workday ... I went out pretty fast."

Tanya popped an orange slice in her mouth and poured them both coffee. "I know you've got to work today. Are you still up for church?"

"Yes. After we eat, I'd like to take a quick look at the files I picked up yesterday before we head out to church, then I can get back to them in the afternoon," he said, scooping the eggs into a warmed bowl. "Will that work for you?"

"I have no solid plans for the day," she said, placing hot toast on a small plate, also warmed. "Thought I'd visit Sherry this afternoon to give her folks an extended break. They have not left her side all week."

The couple sat down at the table for breakfast, enjoying Nick's cooking and their time together. The eggs, toast, and fruit were yummy. They munched for a few moments, then Tanya had another idea.

She took his hand and pulled him toward the bedroom. "Church can wait. Your files can wait. Let's make time for us." Nick did not argue.

Bay Med buzzed like it was under attack by swarming mosquitoes with Sunday afternoon visitors. Tanya took the stairs up to Sherry Conaway's floor rather than wait for swamped elevators. She had some good news to share with the teenager and she hoped it would brighten her spirits.

Again, Danielle greeted her in the hallway outside Sherry's room with a hug. The mom reported that her daughter's mood had improved through the morning after a rough night.

"Sherry had more spotting and some cramping, which kept her awake for several hours," Danielle said. "But she slept late and was more upbeat during breakfast. I'm concerned about the cramping, but she seems OK now. She asked if you were coming by today."

Tanya said she planned to stay most of the afternoon. "Nick is working so I'm here as long as you like. You and Ben can disappear for awhile. Have a nice dinner—do whatever suits you. Have some fun."

Danielle squeezed her hand in thanks, leading her to the door. Ben stood as Tanya entered, glad to see her, and Sherry smiled and opened her arms for a hug. When they embraced, the teen thanked her again for the outfits she'd brought.

"I showed the nurses each of the tops," she said, beaming. Ben and Danielle inched their way toward the door. They watched their daughter and her school counselor, easing out into the hallway without being noticed. "They thought they were cool. One even said that they weren't found around the Tri-Cities. I love them and can hardly wait to wear them."

Tanya smiled. The remark gave her an opening to bring up Central High. "Have you thought about returning to school? Your friends ask about you every day," she said. "You'd be welcomed back with open arms."

Sherry replied she'd been thinking about it since Tanya brought the sack full of cards. The personal notes were very sweet, she said, but the feelings behind them would fade once she returned to school and the whispers started.

The counselor reminded her that she would not be the only pregnant teen in high school. "I know you're aware of other girls at Central who are in your situation. It's not that unusual these days."

Sherry considered her words before responding. "Yup, and I know what's said behind the backs of those pregnant girls. Central is like the capital of Mean Girl City. Some of those bitches will be unmerciful—and it won't all be behind my back."

Tanya said she understood, but hoped Sherry would reconsider. "You know, you're really not that far behind. You're a smart young lady. You can still catch up and finish the school year in good shape to graduate on schedule."

Another long pause. "You're right about the bookwork. I think I could catch up and the extra reading would be good for me to focus on. But I also know that the further I go, the more my pregnancy will show. It won't be long, and I'll have a pretty good bump showing."

"That will happen gradually," Tanya said. "You'll adjust, they'll adjust, and you'll fit in as time moves on."

Sherry laughed out loud and clapped her hands as she sat up in bed. "Sure, and when Halloween gets here, I can get the pregnant nun costume and wear it with pride."

Sherry howled at the joke, and Tanya did her best not to laugh, surrendering to a broad smile. The teen was smart and clever. The counselor decided to press ahead with the good news she'd brought the patient.

"Speaking of school," she said, sitting on the side of the bed. "I checked for an update on the wonderful financial support you're getting. The civic organizations, the school, the booster's club, the church—they're raising tens of thousands of dollars. You're over $100,000 and the amount is still growing."

The teenager covered her open mouth with both hands. Tanya thought her astonishment might make the young lady's eyes pop out of her head. "Oh … My … God! Oh my God!" she repeated, staring into the distance. "I can't believe it!"

"You've got a mountain of support out there," Tanya said. "People want to help, they want you to have a wide path forward. We've got to start planning for college; you can go anywhere you want. We just need to get you caught up on the time you've missed and concentrate on keeping your grades high. Your future is bright."

The talk about college and her future prompted her morale to soar. Excitement filled the air as Tanya reached into her handbag and pulled out more than a dozen brochures from universities across Michigan.

They spent the next three hours discussing each school. Tanya organized the stack by each university's specialties. Then they discussed the positives and negatives for each. Sherry knew students from Central who were now attending each college.

It turned out to be a good day for both the student and the counselor.

Sunday afternoons at Shady Lane were devoted to matinee presentations of classic movies. Men and women of the facility regularly enjoyed warm popcorn and squeezing into the assisted living facility's auditorium for a big-screen trip down memory lane. The auditorium easily transformed into a cozy movie house for about 100 residents and their guests, who looked forward to a digital movie in vivid color with surround sound suited to accommodate any hearing aid.

On this day, *Saturday Night Fever,* the 1977 classic starring a young John Travolta in his white leisure suit and featuring iconic dance moves from the era, would fire up residents, many of whom recalled the film from their youths.

Leona, Penny, and Harriet juggled iced soft drinks and popcorn boxes as they maneuvered for prime seating in a middle row of the makeshift theater. When the idea of the matinee was first suggested to Leona, she hesitated. The earlier commotion surrounding her uninvited visitor had left her unsettled, but she caved in to the pleadings of her friends, especially when they said they'd invited Dave and he agreed to attend.

The friends saved two seats for the burly reporter, planning to use one space to hold their handbags and sweaters. Dave entered the auditorium and found the three friends despite the dim lighting. He slid in next to them as Bee Gees' hits from the '70s played quietly over the speaker system. Each lady greeted him with a quick hug and peck on the cheek.

Dave said he'd seen the movie several times over the years but still loved watching it. "This film never gets old," he said, accepting a box of popcorn from Harriet. Penny passed him a pop with a straw already inserted in its plastic top. "Love the music. This is what really kicked off Travolta's career. Before this role, he was just a side character in **Welcome Back, Kotter.**"

The reporter munched on some popcorn and leaned toward Leona, asking her how she was doing. "Were you able to sleep in at all after being awakened so early? You were pretty shook up earlier."

"Not really," Leona said, sipping from her drink. "I rested but could not find sleep after what happened. The girls really wanted to see Travolta. They thought it would be a good distraction for me, and once they said you were coming—well, that sealed it. Happy you weren't too busy."

Dave patted her hand. "I'm glad you felt up to the movie. I promised I'd help my partner, Nick, later this afternoon, but I've got plenty of time now. Thanks for inviting me."

The auditorium filled up quickly. Residents in wheelchairs were rolled up front, those with walkers were offered aisle seats, and folks with canes, which comprised about a quarter of the attendees, squeezed in where they could find comfort.

Within a few minutes, the soundtrack quieted slowly, and the day manager of Shady Lane appeared from a side door near the front. She was middle-aged, slim, well-coiffed, and dressed in a white pantsuit.

The music stopped and the business lady welcomed the crowd to Matinee Sunday, one of the facility's most popular events. She asked all to make sure their cell phones were turned off. She assured attendees that staff members were on hand in case anyone needed assistance making their way to restrooms in the darkened setting. "Just raise your hand, and you will receive immediate help."

The day manager said she hoped everyone enjoyed the movie, pointing to her outfit and commenting that she selected it in honor of the great performance by Travolta in the movie. With that, she exited through the same door she used for entry. The lights dimmed slowly to almost black, and the movie's electrifying color erupted on the screen with the Bee Gees blaring from the surround sound.

All eyes focused on the big screen as attendees settled in for the two-hour matinee. Dave checked with his ladies to make sure they were comfortable, then slid down in his seat, put his head back and prepared to be entertained.

About 40 minutes into the show, the row Dave and his friends were seated in stirred. Someone was up and walking sideways toward them,

Mackinac Murder 163

intent on making it to the aisle. **Restroom break**, Dave thought. He prepared to stand if it was necessary for the attendee to pass. The man squeezed through, bobbing up and down as he walked, without stepping on anyone's feet.

When he made it to the end, he scooted up the aisle. Leona leaned over to Dave and grabbed his hand, whispering as loud as she could: "That's him. That's the man who stood over my bed with the pillow. I'm certain of it. I could smell him. Same guy."

Dave stood and churned up the aisle, careful not to run and cause a disturbance. When he stepped out of the auditorium, he caught sight of the men's room door closing. He ran to the door. It was locked. He waited, pacing in the hallway.

After what seemed like an eternity, he heard the door lock click. The door swung open, and a man emerged, drying his hands on the sides of his pants. It was Captain America. Dave nodded, doing his best not to appear stunned. The captain smiled and headed down the hall toward his room. The reporter checked the bathroom to make sure no one else was inside.

With the lavatory cleared, he took out his cell phone, fired it up, and called Detective Ripley, who answered on the third ring. Dave could hear the Lions football game in the background. Dave explained his call and gave the officer a summary of what had transpired at Shady Lane during the last day.

"You know it's Sunday, right?" Ripley asked. "Based on what you've said, I doubt we get any kind of search warrant."

Dave persisted. "Just question the guy, please. See how he responds. You can say he was identified. See what he's got to say for himself."

Reluctantly, the detective said he'd be at Shady Lane in 30 minutes. Dave thanked him and then walked to the facility's security office. Earlier, a shift change had pushed Wayne out the door and brought in Greg. Dave asked for a few moments of his time. He sat in a chair across a steel desk from Greg, giving him a full update and letting him know that Ripley was on his way.

Greg went into his files to search for the room number of the resident everyone called Captain America. He found the file but cautioned Dave. "Now, you know we can't go in on our own without a search warrant. Privacy. The resident has to authorize it."

The reporter nodded in understanding as they went to the front door to wait for Ripley. Dave could see the guard was nervous. He made small talk, hoping to get the young man to relax—it didn't work. He paced. Finally, Ripley arrived, pulling up to the front door.

While the three men talked, the movie finished. Residents flowed out of the auditorium, scattering in all directions to their rooms. Ripley suggested the three go to the suspect's room and simply ask to talk. Greg agreed, insisting that anything the resident did had to be completely voluntary.

They walked to the door. Greg knocked, identifying himself. When the door opened, Ripley and Dave were introduced.

The detective asked if the suspect would be willing to answer a few questions. He nodded and invited the men into his room.

"Did you enjoy the movie?" Ripley asked. "It's a classic. Did you find it enjoyable?"

"One of my all-time favorites," Captain America said, grinning widely.

The visitors chuckled, agreeing with him.

"The movie had a full house," Ripley continued, watching the captain's facial expressions. "One of the women in attendance identified you as the man who entered her room without authorization last night."

No response. The captain stared blankly straight ahead.

The detective pushed harder. "Did you go into Leona Hayden's room and approach her with a pillow in your hands?"

He considered the question, biting his upper lip, before answering. "Yes, I did."

The three were stunned by his response.

"Why did you do that?" Ripley asked.

"Leona asked me to help her," he said as if it were a matter of fact. "She called me into her room, and I went in to help her."

Ripley kept going. "How did she ask you to come in? What did she say?"

He smiled, widely. "Well, by telepathy, of course. She spoke to me with her mind. Asked me to come help her leave this world."

"Telepathy? You mean you communicated with her without speaking to her?" the detective asked. Greg took notes ferociously, his mouth open, aghast at what was being said.

"That is correct. Everyone here knows I have special powers. I'm Captain America and I provide justice and peace to all. It's my duty. Comes with the job."

Ripley paused to collect his thoughts and allow Greg to catch up. "How did you get into Leona's room after hours?'

Again, the wide grin. "With this," he said, pulling a key from his pocket. It was attached by a small-link chain to his belt. He held it up in the air for all to see. "It opens all the doors."

"Where did you get a key?" Ripley asked, looking at it closely, just inches from his face.

"I used telepathy to get Wayne to give me a key. And he left it right out in the open on his desk, just as I'd asked him to do. I took it, made a copy at the hardware store down the street, and put it back before he returned from lunch."

Dave couldn't contain himself anymore. "Did my mom use telepathy to ask you to take her life? Did you go in her room and put a pillow over her face until she quit breathing?"

"Why, yes, she did," he replied. "She made it clear she didn't want to go on. She wanted out of this world. I granted her wish and gave her peace and justice."

Dave burst into tears and left the room, afraid of what he might do to the captain if he stayed in his presence. He stood in the hallway, his face in his hands. His mom, in her own nightmare of dementia, loses her life to a man who hears voices and thinks he has special powers. A nightmare within a nightmare.

Chapter 16

Sunday Afternoon
Nick and Tanya's apartment, Bay City

By early afternoon, Nick jumped on his laptop to delve into the Reggie Thorpe files. With a cup of coffee at his elbow, he clicked open the email. He scanned the titles of each file: Hamilton, Ontario. Owen Sound. Fishing trawlers. Bay Port. Argyle. Sugar Beet trucks. Midland tankers. Three rivers. Saginaw Bay. Lake Huron. Mackinaw City. Line 5. Mackinac Bridge. Whitmer. Publicity.

He double-clicked the first file and looked over the cryptic notes, separated by bullets. Stunned, he opened the other files one by one. As he read, absolute horror roared through his body. 'The Plan' was catastrophic. It was diabolic. It was evil. The only question unanswered: When? The words of Tommy, the Argyle Marine Corps veteran, echoed in his mind. It might be happening right now.

He went through it again to make sure he understood it completely. Here's the summary of what he discovered:

- Hamilton—Ontario Recycling Center. Radioactive waste storage from Canadian hospitals. 20 grams of Cobalt 60 skimmed from stockpile over five years. Two 100-pound lead storage castles. Paid for by Patriots Jenson and Pierce.
- Owen Sound Harbor. Two 60-ft. trawlers set to haul lead castles in Styrofoam-lined fishing wet wells. Shipping date and time not set, dictated by Lake Huron weather conditions.
- Bay Port, Michigan, port. No harbor master. Deep channel suitable for commercial fishing vessels. Unmonitored docks maintained by the Department of Natural Resources. Busy with sport fishing only in early morning and early evening. Rarely used midday.

Mackinac Murder   167

- Argyle Patriots located and stockpiled 8,000 pounds of ammonium nitrate fertilizer and high-grade diesel fuel over past five years. Transporting bomb mix in two single-bottom, 20-ton sugar beet trucks to Bay Port. Mix completed by Patriot leader Meade.
- Cobalt lead storage containers loaded on sugar beet trucks with bomb mix in Bay Port public park. Electronic detonation cords bound to 12 sticks of dynamite in each truck. Detonator programmed to two cell phones. Trucks handled by Patriots Jerry, Travis, and Leon. They are to wait for dispatch signal after dark.
- Upon dispatch, first truck to go to Mackinaw City region of Line 5 Lower Peninsula site. Driver to place truck in water over top of pipelines and vacate area. Once detonated, blast will rupture Line 5, dumping millions of gallons of oil into Lake Michigan/Huron, Cobalt 60 to fry and spread in air, Mackinac Bridge to sustain serious damage, perhaps collapse.
- Upon dispatch, second truck to travel to Dow Chemical facility in Midland. Two patriot members of Dow security force to grant entry of blast truck to chemical storage tankers. Upon detonation, blast will cause raging chemical fire, and spread Cobalt 60 and deadly chemical fumes throughout area and pollute Chippewa and Tittabawassee Rivers.
- Potential casualties from both blasts due to Cobalt 60 exposure: 5,000 dead in northern Michigan; 15,000 dead in Midland, Saginaw, and Bay City. 100,000 injuries in both locations from radiation exposure. Oil pollution of Lake Michigan and Lake Huron causing extensive damage to waters of Mackinaw City, Mackinac Island, Escanaba, Cheboygan, Harbor Springs, Charlevoix, Petoskey, Traverse City.
- Letter dispatched to Governor Whitmer, giving her 6 hours to deposit $500 million in a Grand Cayman account or detonation will occur. No negotiation. No delays.
- Publicity. Scalp of Patriot-traitor Stapleton nailed to Mackinac Island Community Hall Building to become viral public event, which would draw worldwide attention to Line 5 controversy and dispute between oil company and environmentalists and Native Americans. World to focus on Michigan and catastrophic event as 6 hours tick off the clock.

Horrified, Nick called Michigan State Police Det. Sgt. Basil Newcomb, the latest criminal investigator assigned to coordinate the Eric Stapleton murder on Mackinac Island and the discovery of his storage unit/dungeon outside of Bay City.

Newcomb worked out of the West Branch state police post and lived near East Tawas. Nick had met the highly regarded, veteran detective but had not worked with him previously. A weekend trooper answered the phone at the post. It was no surprise that Newcomb was not working on a Sunday afternoon. Nick made it clear a message must be passed to him immediately.

"This is a matter of life and death for thousands of people in Michigan. I need to speak with Det. Sgt. Newcomb right away. I'm a reporter with the *Bay City Blade*. He knows who I am. You must find him, even if you have to send somebody to his house or wherever he might be today. This cannot wait."

The trooper said he understood and would do his best to pass the message. Nick repeated his cell phone number twice. "I know he's got my number, but make sure. Also ask him to check his email. I've sent him files that will back up my concern and my alarm. And one more thing: if Newcomb can't be found, then connect me with somebody with equal position or status with the state police. Am I making myself clear? Do you fully understand?"

"Yes, sir," the trooper responded. "I will get on this right now."

Nick hung up. He needed help and reached out to Dave, who picked up his cell on the second ring.

"Hey, Nick, great news. We caught my mom's killer," he said. Nick could tell his words expressed joy but were tinged with sadness.

"No kidding. Glad to hear it," Nick said. "Was it a Shady Lane staffer?"

"Nope, a resident. A guy off his rocker, hearing voices," Dave said. "I got lucky with Ripley. My mom's friends helped corner the guy, and our detective friend came when I called him—on a Sunday afternoon, no less. The guy confessed to my mom's death. And I heard later that he owned up to the two previous deaths at Shady Lane that were laid to natural causes."

"Good deal. Delighted to hear this news, buddy," he said. "But speaking of work on a Sunday afternoon, can I call on you to help with the Stapleton case?"

Dave said he was ready to roll. "Feeling a lot of relief now, so I'm eager to help. What do you need?"

Nick explained briefly that the Stapleton case was breaking open and the ramifications were catastrophic. He said he was trying to get the state police to act on information he had discovered but was concerned about how long that might take.

"Have you got any connections—any trusted sources—at Dow Chemical?" Nick asked.

"I do have an old girlfriend in Midland," he responded. "Last I heard, she had a pretty sweet job in community relations. We busted up on good terms. I can give her a call.

"She's sharp and a great spirit. I know I can speak with her frankly and alert her to a problem. How big is this, really?"

Nick paused. "Well, my guess is this is something Dow has never been confronted with. Huge. Thousands of people could be at risk. Could you reach out to her? I will provide details if she's willing to help."

Dave said he would be back in touch as soon as he could. Nick checked his watch. He hoped to hear back from Det. Newcomb or someone else with the state police at any time. While he waited, he decided to pay Reggie Thorpe another visit.

As the reporter drove to Thorpe's East Side apartment, he thought through the case and what he'd found so far, turning it over and over in his mind like a clothes dryer tossing around wet jeans.

The big unanswered question in the investigation of 'The Plan' was when it was supposed to happen. The outline in the Thorpe files said enactment was dependent on Lake Huron weather, dictating the time when the Cobalt 60 could be shipped safely. Before leaving the *Blade* newsroom, he checked the National Weather Service for Lake Huron conditions during the past two days: on Friday, the service reported light, easterly winds, two- to three-foot waves, high of 60 degrees, no discernible rain. The Saturday report was essentially the same with a fifty percent chance of rain. Waves on the big lake had not been flat as a pancake, but certainly were manageable by big fishing trawlers.

The Thorpe domain came into view. Nick drove by slowly, checking it out. Looked just like yesterday, he thought, with dim lighting coming from the picture window, the front door opened slightly. He parked the Firebird in a safe spot down the street and hoofed it quickly to Reggie's porch.

Nick could hear music playing through the screen door; he approached and knocked, causing it to rattle. He stepped back, peering through the front picture window. Dark, except for the desktop computer screen. He tried banging on the door again with no response.

Nick walked down the front steps and checked the street in both directions. No sign of Thorpe. He decided to try the screen door. It was not latched. He opened it and stepped inside, pausing to listen while he held his breath for a moment.

"Reggie, you here? Got a minute to talk?" No response. An orange cat whisked through the living room toward the kitchen. He waited for a few seconds, then repeated his declaration. Moving quickly and quietly, he stepped out of his loafers and followed the cat. No sign of the pothead Patriot in the back of the apartment.

The reporter hustled back to the living room and went straight for the computer. Thorpe's email files covered the screen. Nick scanned the subjects of each, going back nearly one hundred files to when he visited the apartment a day earlier. He found a file named "Whitmer letter," which had been sent early in the morning from jjmeade@gmail.com.

Nick glanced around the room. Quiet, save for the cat, which had followed him back to the living room, swirling between his feet and ankles, purring. He clicked on the file. It was a blackmail letter with a Monday deadline. He copied it and sent it to his email, Dave and Clapper's email, and Newcomb's online address. When finished, he deleted the sent files.

He reached down and scratched the cat behind the ears, pushing the feline away from his path, and dashed for his loafers. Just as Nick stepped out on the porch, he came face-to-face with Reggie Thorpe, who carried a six-pack of beer under his arm and a Sunday copy of the *Bay City Blade* in his right hand.

The reporter smiled, looked at the newspaper, and asked, "Just thought I'd stop by today to see if I could interest you in home delivery of the *Blade*! We're offering a onetime deal this week. Pay for three days and get seven days of home delivery—right to your doorstep."

Thorpe, puzzled, looked past Nick to his front door. "Were you just in my place? What kind of salesman bangs on doors and just walks into a place on Sunday? You one of them jezebel witnesses, handing out preacher work?"

"No, I'm not a Jehovah's Witness," Nick said, brushing by Thorpe. "I'm with the *Blade* and I was here yesterday. Remember, I visited and we talked before you took a nap in your tub."

Thorpe was befuddled. He turned as the reporter headed down the steps. "What? You was here yesterday?"

"Yup. We had a nice chat. I've got one remaining question for you. Did you kill Eric Stapleton on Mackinac Island? Knock him off his horse and snap his neck?"

"Not me. Eric hired me. He was my friend. I had nothing to do with his killing," he said, backpedaling. "I had nothing to do with him dying. I only lifted his scalp, which I had orders to do because I'd skinned rabbits, gutted deer. Good publicity for the cause."

"Did Jerry Meade take Eric out?" Nick asked, his hands on his hips.

"Now, don't put no words in my mouth," he responded. "I ain't saying nothing about Jerry."

"My advice, Reggie: get yourself a good attorney. You're going to need one.

"I'll make sure the state police know you have been helpful. They'll be here this afternoon. You might want to sober up and tell them everything. And don't think about running. You're going to be the Most Wanted man in America. Nowhere to hide."

On the way back to the newsroom, Nick placed a call to the C-Man.

This story was, literally, on the verge of exploding. He had to alert his managing editor to the dire circumstances he'd discovered. Clapper answered his cell on the third ring.

"This better be important Steele. I've got a house full of relatives here for our anniversary dinner. What's up?" he snapped, his voice dripping with impatience.

The reporter got right to it. "I've just confirmed that two highly explosive dirty bombs are headed toward Bay City. I've got a call into the state police. I believe I know the destinations of the two bombs, but they are hidden in the bottoms of two sugar beet trucks—among about 500 similar trucks buzzing around throughout the area."

"Damn—I'd say that's pretty important," he said, focusing. "Where are you?"

Nick said he was on the way to the newsroom. He added that Dave was on his way, too. "One of the bombs sounds like it's going to Dow Chemical. Dave has got a contact at Dow who is going to meet us. We've got to find a way to head this off without causing widespread panic."

Clapper said he would wrap up his family celebration quickly and meet the reporters at the office in 30 minutes.

Dave and a woman who looked half his age crossed the street at the *Blade* building when Nick pulled up, parking the Firebird in the publisher's reserved space just to the side of the entry. Dave introduced his friend.

"Nick, this is Dana Harrington. She works at Dow Community Relations," he said. The two strangers shook hands. The reporter said he was glad to meet the Dow rep. She smiled and nodded. Dana was dressed Sunday casual, light tan slacks and a golden hooded sweater and tan, flat shoes. A laptop case was strapped to her shoulder. The three shot up the steps to the newsroom, Nick talking as they moved.

"We've got a highly volatile situation on our hands, Dana. Dave vouches for you, so I'm going to trust you to handle this discreetly and with the utmost expediency."

The newsroom was empty, cool, and dark, a single set of fluorescent lights lit up the bank of reporters' desks at the far end of the newsroom. They pulled up at Nick's desk, dragging chairs around his desktop computer.

Nick gave Dave and Dana a quick summary of the situation, focusing on the Dow part of the potential calamity. "Now, I understand that two Dow employees who work in security are going to open the gates tonight for a multi-ton, multi-axle truck to take a highly explosive dirty bomb onto Dow property. We don't know where on the property, we don't know who the security guards are. That's where you come in, Dana."

She said she understood and pulled out her laptop. Nick logged onto his computer and inserted the thumb drive he'd received from Randy. He copied both files—the list of patriot members and the list of Underwater Solutions employees—and emailed them to Det. Newcomb.

Nick turned to Dana. "Here's a list of the Michigan Proud Patriots, the men and women who built the bombs and plan to blackmail the state of Michigan tomorrow; their plan is to demand a big payoff from the governor, or they ignite the bombs. Looking over the list, I see no patriots from Midland, but I do see one in Oil City and one in Sanford. Can you find out if these two men work at Dow, and do they work security?"

Dana looked over the reporter's shoulder at the screen. She noted the two highlighted names, and said she had a way to find out. She added that she could also cross-check all the Patriot names against Dow employee files.

"Excellent," Nick replied, looking at the big newsroom deadline clock. It was 3:05 p.m. "I'm waiting for the state police to call back, but I may also want you to alert Dow executives. It's going to be dark in less than three hours. The bombs go into place after dark."

Dana went to work. The reporters heard her call a friend of hers in Dow personnel. She fired up her laptop and logged into the Dow site.

Nick and Dave huddled just as Clapper entered. They'd never seen him dressed down at work. He sported dark pants with an open collar white shirt, a blue rain jacket, and sneakers. The C-Man warily eyed the stranger working in his newsroom. "It's OK, Drayton. She's helping us," Dave said.

Nick printed out the Reggie Thorpe files so the managing editor could read 'The Plan' himself. When the C-Man finished, Nick planned to give him a printed copy of the Whitmer blackmail letter to bring him fully up to speed. Dave received the same information.

Nick's phone rang. It was Newcomb, who said he was returning home to East Tawas from dinner at his daughter's place near Oscoda.

"Got your messages, and I checked your emails," the officer said. "Cut my visit with my grandkids short. What you sent me is shocking. We are aware of the Proud Patriots, and we've been tracking them for a couple of years. We know they're dangerous, but this is the first I've seen of 'The Plan.' Now, tell me how good your information is. I need to assess how serious this threat is before we jump into action."

Nick responded that he could tell where and how he received the information, but he could not reveal the names of his individual sources. He explained the background of the Patriot membership and Underwater Solutions files and the Thorpe files. He also told the detective about his trip to Argyle and the encounter with Travis and Leon.

Newcomb pulled into his driveway at home. "Tell me about Reggie Thorpe. How reliable is this guy? How good is his word?"

The reporter paused, took a deep breath, and coughed up what he knew. Time was of the essence. He had to play it straight with Newcomb—there was no room for error.

"Thorpe is a drunk and a pothead," he explained. "The first time I met him, he passed out with his computer on. While he snored, I went into his computer files and copied them—that was yesterday. This afternoon, I had the opportunity to get into his place again. That's how I found the Whitmer blackmail letter. It's in your email."

Newcomb considered Nick's words before speaking. "I was afraid you might say something like that. He's shaky, at best. What else do you have?"

Nick said 'The Plan' outline indicated the two targets for the bombs are Dow Chemical and the oil pipelines at the Straits. "Outline shows who is handling the bomb trucks. They go into place after dark. We're checking Dow Chemical right now for a connection to the Patriots. Could you put the pipelines where they enter the Lower Peninsula under surveillance?"

"Yes. We can surveil both locations," he said, still sitting in his SUV.

"We can watch from the air as well—planes and helicopters. Let me make some calls. Please send me the direct line for your boss, Clapper. I need to talk with him. And make sure I've got a copy of the blackmail letter."

Before Nick emailed a second copy of the blackmail letter to Newcomb, he read it one more time.

Governor Whitmer:

You are being given one opportunity to head off certain doom and catastrophe for the State of Michigan. At 3 p.m. today, you will receive explicit written instructions to wire transfer $500 million to an offshore account in the Cayman Islands.

If you do not complete the transfer of all funds by 6 p.m., this is what will happen:

Two dirty bombs will be detonated in two different locations in Michigan. Each bomb carries the explosive kick of the 1995 Oklahoma City bombing with one important difference—each device carries the additional wallop of radioactive waste, Cobalt 60.

The toxic explosion will kill thousands of people in each location. Tens of thousands more will be critically injured. The resulting destruction will be catastrophic: polluting the Great Lakes irreparably for years to come, turning several cities into toxic wastelands, and bringing down one of the state's treasured landmarks.

To prove that we mean business, you will receive a numbered series of photographs of the two explosive devices and the lead castles containing the Cobalt 60 at 2 p.m. today.

At 4 p.m., you will receive photographs of the explosive devices in their respective locations. Any attempt to dismantle or move the devices will result in immediate detonation.

There will be no negotiation and no extension of the deadline.

Start gathering the funds and prepare for wire transfer now.

Our goal is to bring down the illegal, immoral, and unholy government of the United States. This has not been accomplished through its fraudulent election system, so we are taking action that will assist us in achieving this holy crusade.

— The Proud Patriots of Michigan

Nick turned his attention to the C-Man and Dave, who were deep in discussion. Dana continued working her cell phone and clicking through the files on her laptop.

The managing editor and Dave approached Nick, who asked them what they thought about the blackmail letter.

Clapper called it sick. "The idea that Americans would kill and harm Americans and wreck the Great Lakes because they disagree with and don't like the government is twisted. And for them to suggest that they are on some kind of holy crusade is simply deranged. Nothing holy about it."

Dave shook his head. "Disturbed. This is not rational thinking. How can that much death and destruction be justified? Americans taking and ruining the lives of Americans to somehow save America? That's warped."

Nick agreed. "I've looked that letter over three or four times and I'm still trying to make sense of it. This is a group willing to take unthinkable deadly and destructive actions to inflict its will on all citizens. We've got to find a way to stop them."

Clapper said he would assemble a newsroom team to cover the story as it unfolds overnight. He'd already placed a call to the *Blade* editor-in-chief and publisher. The editor was in the midst of a golf fundraiser and the publisher was at a Community Foundation event. They were aghast at the news from the managing editor and asked to be kept informed throughout the night.

The C-Man sought clarity as they moved forward.

"We're missing one key element. We need proof that it's actually happening—that the plot is in place, or in motion. I need some physical evidence. So far, it's just talk. It's on paper, but is it real?"

Nick said that's the same feeling he received while talking to Newcomb. "I think he's got reservations. Is this simply wild BS from some fringe freaks, or is this a real terrorist threat? Once word of this gets out—real or not—it will cause panic, possibly public hysteria."

"Yup," the C-Man said, his hands on his hips. "Think about it. Is Newcomb going to wake up the governor on a Sunday night and hand her a blackmail letter if this is all just crap?"

Dave said he thought they should focus on finding the sugar beet trucks carrying the explosives. He suggested going back to the beginning.

"The bombs were supposedly put together in Bay Port," he said. "That's two hours by truck away from Midland and five hours away from the Straits. Where are they now? Where would your buddies Leon and Travis be sitting with them, waiting for the cover of darkness?"

Nick opened his desk and pulled out a map, focusing on the area and potential route from Bay Port to Bay City.

"These two guys are familiar with Bay City," he said, "but not Bay Port, Sebewaing, Unionville, or the Quanicassee areas. They're from the other side of the Thumb."

Nick drew a large oval on the map around M-25, the direct route from Bay Port to Bay City. He marked each of the communities on the path and the nearby parks where the trucks could sit unnoticed.

"Again, the bomb trucks are going to blend in among dozens and dozens of beet-hauling trucks during harvest seasons," he said. The three newsmen studied the map.

Clapper commented that this aspect of 'The Plan' was actually quite ingenious. "It's like they're playing a gigantic shell game, hiding the bombs in the midst of rolling trucks that all look alike."

Nick nodded. "True, but what works in our favor is that these Argyle guys don't know these side roads. They're going to stick close to the highway and try to hide where they won't stick out."

Nick marked two locations near Bay Port, three in Sebewaing, one in Quanicassee, two in Bay City.

"Bay Port has a bar and a roadside park big enough to handle two trucks on a Sunday afternoon," Nick said. "Sebewaing is home to a big sugar beet processing plant. There are three areas I know of where two trucks could pull off the highway and just sit quietly. Quanicassee has a large drive-through parking lot at a boat sales and service business— nobody would be there on a fall Sunday. And we've got another big sugar beet processing plant on the West Side of Bay City. Euclid Avenue in the South End leading up to the plant would be a good place for big trucks to sit and hide."

Nick looked at the deadline clock. Two hours before sunset and darkness. He said he had met Travis and Leon and could identify them. "I've got time to run to Bay Port, work my way back to Bay City, and check out each of the locations for the trucks. What do you think?"

Clapper urged him to go ahead and give it a try but cautioned him against taking any action. "These people are dangerous. We're not the police. You should not intercede. If you spot them, report back, and we'll alert the cops—that's their job. Don't take chances."

The C-Man indicated he and Dave would stay in the newsroom with Dana, work the phones, and wait for word from the state police.

Dave wished Nick good luck as he dashed through the door.

"Telling Nick not to take action is like telling a bird not to fly," Dave said. "I hope we're not going to regret letting him run out that door. His whole life as a reporter has been about taking chances."

Nick revved the Firebird and pulled out of the parking lot, heading east toward Bay Port. He called Tanya on his cell phone as he hauled ass down Center Avenue, daring the speed limit all the way. She didn't pick up. He left a message that the Stapleton story was running hot, and he would be tied up, perhaps working very late.

As he drove, his mind worked through the story. The catastrophic event appeared as though it was running toward a deadly ending. Had they overlooked something that could stop it?

If they ran out of time to stop it, what would the governor do? Nick recalled that Gov. Whitmer was no stranger to the activities of extremists. In 2020, she had been threatened with a kidnapping plot by a handful of militia members who called themselves the Wolverine Watchmen. The plot was foiled by the FBI and the extremists arrested.

How would she react to this threat? Would she authorize payment to terrorist blackmailers? Would she refuse to pay and run the risk of letting crazy people make good on their threat? What if she paid and the bombs were detonated anyway? What if one or both triggered accidentally?

His mind raced ahead to the possibility that the bombs detonate.

What would be the true toll of such a calamity? How many would die, how many would be injured? How would rescue teams go into areas laced with radioactive waste? How many first responders would be killed or injured?

And what about the environmental consequences from the blasts? They were almost too much for his mind to grasp. A few years ago, the University of Michigan had conducted a study of the possible effects of an oil pipeline rupture. Millions of gallons of oil would flow freely with the currents of Lake Michigan, causing horrendous damage to the lake and the fisheries all the way from the Straits of Mackinac to Traverse City. Now add radioactive waste to the air. The potential damage would be unthinkable.

Nick drove through Sebewaing slowly, eyeing every large parking lot for idling sugar beet trucks. He saw nothing out of order, even when he drove by the beet processing plant. Lots of trucks, but they were all in line to drop their loads of harvested beets—none sitting without purpose.

He continued on toward Bay Port. As he did, he thought about the Mackinac Bridge. 'The Plan' outline suggested it would be damaged or possibly come down as a result of the blast at the pipeline. Mighty Mac is an iconic and treasured landmark for Michigan residents. Nick thought that damage or destruction of the bridge would also deal a psychological as well as physical blow to the whole state.

As Nick approached Brown Roadside Park, a rustic rest stop for travelers south of Bay Port on M-25, he slowed down the Firebird. Large oak trees gave the park—its picnic tables, pit toilet, hand-pump well, and grills—plenty of shade. From experience, Nick knew that long-haul truckers also enjoyed the park's solitude for quick naps or overnight sleep. It was one of the locations he'd marked on the map in the newsroom.

The turn off sign for Brown Park came into view on the right. Nick slowed further, easing off the gas and causing the 'Bird's big V-8 to rumble down. Two multi-ton, multi-axle beet trucks sat about fifty feet apart, parked lengthwise across diagonal one-vehicle parking spaces. Light smoke puffed from the trucks' big diesel engines. He drove by, slowing to a crawl on M-25.

Nick turned into the rest stop and slowly rolled by the trucks sitting on his right. No sign of activity in the truck cabs. As he passed the second truck, he saw a head pop up in the cab through his rear-view mirror. Travis, he thought, and continued moving back out on M-25. Now, he could see two more heads moving in the other cab. **Leon in the other truck, he thought, but who was with him?** The reporter decided to make another pass through the rest stop, just like the first, to make sure he'd correctly identified the drivers.

As he pulled up even with the trailer of the first vehicle, the second truck lurched forward to its left, cutting Nick off. He stopped just as the first vehicle jerked to life, ramming into the side of the Firebird. He heard the diesel roar and the big truck shoved Nick's car sideways, crashing through two picnic tables and shearing off a cast-iron grill on a pedestal cemented into the ground. Nick's head bounced off his window, causing dizziness. The diesel roared louder and slammed the Firebird, now smashed on both sides, into the side of a tree. Nick's head smacked the door frame. He blacked out, blood trickling down the side of his head closest to the broken window.

Coming to, groggy and dizzy, he raised his head high enough to see Travis, Leon, and Jerry Meade peering in through his shattered passenger-side window. He couldn't make out what they were saying through his fog. He heard them laughing, he looked up again just as they gave him the finger with both hands. They ran off to their truck cabs. He blacked out again.

Chapter 17

Sunday Night
Bay City Blade newsroom

Dana and Dave finished cross-checking both thumb-drive files with Dow Chemical employee roles. It was a time-consuming and exhaustive process and would not have been possible without the help of an unnamed associate of Dana's in the company personnel department.

They came up with the names of two employees who were also listed in the membership rolls of the Proud Patriots of Michigan. Now, Dana was checking with security scheduling to see if the two men were working this weekend.

Dave left her side to find Clapper, who was in his office and talking on the phone with Det. Newcomb. The reporter stood just outside the office listening to the C-Man's side of the conversation. He pretended not to eavesdrop, but it didn't fool the managing editor, who didn't seem to mind.

Clapper hung up and smacked his hands on the desk. He told Dave that Newcomb had Reggie Thorpe picked up and questioned by two troopers. The Underwater Solutions employee confirmed what he'd told Nick, surrendering his computer to the officers without a warrant.

The C-Man said the detective had also assigned a dozen unmarked state police vehicles to surround the site of the oil pipeline's entry into the Lower Peninsula. They were ordered to pull over any multi-ton, multi-axle trucks driving through the area.

The editor asked Dave if he and Dana had any luck matching up the Patriot membership with Dow employees. The reporter was almost giddy.

"Yes, Dana got two hits. One employee who lives in Saginaw and another who lives in Bay City," he said, giving a thumbs up signal to the chief. "She's checking to see if they are on security duty tonight."

The two newsmen heard a shriek of joy. They moved to the open newsroom and spotted Dana smiling and standing with one arm thrust into the air as if she'd just hit the lottery. She clicked off her phone.

"YES! YES! I got it," she shouted, jumping up and down like a school kid. "Both guys are working tonight—all weekend, really—and here's the gate they're assigned to."

She jotted down the names of the guards, their home addresses and phone numbers, and the gate they'd been charged with guarding, thrusting the sheet of paper toward Clapper. "And remember, you have no idea where you got this information. I'd probably get fired, my friends, too. These are employee records and information—all confidential."

The C-Man nodded. "Don't worry. I'll make sure you're not fired or harmed in any way. In fact, I think you deserve a medal. Thank you. I'm going to give this info to Det. Newcomb, without revealing the source, and have him call Dow Chemical executives to get access to this security gate and the two guards. Hopefully, we can stop the bomb trucks before they get into place."

Clapper returned to his office to call Newcomb. Dave walked over and gave Dana a high five.

"What you did was both remarkable and courageous," the reporter said, smiling broadly. "I knew you'd be great when I called you, but I had no idea you'd be this terrific. Can't thank you enough."

"Aww, thanks," she said, smiling broadly and soaking up the praise. "I can't remember a time when I had this much fun working. Mind if I stick around to see how it works out?"

"I'd be disappointed if you left," Dave said, looking up at the deadline clock. Three hours had lapsed since Nick left the newsroom bound for Bay Port. "Wonder what's happening with my buddy. Think I'll give him a call."

No one answered Nick's phone. It went to voicemail.

A nurse heading home from her shift at Scheurer Hospital in Pigeon drove by Brown Roadside Park and noticed a crushed gold 1968 Firebird resting on the side of a giant oak tree in the sleepy rest stop.

Beverly Zimmer, a veteran registered nurse who lived in nearby Sebewaing, had driven past Brown hundreds of times and had never seen it hosting a wreck. She pulled into the park and drove by the Firebird slowly. When she spotted a man bleeding and slumped against the driver's side window, she called 9-1-1 and stopped to see if she could help.

Beverly reached through the broken passenger-side window and checked the man's pulse. It was strong. He moaned and lifted his head from his chest. Drool seeped from his lips as he lifted his right hand to wipe it away. The nurse urged him to remain still. In a soothing voice, she assured him that help was on the way.

The man asked for Tanya. He said he had to call the office. Beverly said both would be contacted in due time. Right now, she asked him to be patient, remain still. "We've got to figure out how banged up you are. EMS will be here in minutes. We'll get you fixed up."

"Am I still in the park? My name is Nick Steele," he said in a halting voice, his eyes scanning just above his dashboard. "Will you call the *Blade* newsroom? Tell them I found the trucks—they must be on their way to Bay City. It's dusk now."

From memory, he gave the woman a phone number: Clapper's direct line. She pulled out her cell and called.

"Clapper, speak!" the managing editor barked.

"I'm a nurse. I found Nick Steele in his wrecked car, hurt," she said in a hurried voice. "He insisted I call you. Says he found the trucks and they're on the way to Bay City."

"Holy shit," the C-Man exclaimed. "What happened? Was he in an accident? How bad is he hurt?"

Beverly said she discovered his smashed-up car in a roadside park on M-25. She reported that he looked like he had a head injury and possibly others. EMS is on the way, she continued. He also asked for Tanya.

Clapper thanked her. He asked where first responders would take him.

"Scheurer in Pigeon is the closest," said the RN, as she looked in on

Nick, who rested against the car door, his eyes closed. "That's where I work."

As an ambulance pulled up, lights flashing and siren blaring, the nurse gave Clapper a number to call to check on Nick. He thanked her again. She clicked off.

A rescuer rushed up. He recognized Beverly and asked her for an assessment. Nick tried to sit up, spurred awake by the noise and lights. He'd heard her on the phone talking with the newsroom. He gave her a thumbs up with his right hand and slurred the words: "Thank you."

"Looks like multiple injuries, including a bleeding head wound," she said. "But he asked me to make a call and remembered the number—that's a pretty good sign. You've got to get in there and check him out."

As the two spoke, a Huron County Sheriff's Department cruiser pulled up, responding to a 9-1-1 dispatch. It was Deputy J.D. Ratchett. He immediately recognized the gold Firebird; Nick had allowed him to drive it once, a rare privilege. He rushed to the side of the smashed-up vehicle. Seeing his friend, crumpled in the driver's seat, he called out.

"Nick, it's Booger. Hang in there, buddy," he said, his eyes watering. "We're going to get you outta there." The deputy called Tanya. She had heard from Clapper, said she was on her way.

The rescuer tried the door—it was jammed shut. He chipped broken glass out of the busted window frame and went, headfirst, inside the two-seater muscle car. The young guy, slim and nimble, squirmed his legs inside.

Before releasing Nick's seat belt, he began an examination. He used a small flashlight to check Nick's head wound and his eyes. The reporter talked during the whole checkup, asking if his injuries now meant he'd never be a leading man in a movie.

The young rescuer chuckled. He moved down Nick's body with gloved hands, asking where he hurt. The reporter howled when his left arm was moved. He moaned when his ribs were checked. He flinched when his left leg was nudged.

"Can you feel your legs, can you wiggle your toes?" the young guy asked. Nick nodded and demonstrated with a slight sitting march of both legs. The seat belt was unbuckled. The rescuer's partner stood at the passenger-side door, elbowing Booger out of the way. They conferred while Beverly called home, reporting that she would be a little late.

"You're a tough guy," said the rescuer sitting next to Nick. "We're going to get this door open and slide you out. Legs first, over the console. Then I'm going to have you hug me, and I'll pull you across."

Nick nodded. The two EMS guys and the deputy went to work on the passenger-side door, pushing from the inside and pulling from the outside. On their third exertion, the door popped open with the groan of grinding metal.

Within 10 minutes, the two young guys had Nick on a stretcher. The reporter said he hurt but was doing OK. Before they strapped him down, he rose on one elbow to check out his prized Firebird. Its scraped and smashed side broke his heart. He could only imagine what the side leaning against the tree looked like.

"Those sons of bitches," he muttered, referring to Travis, Leon, and Gold Chains, who he recalled giving him double fingers through his window. "Now they've pissed me off."

"Don't worry too much about them boys, my friend," the deputy said. "We'll track 'em down."

They loaded Nick in the ambulance and whisked him away, lights flashing, siren screaming.

Dave took the news about Nick hard. His nerves had been frayed with the drama surrounding his mother's murder in a nursing home, and now his best friend had been injured and was on his way to the hospital. His heart told him to rush to the Pigeon hospital, check on his buddy, and comfort Tanya, but Clapper ordered him to get to work.

"Balz, get your head out of your ass. We've got a job to do," the C-Man barked. "Nick is getting cared for. The best thing you can do is work on Nick's story and help him by bringing it home. Take your sweetheart there and get over to Midland with a photographer."

The jarring words of the managing editor rocked him. He wasn't sure how to respond. "Ah, she's not my sweetheart," was all he could muster.

"Yeah, right. I got eyes. Now, get moving. And stay out of sight until the troopers get that beet truck stopped before it goes onto Dow property. They've taken the two guards into custody. Cops are undercover, waiting. I want a story on the arrest and disarming of that bomb truck."

Quietly, Dave asked Dana if she wanted to ride shotgun in his F-150. "You know your way around Dow property. I'd really appreciate it."

She smiled broadly. "I'd love to—I'll drive. I know all the side streets around that gate. I can give you the landscape and help your photographer get into position. We want to stay safe, stay out of view, and be ready for anything."

Dana was proving to be invaluable, reminding Dave why he'd liked her so much. She was sharp, on top of her game, and had great news instincts. "Sounds good. I think you may have missed your calling."

The three left the *Blade* through a side door. Clapper returned to his desk to assemble staff members needed to cover the story through the night and get ready for morning publication. That task would be challenging under any circumstances, but now he had to get it done without Nick Steele, the driving force behind the story.

When Tanya arrived at the Pigeon hospital, Deputy Ratchett was just leaving. He stopped to talk with her.

"Nick is pretty banged up, but they say he's going to be fine," Booger said, adding that the same thing could not be said of the Firebird. "She's pretty much wrecked."

Tanya frowned. She said she watched Nick's prized car being loaded onto a flatbed truck when she drove by Brown Park.

"I stopped and asked the driver to take it to a shop in Essexville," she said, looking over the deputy's shoulder. "What did the docs say about Nick?"

Ratchett said testing was still underway. "He's in there talking up a storm to anyone who walks by his room. Seems good to me. He told me about the clowns who rammed him with beet trucks; it's all in my report. They're right in the middle of a story he's working on. I'm sure he'll fill you in. Room 113."

Tanya thanked him and hustled down the hall. She found Nick talking with Dave on his phone. He was giving his buddy background information on the Argyle Neanderthals and Gold Chains, the guys who he discovered driving the bomb trucks. He clicked off when he saw Tanya.

She went to the side of his bed and kissed him on the cheek. He grabbed her arm with his right hand and pulled her close.

"Thanks for coming," he said, kissing her back. "You gotta bust me out of here. This place is full of sick and dying people. I'm all right. Little headache, bumps, and bruises."

Nick pushed himself up in his bed with his legs and right hand. He winced. A four-inch square white bandage was stuck to the upper part of his face on the left side, just above his eye. His left arm hung in a sling by his side. His ribs had been wrapped.

She shook her head. "Let's see what the doctors say. You've been hurt. You don't need to rush this. Let yourself heal up a little bit."

A doctor came into the room carrying a chart. Tanya wondered if he was old enough to drive. Nick noticed more pimples than chin stubble. He had dirty blonde hair and was so slender that his white lab jacket hung on him like a flasher's baggy raincoat. Doogie, Nick mused. Howser, Tanya reflected.

"Mr. Steele?" said the young guy, studying the chart. His blue and white name tag labeled him as Dr. Carter. "How do you feel?"

Nick smiled. "Knocked around some, but not too bad. You people have done a lot of poking and prodding and x-rays. What did you find?"

"A concussion, two cracked ribs, a sprained shoulder. Your head wound is superficial so you shouldn't have scarring," the doc said. "I'd say, you were lucky—especially for a man of your age."

Nick took exception. "My age? What's that supposed to mean?"

"When we get older, we tend to become more brittle," he responded, sheepishly. "With a car accident, you could have been hurt much worse."

"It was no accident," he responded. If his head was a teakettle, steam would have been rolling out of his ears. "I got blocked and then rammed by some lowlifes driving diesel trucks."

Tanya had wondered about the nature of the crash. Having seen the Firebird, now she understood. Tree on one side, truck on the other—crunch. She asked Doc Doogie about the prognosis. "What do you recommend?"

"Rest. The more, the better," he replied, holding the chart flat against his chest. "I think we should keep you overnight. Keep a close eye on your concussion and watch for any internal bleeding."

Nick protested, raising his good hand and his damaged limb partially. "I really do not want to stay overnight. I need to get back to work. How about cutting me loose in Tanya's care? She'll crack the whip, keep me in line."

Doubtful, Tanya thought, but a provocative concept.

"Well, of course, we can't keep you against your will," the young doc said. "But it's imperative you get rest. You should sleep. No strenuous activity. And no driving. You may have moments of dizziness, disorientation, confusion."

Nick said he understood, explaining that he thought he'd get better rest at home. "This place is like a train station. People coming and going. Noise. Nurses popping in every few minutes to see if I'm still breathing. I want to go home, and I promise to go straight to bed. I am tired."

Tanya nodded. She understood. She'd seen firsthand the hospital train-station effect when visiting Sherry Conaway every day during the past week. It was tiring just watching the traffic in and out of the teenager's room. Now, her chief concern, which she did not voice, was containing Nick. She wasn't sure how long she could hold him back. He's a hard charger; it's just his nature.

When Doc Doogie left the room, Nick asked Tanya to help him get dressed. "Let's go before they lock the doors."

It was 10 p.m. when Dave spotted the sugar beet truck lumbering down Midland's Washington Street heading on an arrow's path for Dow Chemical's Gate 32. Dana had explained that this entry point gave access to the company's Industrial Park where large outside storage tanks, silos, boilers, condensers, oxidation units, scrubbers, and thermal heat recovery systems were maintained. Chemicals included a wide mix of potentially toxic mixes including DOWTHERM A or biphenyl, diphenyl oxide, dioxins, and ammonia.

The Proud Patriots had done their research, Dave thought. An Oklahoma City-style blast, with an added kick of Cobalt 60 radioactive waste, could cause a horrendous chemical fire and deadly toxic fumes to kill and harm thousands across Michigan's Tri-Cities, depending upon which way the wind blew off Saginaw Bay.

Tension mounted as the big truck approached. Dave took Dana's hand as they watched, hunkered down in the front seat of her Chevy SUV. She squeezed back. They both held their breaths as the truck inched past them.

Gate 32 did not open. The truck brake lights lit up, wheels squealing, its hydraulics hissing. The diesel stopped, idling quietly for minutes, which seemed like ages to Dave. The driver's side window of the cab rolled down. A head popped out sideways. Based on Nick's earlier description of the Argyle Neanderthals, Dave guessed it was Leon. He shouted at the guard shack. "Where's Terry and Walt? Thought they were working tonight."

Dave and Dana stepped out of her vehicle and approached cautiously so they could observe and hear. The *Blade* photographer, placed in an adjacent building's upper-level window with Dana's help, hung out over the street snapping photos from an ideal bird's eye vantage point.

The shack door opened, and two guards stepped out. They approached the idling diesel on both sides, hands on weapons. The guard on the passenger side of the cab mounted and drew his weapon before pulling open the cab door, catching Leon by surprise. The guard on the driver's side completed the same maneuver. The diesel shut down. Leon stepped out, hands raised. The guard ordered him to the ground, face down. He was identified as Leon Schmidt, handcuffed, and dragged off to the back of an unmarked SUV.

Unmarked state police vehicles swarmed the truck. Two trucks pulled up carrying spotlights in their beds. A state police bomb dismantling crew moved in on the truck, shields up. Slowly, they started the process of picking the truck payload apart, searching for detonation devices.

Dave called the office and let Clapper know what happened. Disaster averted.

The C-Man was excited and relieved. He asked Dave to run north on I-75 just past Standish where troopers had pulled over a sugar beet truck with a faulty headlight on its driver's side.

"Newcomb told me his guys discovered gold paint on the front fender where the headlight had been damaged—the lamp flickered on and off as the truck headed north," Clapper said. "A gift from Nick. The driver was identified as Travis Dickinson from Argyle. He's in custody and the bomb squad is all over the truck. They'll be there for awhile. Get up there and get me a firsthand account. Both bomb trucks stopped before midnight and before they could do damage. I'm so relieved."

Dave asked if the managing editor had any news about Nick. The C-Man said Tanya had called him while driving Nick home from the hospital.

"He's going to be OK," Clapper said. "Tanya says he's beat up and tired, needs rest at home. If I was a betting man, I'd put money down on him coming in here in the morning. We'll see."

Dave and Dana jumped in her vehicle and headed north, toward I-75 and Standish.

"Are you willing to check out the second bomb truck?" Dave asked. "It's getting late. Are you up for this?"

Dana laughed. "Try and stop me. Let's go."

Chapter 18

Monday Morning
Nick and Tanya's apartment, Bay City

At 4:42 a.m., Tanya's cell phone howled to life. She flipped over in bed and grabbed the device, hoping to quiet it before the racket awakened Nick. She had only partial success. He groaned, his achy body squirming for a new comfort zone.

"Hello," she whispered into the cell, cupping the phone and her mouth with her free hand. It was Danielle Conaway. She was weeping and trying to breathe at the same time. Tanya recognized her plaintive voice and feared the worst. "Yes, Danielle. What's up?"

Nick could hear the muffled, limited conversation. The two women talked for several minutes. He almost drifted back into another deep sleep when he felt Tanya's weight shift in the bed. She placed the cell phone back on the nightstand before rolling back into Nick's good side, snuggling next to him. He felt her body shudder. She took a deep breath and let it out slowly, sniffling at the end.

He sensed something was wrong and pushed grogginess aside. "What is it, Tanya? What's troubling you?"

She didn't respond immediately, trying to control her emotions. Then, she let it out, allowing her words to land and settle. "We lost our baby."

It hit Nick hard, and he understood Tanya's disappointment. He knew she had invested in Sherry and the Conaways, trying her best to help them through this very stressful and difficult part of their family life. He also knew she harbored hope that if Sherry carried the baby full term, there was a chance—albeit a remote chance—the Steeles might be able to adopt an unwanted newborn.

"That was Danielle," Tanya whispered. "Sherry miscarried. She lost the baby tonight after serious cramping and bleeding. She said it all happened pretty fast."

Nick had feared the sad news since it was learned the teenager was pregnant. Sherry had suffered even before the moment of her baby's unwanted conception. Abused physically and mentally. Starved and deprived of water. Alone and hopeless. Barely surviving while consumed by fear. What chance did her unborn child really have?

"How's Sherry doing?"

"Danielle says she had a very rough time all night, but was resting now," Tanya said. "They think she's going to be fine physically. They'll watch how she handles it emotionally. I'm thinking this is going to be a big relief for her."

Nick grunted. "I can see that. From what you've told me, it sounded like she was not looking forward to having this baby—adoption or not."

Tanya took a deep breath and sighed heavily. "I know I'm being silly, but I just had it in my head that if Sherry did not want the baby, that maybe, just maybe, we could take the baby. That was so stupid on my part."

On her side, she snuggled closer to Nick, careful not to hurt him more than he'd already been damaged. He took her hand in his right paw, the good one, and squeezed gently.

"You weren't being stupid, you just wanted to be a mom," he said, quietly. The two laid in the dark, comforting each other. He stared at the ceiling. She focused on the side of his face, her nose inches from his ear. He felt her warm, light breath, and was so thankful, once again, to have her love.

"Time is not my friend," she whispered, "on the idea of becoming a mom. I know it. The clock is running out. I absolutely love being a counselor and working with kids, helping them in the best way I can. I was hoping, and dreaming, of doing that with my own child."

"Oh, honey, that's one of the many things I love about you. I see it. Everyone does. You're great with young people. You're a natural. They respond to you."

"I guess I should be thankful, and happy, with that," she responded. "I'll get over it."

They laid quietly for several moments until Nick stirred, asking if he could run a wild idea past her—something to chew on for a bit. She nodded, her nose brushing his cheek up and down.

"What would you think about looking into the idea of becoming foster parents?" he asked, trying to turn sideways but giving up on the notion because it hurt too much. "There are thousands of kids who need help. Through no fault of their own, these young people—all ages—are struggling in troubled families. They need steady hands, stability, and love while their families are getting back on track. You'd be great at it. I think it could be good for us, too."

Tanya nodded eagerly. "As a counselor, I've seen how terrific foster parents can be—what a positive effect they can have on kids who are in trouble, trying to find their way. I didn't think you'd be open to it. It's a tremendous responsibility, but it can be wonderful."

"Let's check it out," he said. "I saw online where the state has a training program. I'm open to it."

Tanya snuggled even closer. "I know who to call, how to get started. Thanks for being so fabulous."

They laid together quietly. Tanya relaxed. She almost dozed back off to sleep when she felt Nick shift, then strain to sit up.

"I can't sleep," he said, his feet on the floor, rotating his head, flexing his shoulders. "It's 5:30. I want to go to the office. We've got stories to write—a paper to put out. I want to be part of it. This is still my story. Will you drive me?"

She knew it would be futile to argue. She boosted herself to the edge of her side of the bed. "Let me get dressed, then I'll help you."

Dave had been up all night, gathering information and conducting interviews for articles that everyone in the *Blade* newsroom believed would be the state's biggest and most important story of the year—perhaps in its history.

Extremists, armed with catastrophic munitions, were bent on blackmailing the State of Michigan into a gigantic payday that would fund terrorist acts throughout the nation aimed at destabilizing and bringing down the U.S. government. The blackmail plot was stopped before it could be put into place as a result of an investigation by the *Bay City Blade*.

The plot, though formidable when it was hatched, had become a fantasy—a pipe dream of terror.

Fatigue was setting in on Dave, as well as two other reporters, three copy editors, two graphic artists, and two photographers—all working on the package of articles and artwork. Clapper had managed to expand the A section of the Monday newspaper from twelve to sixteen pages, all devoted to the story, photos, and graphics.

At 6:30 a.m.—four hours before deadline—Nick hobbled into the newsroom. Tanya had helped him up the stairway, one step at a time. All activity stopped. The cavernous room went silent as Nick walked to his desk, his left arm still in a sling and the left side of his head swollen and bruised.

Clapper watched him. "Steele, you should be at home in bed, not here."

The reporter was resolute. "Nope, this is where I belong. Now, how can I help?" he asked, checking the giant deadline clock. "What needs to be done?"

The newsroom roared back to life, enlivened by his energy and dedication.

The C-Man walked up to Nick's desk to give him an update. He reported that Newcomb had alerted the governor to the gravity of the situation as the bomb trucks rolled toward Bay City. He sent her the blackmail letter when the trucks had been seized and the bomb squads had dismantled the explosives. The governor would issue a statement at 9 a.m. and be available for an interview.

"Are you up for interviewing the governor? This is your story, Nick," Clapper said. "You know more about it than anyone else. You don't have to do any writing—just help everyone else put this project all together."

Nick said he would do his best. Dave rolled up, his eye still puffy and holding hues of being blackened a week ago. Instead of writers, the two reporters looked like tested cage fighters. They conferred and planned their next steps. Then Dave leaned into Nick's personal space, put his arm around the damaged but not defeated journalist's shoulder and whispered, "So glad you're OK, and even happier that you're here. I wouldn't even want to attempt this without you leading the team."

Nick laughed and nodded. "Let's see how you feel after deadline. We've got a lot of work to get done."

Lennie, the *Blade's* chief photographer, brought a dozen proof sheets of small images to Nick's desk. He wanted to show him the array of potential photos available for publication. The big job would be winnowing—selecting the right images, the most engaging and captivating photographs—to help tell the overall story. Clapper joined them in the give-and-take discussion. Some would be great for print and many more would go online with the digital story.

The clock ticked as the buzz and hubbub of the newsroom rose, ebbing and flowing into crescendos of creativity. Time evaporated as split-second decisions were being made across the newsroom about what information was going to be published and how it was going to be presented to readers.

At 8:05 a.m., Newcomb called Clapper with another important development in the ever-changing story. Jerry Meade, one of the architects of 'The Plan' and the extremist who allegedly killed his former accomplice, Eric Stapleton, had been arrested while trying to cross the border into Canada at the Blue Water Bridge, the nearly two-mile twin span over the St. Clair River linking Port Huron and Sarnia, Ontario.

Border security had been placed on alert for the possibility that members of the Michigan Proud Patriots would flee once their plan collapsed in a heap after discovery. Meade was near the top of the watch list.

Newcomb reported that the extremist conspirator had been discovered hiding underneath bags of dirty laundry in the back of a nondescript cargo van. Meade carried false identification but his photograph, copied and distributed from Underwater Solutions publications, betrayed him.

Gold Chains had abandoned the beet truck at a rest stop just before it got on Interstate 75, heading north toward Mackinaw City. The cargo van had been planted at the rest stop so Meade could flee and monitor developments from Canada after the governor received the blackmail letter.

Newcomb offered exclusive interviews with border security officers who captured the fugitive and state troopers who took him into custody. Meade, who had waived his right to remain silent and access to an attorney, was eager to take credit for 'The Plan' and spread extremist propaganda.

Clapper assigned a reporter to take Newcomb's call and conduct interviews. A photographer from the *Detroit Free Press* had been alerted to the arrest and raced to capture images. News of 'The Plan,' and how it had been thwarted, had begun to leak like the sinking *Titanic*. News outlets from across Michigan and the Midwest had begun calling Clapper for comment.

Newcomb, grateful for the *Blade's* role in disrupting the domestic terrorist plot, referred all news inquiries to the C-Man.

At 9 a.m., a statement from the governor's office arrived at the newsroom via email. Nick read it and called the governor's office, speaking with her for nearly 10 minutes. She gushed praise for the state police coordinated efforts to find and stop the bomb trucks. The governor thanked them for their courageous efforts to dismantle the explosives and safely handle the radioactive waste. She condemned terrorist acts. And she correctly credited the *Bay City Blade* for uncovering the heinous plot and working with authorities to avoid a deadly calamity.

Reporters and editors worked feverishly to make deadline. When the presses rolled, the front page contained four articles, two photographs, and an infographic. The main story focused on how the two bomb trucks were tracked down, the drivers arrested, and explosives dismantled. A sidebar revealed 'The Plan:' where, when, and how it was hatched. A second sidebar profiled the terrorists—Eric Stapleton, Jerry Meade, Reggie Thorpe, Leon Schmidt, and Travis Dickinson—and their roles in 'The Plan.' The fourth story looked at the targets of the terrorists—the Line 5 oil pipelines and Dow Chemical—and what the human, economic, and environmental toll of the blasts would have been.

The photographs on Page 1 showed the nighttime arrests of the Argyle Neanderthals, their beet truck bombs, and the heroic efforts of the state police to stop and dismantle the bombs. The infographic detailed and compared the bombs assembled in 'The Plan' to the infamous Oklahoma City blast in 1995.

The inside pages of the A section carried the jumps of stories from Page 1, multiple photographs as well as articles about the Stapleton murder, the Sand Box as a meeting place for the terrorists, and the dungeon for Sherry Conaway.

Another article focused on the role of Mackinac Island in the plot, including a look at the rental cottage for Underwater Solutions employees, the posting of Stapleton's scalp, and the declaration on the island's Community Hall. Inside pages also detailed the Proud Patriots and other known extremist groups in Michigan.

The publisher of the *Blade* ordered the pressroom to kick out an extra 10,000 copies of the Monday newspaper, figuring reader demand for the product would easily exceed its normal daily run of 45,000 copies. Demand for the online edition of the *Blade* instantly jammed and slowed to a crawl upon publication.

The overnight reporting team that Clapper assembled was exhausted. He thanked them for their hard work and dedication. He also posted a notice on the employee bulletin board that all *Blade* employees would be excused from work if they chose to attend the funeral of Dave Balz's mother, which was scheduled for 1 p.m. Tuesday.

Several journalists stopped by Dave's desk to express condolences and let him know that their families would be in attendance for the service. Nick did the same thing, asking his friend if there was anything he or Tanya could do.

Clapper, who carried a single sheet of paper in his hands, encouraged all members of the overnight team to go home, get some rest, and be ready to publish another great newspaper on Tuesday. Everyone, that is, except for Nick Steele.

He sauntered to the reporter's desk and lifted the sheet of paper so he could read it as he spoke.

"Steele, there's no way this expense account is going to get past the number crunchers in accounting. Who is Randy? What's his last name?"

he asked, squinting at Nick's request for reimbursement.

"I don't know," he replied, fidgeting with an ink pen. "Randy is a woman, and she was my key source in opening up the terrorist bomber plot."

"You don't know her last name? And you've got contractor written under occupation. What kind of contractor? The bean counters are going to want a company and an address."

Nick waved for the C-Man to come closer so he could speak in a hushed tone. "Randy is a call girl. She gave me the thumb drive and tipped me to Reggie Thorpe. We wouldn't have broken the story without her."

Clapper was stunned. "A hooker? You used the services of a prostitute to break the biggest story in the state of Michigan?"

"Information only," Nick said, getting a feeling of déjà vu with this conversation. "She asked to be paid for her time. Two hundred dollars for two hours of discussion—talk only."

"A hooker?" Clapper repeated, his eyes squinting, his mouth hanging open.

Nick tried to explain. "I don't make judgments. I take people at their word, at their actions. She never lied to me, not once. Everything she said was as right as rain. She didn't want anything but to be paid for her time. She was smart enough to know she was dealing with some bad, dangerous dudes, and responsible enough to want them stopped because they wanted to hurt people."

Clapper put the expense form on Nick's desk and beside Randy's name, he printed the letters "I-d-u-n-o." So, she became Randy Iduno. Under occupation, he added the word "Independent" beside contractor, and then under the company address, he added his own home mailing address.

"OK, we'll run this up the flagpole and see if accounting salutes," he said. "If it gets rejected, I'll give you the two hundred smackers out of my pocket."

Nick thanked him. Noting Clapper's generous mood, he pressed further. "One more thing," he said, "is the condition of my Firebird.

"I've got insurance, but I doubt it will cover the amount of damage it received from the Argyle boys. They're headed for long prison stretches, but my Firebird is probably doomed."

The C-Man smiled. "It's taken care of. The publisher called the Essexville body shop herself this morning and ordered full restoration, regardless of cost."

The reporter was surprised and pleased.

Clapper added a final word of advice: "If I were you, I wouldn't mention the payment of money to a call girl to Tanya. Knowing her, I'd bet it wouldn't sit well."

Nick laughed. "Drayton, you are wise beyond your years."

Acknowledgments

Many hands pitched in to help create this novel. I cannot thank my team at Mission Point Press enough for the support and guidance in completing this story. Once again, my legal eagles—retired Bay County Circuit Judge Harry P. Gill and my son, Michael D. Vizard, a Flint-area attorney who speaks for those who have no voice or power—offered great advice navigating the law through the story's twists and turns. I would be remiss if I did not thank my brothers, Frank and Mike, for introducing me to the community of Argyle, Michigan (a key locale in this story) and the backroads of The Thumb.

About the Author

Dave Vizard is a former award-winning journalist who absolutely loved his 35-year career in Michigan newspapers. He is a former managing editor of the *Bay City Times*, editor of *True North Magazine*, columnist, and a labor reporter for the *Flint Journal*. The plots and storylines in the Nick Steele Mystery Series rise from his experiences as a newspaper reporter and editor. Dave writes from the home he shares with his spouse, Barbara, near Lake Huron in Michigan's Thumb region. His works can be found at davevizard.com and he can be reached at davidvl652@gmail.com

Milton Keynes UK
Ingram Content Group UK Ltd.
UKHW041456121024
449426UK00001B/158

9 781965 278185